D0914718

A Whole Song and Dance

Sarvenaz Tash

HYPERION
Los Angeles   New York

First Edition, April 2023
1 3 5 7 9 10 8 6 4 2
FAC-004510-23048
Printed in the United States of America

This book is set in Excelsior LT Std/Adobe Systems
Designed by Zareen Johnson

Library of Congress Cataloging-in-Publication Data
Names: Tash, Sarvenaz, author.
Title: A whole song and dance / Sarvenaz Tash.
Description: Los Angeles ; New York : Hyperion, 2023. •
Audience: Ages 12–18. • Audience: Grades 10–12. • Summary:
A freshman at NYU's Tisch School of the Arts, Nasrin is seemingly
living her dream, except her parents think she is attending
business school and it gets harder and harder to keep lying
to them, especially after they surprise her in New York.
Identifiers: LCCN 2022012378 • ISBN 9781368077552
(hardcover) • ISBN 9781368093521 (ebook)
Subjects: CYAC: Secrets—Fiction. • Theater—Fiction. •
Universities and colleges—Fiction. • New York (N.Y.)—Fiction.
• Iranian Americans—Fiction. • LCGFT: Novels.
Classification: LCC PZ7.T2111324 Wh 2023 • DDC [Fic]—dc23
LC record available at https://lccn.loc.gov/2022012378

Reinforced binding

Visit www.HyperionTeens.com

SUSTAINABLE FORESTRY INITIATIVE   Certified Sourcing

www.sfiprogram.org
SFI-01681

Logo Applies to Text Stock Only

*To my maman and baba, who always
supported my wild, impractical dreams*

*And in loving memory of Mahsa Amini
and the countless brave, fierce, and
unshakable women of Iran*

CHAPTER 1

How to Succeed

✪

I'm idling in my car even though I pulled into my driveway at least ten minutes ago, nervously tapping my hands on the steering wheel in time to the *How to Succeed in Business Without Really Trying* cast recording. My stomach is flipping like a full-blown *Newsies* routine, and my perfectly ordinary front door has never looked so intimidating.

To give myself an extra shot of courage, I pick up my phone and read the impossible email just one more time.

Dear Nasrin,

Congratulations! You have been accepted to the Drama BFA program at NYU Tisch School of the Arts. Welcome to New Studio on Broadway.

I close my eyes and focus on the visualization technique I use to calm my nerves every time I'm about to step onto a stage.

First, square breathing: in for two, hold for two, out for two, hold for two. Repeat four times.

Next, my three words of intention: how I want my audience—in this case, my parents—to feel once I've performed. The words are technically supposed to be verbs. So, okay, I want to charm, excite, and...uh, prouden? Is that a word?

Lastly, and arguably the easiest part for me: remind myself to speak calmly, slowly, and with passion. I also need to remember the most important truth bomb in my arsenal: that the NYU musical theater department only has a 15 percent acceptance rate. If there's one thing my parents can get behind, it's percentages.

This is it. I'm going to use all my performance acumen and all my courage and come clean: *Maman and Baba, I applied to Tisch, the art school, not Stern, the business school. I got in! And I'm going to study theater and spend the rest of my life performing.*

I'm going to tell them. *Today,* I think, just as my stomach does another Tony-worthy backflip and the arched glass in my front door seems to frown even wider. Or maybe...sometime this weekend. Because I think there's an Iranian soccer match on tomorrow and then they'll be feeling particularly relaxed.

Don't get me wrong. It's not that my parents aren't supportive. Maman and Baba paid for and drove me to every voice lesson or dance class, attended every single one of my performances whether I was playing a background tulip or had the lead role, and cheered harder than anyone when I took my bows, from age four until now. They love that I love to perform.... They also really, *really* want me to go to business school.

I listen to Daniel Radcliffe belt out some more tips about how to walk into a conference room, soaking in my ironic choice of pump-up music, before I finally turn off the car. It'll be okay; I have a whole weekend to tell them.

But when I step into the door, Maman and Baba are both lying in wait in the foyer. Their eyes are wild and bright, and when they land on me, my parents let out a joyous exclamation, as if they've been standing there all day. I glance back at my treacherous front door uneasily, wondering if they've been staring out at me sitting in my car.

"Nasrin, I'm sorry," Maman says, and that's when I notice that she's clutching my iPad. "I promise I wasn't prying. It's just, the alert popped up on here this morning and I've been waiting for hours to have you read it...." She hands the tablet over to me.

"It's from NYU!" Baba butts in. "We just saw it was from NYU."

So much for that soccer match.

"Did you get in? Are you going to be a Sternie?" I look at my dad's smiling face, how his dark mustache is bobbing up and down with anticipation. Then I turn to Maman, her brown eyes blinking madly behind her funky purple-and-pink glasses.

Maybe this would've been easier if I'd just let them overhear my Zoom audition. But I specifically asked my theater director to let me borrow the school auditorium for it. Probably because a large part of me never expected it would lead to this moment. I mean, come on. Fifteen percent.

I take a final deep breath and finish it off with my good-luck ritual—two taps on the silver necklace that's hanging from my neck, the pendant a tiny rendering of stage curtains. Maman and Baba got it for me years ago, just a few months before that disastrous *Chorus Line* audition that almost made them make me quit....

But no, no. That is *not* what I need to be visualizing right now.

I put all the force of my vocal training behind my voice as I say, "I got into NYU—"

But before I get to finish my sentence, both my parents are hugging me and whooping loudly. I'm pretty sure that's one of my mother's tears I feel on my hair.

"We're so proud!" Maman says.

"So proud, jigar talah!" Baba reiterates. "This makes everything worth it. All the sacrifices..."

Maman waves at him. "Let's not get into that now, Nader. This is Nasrin's moment! She did it!"

They both embrace me from either side again, a tight-knit Mahdavi circle that feels as warm as the sun.

They're so happy.

And I'm so happy.

And we're elated over the same thing, really. The same university. Just...a slightly different school within it.

Okay, this is good. This is how I'll ease into the truth. "So, Maman. Baba..."

"We have to celebrate properly!" Baba says, and jumps away from the embrace, the slight chill in his wake scattering my train of thought like stage snow. "I'm making reservations!" He grabs for his phone.

I don't have to ask where. He knows my favorite restaurant. He sorta knows *everyone's* favorite restaurant, given that my parents are the proud creators of RatethePlate.com, currently the number two restaurant-rating site in the country.

"I'm opening up some champagne. Just a little for the special occasion," Maman says, winking at me.

I smile at her, swallowing down my confession for the time being. Because a little alcohol will make it go down easier too, right? I mean, I've never really drank, but I've seen enough act 2s opening on party scenes to get the idea.

"I'm buying us matching sweatshirts!" I look over in alarm to see that Baba has somehow already managed to navigate over to the Stern merchandising page.

I give a small laugh. "Well, maybe let's hold off on that for one—"

POP!

I physically jump, for one bizarre instant thinking that a cymbal has been hit, signaling the first note of my opening number. Traditionally, it would be something called an

"I Want" song, the main character establishing to the audience what their goal is going to be for the next two hours and change. Think "Wouldn't It Be Loverly" or "Part of Your World."

So I want...

...to get into Tisch. The program whose audition I agonized over for months. The program I applied to just to see if I had what it took to make it. I told myself that if I got in, it'd be a sign that theater is what I'm meant to be doing.

And I did. I got in. *Fifteen percent.*

Right, that's it. Remember the percentages, Nasrin. Remember the percentages!

My mom stuffs a skinny glass into my hand, a small pool of pale liquid fizzing at its bottom.

"To our great mind!" she says.

"To our great mind!" Baba echoes, raising his glass and clinking it with mine.

My eyes involuntarily flick over to the wall of my parents' office, where the giant sampler that hangs there is visible even from the foyer. It reads:

Great minds have purpose, others have wishes.
—Washington Irving

Ironically, I'm the one who stitched the words of my dad's favorite quote onto an enormous piece of fabric a few years ago, when I learned how to sew so I could have a better grasp on how to alter my own costumes. The sampler was a Father's Day present, replacing the small framed quote that had been there for as long as I've known how to read.

Everything my parents have ever done seems filled with purpose. For one thing, they left behind their entire *country* in pursuit of opportunity. And when they combined Maman's coding skills and Baba's penchant for sales, they somehow arrived at a magic formula for success. It seemed like one day they were updating their WordPress from the little alcove in their bedroom, and the next, they had a feature in *Wired*. But I know it was "overnight success" by way of ten years of toiling in obscurity.

And that's all they've ever wanted for me too. Maybe not the abject struggling part, as they've made quite clear, but the part where I work hard and eventually get rewarded for it. The first and last time I ever saw Baba with tears in his eyes, through fresh ones streaming from my own, was the month after the *Chorus Line* audition, when he told me in no uncertain terms that theater is meant to be a fun hobby and not a source of devastation. But this acceptance email makes me feel like my wishes have purpose too; one of the premier drama schools in the country thinks I have what it takes to turn them into something concrete—into a career. What could be more purposeful than that?

I smile and follow Maman and Baba's lead by taking a small sip from my glass. The liquid is cool and light, and nowhere near as bitter as I was expecting. I read it as a sign that my confession will be the same. My parents might be surprised by its novelty, but they'll get used to it, accept it, and, maybe even eventually, enjoy it.

I put down my glass. "Maman, Baba. First of all, I want to thank you. It's because of *you* that I was ever able to do this." I get a little choked up because it's so accurate. All those lessons, all that driving me to community theater auditions and rehearsals over the summers...

"Oh, don't be silly, azizam," Maman says. "What are we doing in this country at all if not helping you to accomplish your goals? *You* did all the hard work...."

"Nasrin, look," Baba says, bouncing on the balls of his feet. He thrusts his iPad into my face, and I can see that, fortunately, he's navigated away from the merchandise... though, *un*fortunately, it might be to an even more disconcerting page. "There are so many clubs you can join!"

The Stern clubs page is filled with words like "economics" and "finance" and "investment analysis" that stream through my eyes and get jammed up before they can absorb into my brain. But then there's one that actually makes its way through my synapses: a Stern & Tisch Entertainment Business Association. Okay, maybe this is the opening I need.

I point to it. "This one looks interesting...."

Baba looks down, and his eyebrows knit together as he reads what I'm pointing at. "That one? Well... we wouldn't want you to get tempted, Nasrin."

"Tempted?" I ask, my shoulders slowly creeping up.

"You might see all those Tischies and decide to become a

8

drama major! Remember when you started high school and that's what you wanted to do? Your mom and I were so worried." They look over my head at one another. The sense of relief flowing through them is palpable, like they dodged a literal bullet—naturally, from a gun that appeared in act 1 and, in a Chekhovian progression, went off by the end of the play.

They clink their glasses again, and it's like a lighting cue has darkened the liquid inside to an ominous amber. Suddenly my stomach feels like giant bubbles are sloshing around in it, bouncing together, creating friction and waves upon waves of anxiety. My dad just voiced everything I was afraid of.

But I fall back on my training once again. My tone is entirely calm and relaxed when I say, "But there was never anything to worry about, was there?"

CHAPTER 2

You Can't Stop the Beat

✧

"Listen, there's room for only one Aladdin and Jasmine on Broadway. What do you say we team up and audition for it as a duo?"

I blink at the boy standing in front of me in our Broadway Dance Styles classroom: He's got medium-brown skin and artfully coiffed black hair, and he's looking at me with such sincerity that it's only when he breaks character and cracks a giant smile that I realize he's joking.

"I'm Beckett Banerjee," he says, sticking out his hand.

"Nasrin Mahdavi," I reply as I shake it.

"Let's be best friends?" he says with that same wry expression, and I can't help but laugh.

"Sure, why not? That is...if you're okay being seen with me." I lower my voice to a whisper. "I, uh, only placed level two in dance."

"Son of a gravity-defying witch, me too!"

"Really?" I ask. "Did you also have a decade's worth of ballet, tap, and jazz under your belt?"

"Honey, yes," he says as he laces up his dance shoes. "Plus featured roles in *Matilda* and *Billy Elliott*."

"At your school?" I ask.

"On Broadway," he says casually.

"Hold up, what?" I ask.

"It was a few years ago. My child star days." He shrugs it off dismissively. "But enough about me. Tell me more about you. I feel like I know hardly anything about my best friend."

I laugh again, but surprisingly, I feel the warmth behind his words too—like I really may have just made my first friend at Tisch.

Two weeks ago, I stepped onto the un-campus of NYU for the first time. The late-summer city air was hot and stifling, but I felt like the breeze in my heart was strong enough to make those purple school flags wave proudly above the concrete jungle. I looked to them for courage.

My parents were helping me move in, of course, and the plan was to tell them then, once the stage was set and I could show them that I clearly belonged at Tisch. I had a whole monologue prepared for how I was ready for the hard work and potential rejections of the professional theater world and that college freshman Nasrin was completely different from high school freshman Nasrin. I was even going to float them the idea that I could maybe double-major in business and drama, the perfect compromise for all of us. But, it turns out, moving in is a whirlwind of logistics and nerves and wholly new information being thrown at you at high speed. Plus, if your parents only have a couple of hours before their flight back home because freshman orientation coincides with a major site relaunch... well, it becomes sorta easy to decide against dropping a huge bombshell right before they leave for the airport.

A couple of weeks of grueling dance auditions and frenzied first classes later and I'm still working on figuring out when to tell them.

"Shall we dance?" Beckett asks me as he crooks his elbow in invitation.

I smile at the Rodgers and Hammerstein reference and give him a Lerner and Loewe one in return, hooking my arm through his. "I could do it all night."

Maybe I shouldn't have said that so callously, because now I literally have been dancing all night, and all day, for a solid month, and my muscles are Feeling It. At this moment, as I tap a double traveling time step across the small stage set up in the classroom, the wooden floor reverberates up my metal taps and through my ankles and calves; the soles of my feet can almost sense the grain of the wood even though we're not doing contemporary in Broadway Dance Styles today and I'm not barefoot.

I end the routine with a turn into Beckett's arms. He dips me, and we finish with identical extended hands and wide grins for our riveted audience—or rather, our imaginary riveted audience. Our classmates are too busy practicing their own routines in separate areas of the large studio classroom to pay us much mind, and Alan, our professor, is looking more critical than riveted. He frowns, his hand patting his wild, graying curly hair—a sign that he's not pleased with our performance.

"You need a lot more definition in your taps," he says to me. "I need elegant woodpecker, not malfunctioning jackhammer." Then he turns to Beckett. "Your frame for the dip? Jellyfish arms." He walks over and adjusts Beckett's arms and then beckons for me to slip back into them. "See the difference?" he asks me. "You feel more supported, right?"

I nod.

"Okay, keep practicing. Next." We move over to a corner of the room while two more of our classmates come up to get their critiques.

"*Do* you feel more supported, Nasrin?" Beckett asks me. "I can't help feeling more eviscerated with every class." He slides his eyes over to Alan's grim face and hard mouth as he jots down whatever Elana and Shohei are doing wrong.

"Well, you know. Statistically, only eight percent of us will ever be on Broadway," I say, echoing the chilling words Alan intoned at the start of our very first day of class.

"So I've heard," Beckett replies.

"And, like, since you've already been on Broadway, does that mean the chances for the rest of us are down to seven point nine eight percent?" I ask.

"Nah," he says. "You're only as good as your next job."

Though Beckett often downplays his experience, there's no doubt that it's impressive. But then again, *everyone* here is impressive. It didn't take me long to realize that every single person at Tisch was the star of their high school theater departments, just like me, and that many, like Beckett, already had professional credits to their names. I watch the two dozen of them in this classroom, each concentrating so hard on whatever aspect of their body Alan has told them is lacking, and I send up a silent prayer to Ethel Merman in gratitude for Beckett. I'm not sure I could take the intensity of the first month of drama school without a good friend to lean on—quite literally, as we rehearse our turn into the dip over and over again.

The next morning, I open a bleary eye at the sound of a slamming door and find myself alone in my dorm room. Beatrix, my roommate, is in New Studio with me, though we don't share any classes. We also don't share much of anything else because, as she told me via whiteboard on the first day of freshman orientation, she has taken a vow of silence to save her voice for her classes, and *only* her classes. Presumably, she too was the lead of all her school plays, but I don't think there's enough ink in a dry-erase marker to get her full résumé.

The whiteboard is now propped up right by my bed. It reads:

Didn't you say your Stats TA was going to murder you if you were late one more time? ~Bx

My eyes fly to my alarm clock: 8:30. Crap. Why didn't it go off at 7:00 like it was supposed to? And why the hell would Beatrix not just *wake me up* like a normal human being?

Now I have half an hour to get dressed and book it over to the CAS building for my least favorite class in all of existence. I scurry over to the bathroom, brush my teeth, and throw my long, dark brown hair up into a messy bun. No time to put on any makeup, but my cat-eye liner from yesterday has turned into a smoky eye today, so that'll have to do. I go back out into the room to quickly dress, and I'm out the door in ten minutes flat, which should give me plenty of time to make the twelve-minute walk over to Washington Square Park.

And it would've. If there wasn't a massive traffic jam involving two trucks and half a dozen yellow taxis right where I have to cross on Fourth Avenue. I can't even squeeze through in between the cars. I look longingly at the top of one of the cabs, wishing my life was in fact a musical and I could just *Fame* my way through this jam.

But no, in real life you can't just jump on top of a car, expect a killer '80s synth soundtrack to blare out of nowhere, and grand jeté onto the van in the next lane. Not without the cops showing up, anyway. (And I don't mean ensemble cops who eventually join in on the number.)

So I'm late to class. Only by three minutes, but it's enough to earn me the stink eye from one Max Fletcher.

I should probably give him an apologetic smile; after all, I know I'm the one in the wrong here.

But Max doesn't deserve that from me. For one thing, he's not even the professor, just a TA who's only three years older than me. For another, when he handed me my abysmal test score for my first exam, he included his office hours in neat block letters. I naively assumed that meant he wanted me to go see him so he could help me bring my grades up.

So I went to his office, a big, stupid smile on my face. He was on the phone when I walked in, his head down, so all I could see was a neat mane of strawberry-blond hair and the slope of his freckled nose. "Do you have to call me to tell me this?" he was saying in a pinched voice. "Can't you just email me your disdain?" He paused before saying a curt "Fine, bye" and pressing the button on his phone.

Clearly, I was intruding on something personal. I tried to quietly back out of his office, but Max, without looking up, intoned emotionlessly, "Can I help you, Ms. Mahdavi?"

"Um..." My smile faltered. "You put down your office hours on my exam...."

"Yes?"

"I thought...I don't know. Maybe you wanted to help me?"

He looked up at last. Cold blue eyes, a mouth that was a straight slash across his face. "Help you how?"

I blinked. "Getting my grades up?"

"Sure, I can help you," he said slowly, like he needed to enunciate in order for me to understand him. "It's called studying. Do you want me to pull up the Wikipedia definition for you?"

I flushed, stammering, "N-never mind." And I almost walked out the door. Except that within twenty seconds, my embarrassment turned into anger. What right did he have to make me feel like an idiot for asking him to do his job?

So I turned around and said, "You know, I never knew that TA stood for 'top asshole.' Go figure." And *then* I walked out the door.

Did it feel amazing at the time? Sure. Have I felt ever since like I have a target on my back for the rest of the semester? Definitely.

Now, in the class I had the *audacity* to be late to, he's making a big show of marking something down in his little notebook before he looks away, obviously planning to ignore me for the rest of class.

I slump in my seat as I listen to Professor Pham drone on about something called "fences for outliers." I mean, if that doesn't sound like the title of a Tennessee Williams play, I don't know what does. I wish it *were* a play. I wish I were preparing a monologue instead of...this.

I hate this class, I think as I try to mentally bore a hole through the side of Max Fletcher's ear with the strength of my death stare. I should've dropped it while I had the chance, within the first two weeks of school. I don't need Statistics for my major. I could've used hundreds of other classes to fulfill my math/science requirement.

But it is a required course for the business major my parents *think* I'm pursuing. And I've been lying to them so much that I stupidly thought if I took one course that I could openly talk about with them, it would help mitigate the rest of the guilt.

Because, uh, yeah, sidebar: They still think I got into Stern.

I'm going to come clean soon, though, I swear. I even have a bullet-pointed Note on my phone with carefully crafted arguments and reasons why I need to be at Tisch. I open it now to quickly add a new one: I HATE STATS.

It's at that exact moment, of course, that Max Fletcher deigns to look my way again. He rolls his eyes and shakes his head.

Perfect.

I slump down farther in my seat and spend the rest of class pretending I'm auditioning to be Jean Valjean to Max's Javert, death-staring *en français.*

CHAPTER 3

Friend Like Me

✦

As I walk into the following week's Ballet class, Beckett greets me with a high five and his typical pep talk: "We can do this."

I nod. The mantra has become one of our Monday-morning traditions, a strategy for making it through the long day ahead of us. We start the morning off with Ballet, and then an hour and fifteen minutes of Sight Singing followed by two and a half hours of the benignly titled Acting—a name that gives *no* indication of how intense a class it really is. Everyone thinks drama students are, well, *dramatic*. But in reality, we're mostly keeping up a cheerful facade of "We're so lucky we get to do what we love," when the actual work we're doing is mining our emotional devastation for laughs/tears/applause.

We've just entered the Sight Singing classroom, grabbed our music stands from the corner, and settled into a pair of chairs, when a girl named Jo plops down next to us. "Are you two twins?" she asks in a chipper voice.

Beckett and I don't even look at each other. She's definitely not the first person to ask this. "Nope," Beckett says politely. "Just good friends."

"Ah," Jo replies. "You look so much alike."

Beckett waits until she leaves to grab her own music stand before he turns to me with a roll of his eyes. "There's almost two thousand miles between India and Iran. But, sure, why not."

"You could even say there's a . . . *whole new world* between them," I reply.

"Ba dam cha," Beckett says. "She'll be here all week, folks."

I curtsy. "I'm not so offended to be mistaken for your sister. You're good-looking enough." I bat my eyelashes.

"Don't flirt with me, Mahdavi. I'm taken."

"You're kidding!" I exclaim. "Is that why this beautiful face takes up your entire phone's wallpaper?" I swipe his phone from his hand and press the button to wake it up, showcasing the beaming visage of Oliver Tanaki.

Beckett has taken on the gargantuan task of trying to make a long-distance relationship with his high school boyfriend work. Despite our fast friendship, I've kept my qualms about this to myself so far. But looking at his face now, I'm guessing that its frown lines might be Oliver-related. I don't outright express this, though, instead asking an open-ended "What's wrong?"

"Oliver's missed our last two FaceTime dates," Beckett says. "He says he's busy...."

"Well..." I start carefully. "He's premed at Johns Hopkins. He probably *is* busy...."

"I'm also busy, being Drama at Tisch School of the Arts," Beckett replies grumpily.

"Of course you are," I say. "I'm just saying...I mean, do you think he's lying?"

"No," Beckett grouses. "That's the problem. I think we're both...really busy. Maybe too busy to keep this up."

I nod sympathetically. Despite my misgivings about the probability of this relationship surviving, I don't *want* to be right. I've never met Oliver in person, but he and Beckett look like a magazine cover together. Besides, the way Beckett talks about him, cheeks slightly flushed, his voice going up in pitch as he enumerates all Oliver's best qualities—I've never been in love myself, but I've studied it in enough shows and movies and songs to know it when I see it.

"Just call him and talk it out," I say. "The only way this is going to work is if you communicate. Don't be the bottom of act one."

"Act-two finale all the way," Beckett says with a grin.

"Exactly. But, like, *Grease* act two, not *West Side Story* act two."

He nods. "One must clarify when at the altar of the Broadway gods."

The whole class is now assembled in a large semicircle in front of a perfectly arrayed arc of shiny silver music stands.

The professor hands a pile of papers to Jo, who goes around and gives each of us a page of sheet music.

"Ah," Beckett says, looking it over. "Another musical I've never heard of."

We're not sure how the Sight Singing professors find so many compositions that are obscure to even us hard-core musical theater nerds, but somehow they do. "It's a gift," I say, then stop talking as we spend the next hour struggling to suss out the melody of the complicated song.

Afterward, we rush to the café in the Tisch lobby to pick up smoothies before our next class. There's always a line, and we never have more than fifteen minutes. Our quest for nourishment is a weekly struggle with about a 60 percent success rate.

We've grabbed our drinks with three minutes to spare—already a victory—when an incoming text on Beckett's phone immediately sweetens the win. I know from his huge grin that it's Oliver.

"He says we can talk tonight," he exclaims in glee.

"Yay!" I reply, clinking our plastic cups together.

In Acting, our petite professor, Clara Hodgens, calls the class to attention with just the gravitas of her classically trained voice. I recognized Clara from day one and have been doing my best to hide my fangirling ever since. She has a ton of credits in film and TV, where she is known as a character actress—as in, she gets all the quirky side roles—but of course I knew her mostly for her impressive career on Broadway, where she's known as a powerhouse lead actress. Funny how you can get cast so differently in those two mediums without it having anything to do with your skill level or talent—just how kind the camera is to your face.

"We're going to be doing the Meisner repetition exercise again, so please pair up," Clara says. There's nothing about her gentle stance or serene expression that hints that she's projecting her voice, but her mellifluous tones echo around the airy classroom as if she were miked. "As a reminder, I'll be giving you one phrase to repeat to one another, to the point where the words themselves will lose meaning. Instead, pay attention to the emotions, and respond to what your partner is doing, how they look, or what the inflection is in their words."

Beckett and I turn to each another automatically and wait for Clara to make her way around the room. When she gets to us, she gives a nod of encouragement as she assigns us our phrase: "You are such a liar."

"Huh," Beckett says. "You *are* such a liar."

He smiles. I scowl.

Beckett was so immediately in my inner circle that I confessed the my-parents-think-I'm-attending-business-school lie to him the very first time we had lunch together. It helped to relieve the burden somewhat.

"How are your parents paying the bill, then?" Beckett asked me over Beyond burgers and fries. "It says Tisch on mine."

"Mine too. My real one, anyway." I explained the elaborate scheme: They get electronic bills from a proxy website that I set up after, ironically, watching a coding YouTube tutorial series that my mom sometimes contributes to. "The money goes to my account and I take it to pay the real bill. I have some savings to cover the difference between the Tisch and Stern bills...though it's not going to last me much longer." I made a mental note to add *that* to my list of reasons I needed to tell my parents ASAP.

"Wow," Beckett said. "Is that really better than just coming clean with all this?" He jazz-handed to indicate the jazz hands involved in *all this*.

"No. But also, currently...yes." I squirmed in my chair, thinking there were some things Beckett couldn't be expected to understand. His parents literally named him after a famous playwright. And not only was he a Broadway child star, but Mrs. Banerjee teaches dramatic literature at Hunter College right here in Manhattan. Plus, I know they live and breathe Bollywood as much as they do Broadway. My parents too enjoy a good Bollywood film. There are usually a couple a month dubbed into Farsi airing on the Persian TV network they subscribe to. But...

"They don't want their one and only to live a life of rejection and abject poverty?" Beckett offered softly, and I immediately regretted doubting him; even if he doesn't live it, he *does* understand. After all, it takes real empathy to be an actor as talented as Beckett.

"Yes," I said. "And they worry that I can't handle it because the one time I didn't make the spring musical in my freshman year, I got really depressed. They ended up taking me to a therapist, and it was a whole thing...but when you're

24

fourteen and you suddenly get shut out of the field that is *your entire identity*, you might cry a little. Or, like, every night for three months."

"A reasonable reaction," Beckett agreed.

"Exactly," I replied. "But it was a long time ago. I just need to prove to them that things are different now. *I'm* different now. And the rejection didn't ultimately break me. It only made me more determined."

"I get that," Beckett said. "My parents are sort of on the opposite end of the spectrum. They wanted me to come to Tisch so that I could make the transition from child actor to adult actor, because we all know it's the only thing I really want to do, low points and all."

I nodded and ever since have been a little jealous of him having his parents' full and open support.

Now, at the end of Acting class, Beckett immediately apologizes. "I'm sorry about the line."

I smile at him. "Why? You didn't assign it."

"I know, I just . . . I don't think you're such a liar, Nasrin," he says.

"But I am," I reply with a sigh. "And if nothing else . . . I should at least use the real-life experience to succeed in the acting class I'm not supposed to be taking." I put on my sweatshirt, ready to face an unusually brisk October day. "Anyway, I'm going to tell them. Soon. I've set up a meeting with Clara to see if I can do any sort of business-related double major. And then: boom. I'll have the coup d'état for my list of Reasons They Don't Have to Worry About Me."

Though I started Tisch with the vague notion that I could double-major in business and drama, had I done much research on this before I landed in New York? Nope. If I had, I probably would've realized pretty quickly that NYU doesn't let you double-major in its two top schools, not unless you want to do a track for film producers. So now I've been scrambling to come up with an alternate double major—probably at the College of Arts and Sciences—that might appease my parents. At least I have Clara for my adviser, and I've made an appointment to talk to her about it in a little over a week.

"Or if the double major doesn't work, maybe you can pull off a different headliner for your list. Like...a walk-on role on an Off-Broadway show!" Beckett enthuses.

I laugh. "Perfect. Do you have one of those in your back pocket?"

"Well, not quite," Beckett says. "But I actually did want to show you this." He takes out his phone, navigates over to a page on Backstage.com, and hands it over to me.

It's a casting call for a new web show—a musical one, apparently.

Leila: Female, 18-22

Ethnicity: Middle Eastern/South Asian

Character: A spunky and slightly naive girl ready to take Broadway by storm...just as soon as she makes curfew for her strict parents.

"Huh," I say. "It says auditions are next Wednesday."

"Yup," Beckett says. "You going to submit for it?"

"Maybe," I reply. I'm intrigued, even though I obviously have class on Wednesday. Then again, what are the chances they'll actually call me in for an audition?

I've applied and sent in my headshot before we've even left the building.

CHAPTER 4

Don't Tell Mama

✫

Because anything that makes my life infinitely more complicated is bound to happen, of course I get a call for the audition. And of course my fifteen-minute slot is at 8:15 a.m. in Midtown. That gives me half an hour to book it to Statistics afterward, and that's *if* the audition doesn't run over, which is unlikely.

When I tell Beckett my dilemma, he responds, "Nasrin. What's the number one rule of drama school?"

"We don't talk about drama school?" I offer. "We sing about it."

"Good one," he responds. "No, the number one rule is, we don't turn down auditions. Not at this stage in our career. Even if you don't get the part, you need the experience of going in for a real New York casting call."

"I know. You're right," I say. Maybe some sort of miracle will happen to get me to class on time.

The audition is being held on the fifth floor of a very large, nondescript office building. On Wednesday morning, I wait in a scuffed-up white hallway among at least a dozen other girls who look similar to me, with varying shades of brown skin and dark hair. I'm a little taken aback by how many of them there are, especially considering the casting call was for a low-budget, low-paying, unproven streaming show. *This staggering level of competition*, I think as I take in all these girls clutching their headshots and sheet music, *is probably exactly what my parents are worried about.*

But what they don't understand is that I'm fully prepared to be rejected today. I'm so relaxed that I start imagining all of us in leotards, busting out the opening number of *A Chorus Line*. Except instead of singing "I hope I get it," I could do an impromptu counterpoint harmony of "I'm just here for the experieeeeence."

"This is my first audition!" a nervous girl says to no one in particular. She's chewing gum in time with the tapping of her feet against the legs of her metal chair. It's all very... rhythmic.

No one responds to her, and she looks so despondent staring down at her character shoes that I feel compelled to tell her, "Me too."

"Ohmygod," she says to me in a gush. "I'm Sunny."

"Nasrin," I reply.

"I think...I'm going to throw up," she says.

I smile, thinking she's exaggerating, but she immediately puts her hand to her puffed-up mouth and runs in the direction of the ladies' room.

She makes it inside the door before I hear the unmistakable sounds of vomiting.

"She is never going to make it in this business," deadpans a tall girl doing leg stretches against the wall.

"Well...it is only her first audition," I reply.

The girl rolls her eyes. "Even if she's not okay, she should *act* like she's okay. If she can't even do that...never going to make it."

She bends over her outstretched leg, and I take the opportunity to walk down the hallway and knock on the bathroom door.

"Hey, Sunny," I ask gently. "You all right in there?"

She opens the door, her face flushed. Inexplicably, she's still chewing gum. I sincerely hope that's a new piece. "Fine," she says, with a shrug. "I always get sick before a performance." Now that I take a closer look at her, she does look calmer.

"Um, wow," I say. "That's intense."

"Nasrin Mahdavi?" A tall, middle-aged woman with her blond hair in a bun and a tablet in her hands stands at the door to the audition room.

"Here," I say, walking over briskly. "Hi."

"Hello there. Please come in. I'll take these." She takes my headshot and my sheet music. "I'm Liz, the producer of *Small Town Dreams*."

We walk into the tiny room, one side of which is covered in wall-to-wall windows that look out on a forest of skyscrapers and somehow make the room feel more cramped. Liz walks over to a twentysomething Black girl with long locs who is sitting behind a piano and hands her my sheet music.

"Huh," the pianist says when she sees it. "Nice choice."

I smile at her.

"This is Tru Davis, our lyricist, composer, and music director," Liz says. "And this"—she points to a schlubby-looking white guy in his late twenties—"is Petie O'Donnell. Our director." Liz takes her seat next to him.

"So nice to meet all of you," I say.

"Hi there, Naz-ring, is it?" Petie asks.

"It's actually 'nas,' like rhyming with 'glass.' And 'reen,' long 'e.' So Nasrin." There was a time when I wouldn't have corrected him, but that was about three years and several lead roles ago.

"Got it," he says with a smile, though he doesn't attempt saying my name again. "Did you prepare a scene for us?"

"I did," I say, indicating the two pieces of paper I have left in my hands. I'm off-book already, but Beckett told me that nobody shows up without sides, even if they don't plan on using them.

"Great," Liz says. "I'll be reading the part of your mom." She reaches over and presses the red record button on the camera that's set up next to her table. "Whenever you're ready?"

I take one small, centering breath and tap my curtain necklace twice before I look at Liz and say. "Hi, Mom."

"Don't you 'Hi, mom' me," she replies, in a somewhat robotic voice. "Where have you been?"

"Um...schoooool?" I say this part so comically unconvincingly, it elicits a laugh from Petie.

"Try again," says Liz-as-Mom.

"The...mall?" I say as if it's a word I've never heard before.

"You needed a train ticket for the mall?" Liz asks.

"How did you...?" I gasp.

"Leila. You're holding it in your hand."

I look down at my empty hand and give a visible start. Petie gives a loud snort.

The rest of the scene goes just as swimmingly. I act like a nervous, clueless seventeen-year-old girl who is terrible at lying to her parents, which, let's face it, isn't too far from home. The only thing is, I'm not really nervous at all, since I'm not worried about getting a yes or a no. It's comforting that my goal is already fulfilled by virtue of just being here.

After the scene is over, Liz, Petie, and Tru all give me a round of applause. After a couple of months of getting relentlessly critiqued at drama school, I've forgotten what that feels like. The sweet, nostalgic sound fires up a smile on my face.

"Well done," Liz says. "Ready to sing?"

"Ready," I say.

Tru plays the opening bars of TLC's "No Scrubs," and I proceed to bring it: vocal training and sass, all rolled into one.

I get more laughs and another round of applause when I'm done. A girl could get used to this.

"That was great," Petie says. "Could you tell us a little more about your background?"

"I'm a freshman New Studio student at Tisch," I explain. "To be totally transparent, this is my first-ever professional audition."

"Wow," Liz says, looking genuinely impressed. "You're a natural. But yes, we have all that here." She indicates my CV. "I think Petie was asking about your cultural background."

Ah, the "What kind of brown?" question, as Beckett would call it. He already warned me it might happen, so I shrug it off and answer. "I'm Persian. Iranian. Second-generation. My parents are from Tehran, but I was born in Indiana."

"Great," Liz says as she jots something down on the paper. "And would you be available for callbacks at the end of this week?"

"Of course," I say. I don't even need Beckett to know that's the standard answer, no matter what's actually on my calendar. A big test, a wedding, major surgery? All that takes a back seat to a callback, thank you very much.

"I think you'll be hearing from us," Petie says, smiling. And as I walk out of the room, I realize that might not be BS.

"How did it go?" Sunny asks me as soon as I step back into the crowded hallway.

I'm not entirely sure how to respond. "Really well" seems

rude since we're obviously going for the same part. I settle for "Not bad." And then a sincere "Good luck!"

"Thanks!" Liz calls Sunny's name, and she heads into the room.

I check my phone on the way out. 8:54 a.m. I'm obviously not making it to my 9:00 a.m. class, so I figure I might as well make the most of my rare downtime. I grab a hazelnut coffee from the deli downstairs before heading back on the downtown train.

While the train rumbles along, I text Beckett that the audition went pretty well and that maybe I'll get a callback by the end of the week. He replies with a variety of excited emojis and a Get it, N.

By the time I'm off of the train, it's past ten, so I'm in the clear to text Maman too. (Obviously, she knows the class schedule I gave her by heart already.)

I send her a photo I took yesterday of the awning of Goshneh, the fancy new Persian restaurant that's just about to open on Eighth Street. Any scoop on this? I ask.

Within moments, my phone buzzes with an incoming FaceTime call.

"No trade reviews yet," Maman says when I answer.

"I know," I say as I head over to Washington Square Park. I'll probably need a bench for this conversation. We've been playing phone tag for a few days, so it's bound to be a long one. "It hasn't opened yet. I'm wondering if I should try to get reservations before it becomes impossible. Or . . ."

"Hold on," she says, and I can see her typing away on her

34

laptop. Probably running stats through one of her brilliant, proprietary programs that can magically determine culinary trends ranging from which food is about to get the nitro treatment to which chef is about to get her own Netflix show. "Lack of other Persian restaurants in the area plus the jigooly decor and buzz about Chef Golestan... Get the reservations," she concludes firmly.

"Figured."

"How are you doing, jigar talah?" she asks.

"Well, I can tell you she's *not* sick," a voice says from right beside me, nearly causing me to spill my coffee on a pair of yellow-and-white Air Jordans.

They belong to Max Fletcher, who is standing behind my bench, glaring at me *and* my mother.

"Who's that?" Maman asks.

"Nobody," I say grimly. "Let me call you right back." I hit the red button to end the FaceTime call with more force than strictly necessary.

"Coffee and a chat more important than class today, huh?" Max asks.

"Are you serious right now?" I ask him. "That was a private conversation."

"Then maybe you shouldn't be having it in the park." I notice he has his own large thermos of coffee just as he takes a casual sip from it.

"What *is* your problem?" I say.

"I don't have a problem," he says. "I'm not the one wasting my parents' money by not attending class."

"Wow," I say sarcastically. "It's amazing how you know everything about me *and* my motivations *and* my parents. You're a goddamn genius."

He shrugs. "I have tracked above average my whole life."

"That undoubtedly includes your knack for inciting rage." I can't believe this kid almost told on me to my mom. "You do realize this is college and we're adults, right? Like, whether I go to class is not something you get to have a parent-teacher conference about?"

"You do realize you shouldn't end sentences with a preposition?"

Oh. My. God. Max Fletcher is, hands down, the *most* infuriating person I have ever encountered. And that's saying something considering I once spent a summer filtering through all the trolls on my parents' site.

I open my mouth, but he beats me to the punch. "Anyway. Enjoy your coffee. Maybe I'll see you next week. Though I'm guessing not." And then he saunters away, leaving me sputtering and stewing on the park bench, wishing for a comeback I don't have.

This should be my angry song moment, I think. My "Just You Wait, 'enry 'iggins" or my "I'm Gonna Wash That Man Right Outa My Hair."

Of course, the problem with those songs is that the heroine eventually falls in love with the man she's singing about.

And no way on God's Great White Way is that *ever* happening.

CHAPTER 5

I Hope I Get It

✪

"Say cheese," I say as I hold my phone an arm's length away to take a selfie of Beckett and me. Beckett dutifully holds his *Playbill* in front of his chest so that my Instagram post will have context.

We're sitting on black folding chairs in a tiny theater in Union Square, three rows away from the small stage. The set decor is minimal: two apple boxes bathed in blue light. The whole thing feels about one step up from a student production. And yet, there's a buzz in the air, an anticipation that we're about to witness something transformative.

Beckett was the one who had the forethought to buy tickets to *Birds of a Feather* while it was still in previews. Its composer and lyricist are both graduates of Tisch, and its playwright, Lucia Ramirez, is actually a senior there now.

Beckett already caught its student run last year. "It's gonna be big," he told me, "and you're gonna want to brag that you saw it when it was still in a tiny Off-Broadway theater. Trust me. It's the next *Prom, Hadestown, Hamilton*."

"*Hamilton*?" I asked with a raised eyebrow. "Really?"

"Okay, fine. *Hamilton*'s a once-in-a-lifetime phenomenon, but the show is really good."

And that's how the two of us find ourselves squeezed into the middle of row C, only a few seats ahead of—of all people—Beatrix, sitting with another girl I recognize from the Tisch lounge.

"This is so cool," I say, taking another glance around the theater and realizing I recognize at least one more trio of audience members—I saw them at first-week dance auditions. "The entire creative team was literally in the same school as us last year."

"I know, right?" Beckett says. "Sometimes it's hard to justify all the effort and—let's face it—the money to go to Tisch. But then you see something like this and realize so many people who came out of our school have *made it*."

I open my *Playbill* and look over the bio of the three creators. Beckett's right. Success like this is exactly how I could show my parents that not only can my passion be my purpose, but the means to make a living too. Now I just have to, uh... create a show, star in it, get a bunch of Broadway producers to stage it, pay me for it, and ensure it becomes a massive hit. Piece of cake.

The lights dim, and I hit post right before I tuck my phone

away, ready to put my own worries aside to get immersed in someone else's story for a while.

And *Birds of a Feather* is fully immersive. It's just a bare stage, minimal lighting, and only four actors total, but filled with all these moments that feel small and massive at the same time. Being in a tiny theater, where the whole audience is basically only feet away from the actors, makes the experience that much more intimate. When the protagonist's best friend makes a joke, the ground practically shakes with laughter. When that same friend reveals a massive betrayal right before the lights go out at the end of act 1, the entire audience simultaneously sucks in their breath, creating one of the most powerful sounds I've ever experienced.

"This is amazing," I say as soon as the lights come up for intermission.

"Right?" Beckett says. "I'm telling you, you're going to be able to say 'I was there when.'"

I check my phone and see a bunch of Instagram notifications—likes and comments from some of my high school friends. Great dress! my cousin Minu has written all the way from Tehran. And then there's one from Rate the Plate: Looking beautiful, azizam. Glad to see you're having fun!

"That's weird," I say.

"What?" Beckett asks.

"That my mom didn't switch to her personal account before she wrote this." I show him the comment.

Beckett shrugs. "Well, you know the elders and the social media."

I shake my head. "Normally, yes. But my folks are way more social media savvy than is necessary. They know too much. I basically can't hide anything from them." Beckett gives me a raised eyebrow. "I mean, I definitely have to be careful what I post on social. I think they have an alert set up whenever I post *any*thing."

"So no odes to the purple Tisch flag, huh?" Beckett asks.

"Not yet," I amend.

"But maybe since callbacks for the streaming show went so well . . ." To my surprise, Liz had called me within twenty-four hours of my original auditions and asked me to come in again yesterday.

Despite the fact that the second reading seemed to go even better than the first, I laugh. "I mean, that would be an amazing thing to add to my List, but it seems like such a long shot."

"But they asked all sorts of availability questions," Beckett points out. "And they wouldn't ask those unless they were serious."

Beckett, with his two Broadway roles under his belt, knows so much more about the business side of, well, *the biz* than I do. I know he wouldn't bullshit me, but still. "Come on. How can my first New York audition result in a job?"

"It happened to me. Of course, it was my *third* audition where the problems started." He sighs. "My voice changed. And I grew about six inches."

"I still can't believe those would be problems."

"For a normal middle schooler, no. For a child star,

absolutely." Beckett shrugs. "Anyway, I'm pretty sure you'll be hearing back from the show soon. Exciting!"

"Yeah," I say, not voicing how I really feel—which is that it's kinda nerve-racking to suddenly hope I get this job. I was definitely feeling way more zen about awaiting the outcome when I was sure I didn't have a Snow Queen's chance in Hadestown.

The lights go down to indicate that act 2 is about to start, and I let the show carry me away again to a New York tenement in the early twentieth century.

By the time the final line is sung, there are tears streaming down both my cheeks. I'm on my feet, along with the rest of the audience, before the actors even begin their curtain call. I look over to see Beckett having the same reaction and, behind us, Beatrix and her date too. Beatrix has even drawn a crying emoji on her whiteboard—which she's apparently brought with her.

As we stand up to file out of the theater with the rest of the audience, I grab Beckett in a fit of inspiration. "I think I'm going to tell my parents. Today. Right now."

"Yeah?" Beckett asks.

I nod. "I'm just going to bottle all *this* up"—I move my hands in a circle, indicating the perfect, magic bubble of emotion that this tiny theater just held within it—"and tell them. My passion for it, that's got to be at the top of my list." Except I can't help but add, "Right?" I need validation that this is as good an idea as my drunk-on-live-theater mind thinks it is.

Beckett nods firmly. "Absolutely. Call them right now." He takes a look at the faces of the impatient New Yorkers behind us who are waiting to exit our row. "Well, as soon as you're out on the sidewalk."

And that's exactly what I do. As soon as I'm out the door, I step aside, whip out my phone, and navigate over to my mom's contact. I'm just about to press call when my phone rings.

It's a 347 number, not one that's in my contacts...

I accept it. "Hello?"

"Nasrin Mahdavi?" the familiar voice on the other end says.

"This is her."

"This is Liz from *Small Town Dreams*. I'm thrilled to be the one to deliver the fabulous news to you. You got the part! You're our new Leila!"

Beckett and I get a few stares as we spend a solid minute jumping up and down and screaming in front of the stage door.

"I guess we should try to get tickets to this," I hear a passerby tell her teenage daughter as she takes in our euphoric state. Eventually, a security guard lets us know that we need to move along before the actors start coming out.

Beckett walks me back to my dorm so that he can, as he puts it, "be a part of the triumphant walking-in-a-state-of-ecstasy-through-the-streets-of-Manhattan number you're about to have."

"You do realize we're not actually living in a musical,

right?" I've calmed down slightly but not enough to stop myself from bursting into a fit of giggles.

"Aren't we, though?" he replies. "Look at that literal steam coming up from the subway grate. You can't tell me an unimaginative set designer didn't make that happen."

I look to where he's pointing. "Ooof. And that river of green slime."

"Provocative," he replies.

By the time we've made it to the front of my dorm, I already have an email from Liz that Beckett forces me to read out loud. "'The *STD* set is going to be fast-paced, energetic, and, most of all, fun. But it's only going to work if we have everyone on board. And I already know we've picked the right team for the job.'"

"Uh, *STD*?" Beckett asks.

I double-check the email again before responding. "Um, yeah. That's ... an unfortunate acronym."

"Noted. Anything else in there?"

"It says my first day on set is the day after tomorrow. And the show is scheduled to premiere in four weeks." I look up from my phone. "Whoa. That's fast, right?"

Beckett shrugs. "A little. But maybe not so much in the world of web series. The internet is vast and needs content, Nasrin."

"Fair point," I say as I skim the email one more time. "I can't believe this."

Beckett grins. "Believe it, baby. Nasrin Mahdavi is on her way. So, are you still going to call your parents?"

The long-standing grin on my face freezes. In all the excitement, I've somehow forgotten that's exactly what I was about to do before I got the unbelievable news. I glance back down at Liz's email. "I mean, if the show is going to premiere in *four weeks*, what could be more concrete to show them than that, right?" A purpose premiering on YouTube.

"Right," Beckett says with a grin. "Looks like everything is falling exactly into place."

I'm brushing my teeth the next morning, when my phone's photo memories pops up with a video from last year.

I hit play and watch myself belting out, "Anything gooooooooooooooes!" on my high school stage. There's a sheen on my face that matches my spangly pantsuit. I remember so vividly the focus it took to find the breath for that high note, right after completing a paddle turn that took me all the way from one side of the stage to the other. The video was recorded from the wings by one of my best friends, Allie.

There's thunderous applause from off-screen.

Video me grins from ear to ear as flowers are thrown onstage and Allie shifts the camera so that it shows Maman and Baba standing on their feet in the front row. My dad's beaming, his mustache extra groomed for the occasion. My mom is wearing her fancy glasses, the ones with the tiny rhinestones in the corners of the frames. She's looking indecisively down at the dozen roses in her arms. *To throw or not to throw*, she's thinking, *because what if they get trampled or crushed or never reach their intended recipient and then wouldn't that be a waste?*

The mustard-colored curtain closes on us before she gets a chance to decide.

Backstage, the entire cast can't help but let out a roar, not one of rowdy middle-aged people on a 1930s cruise ship who just got finished belting out Cole Porter classics, but one of high schoolers feeling the elation of their final performance of the spring musical. Joel, the Lord Evelyn Oakleigh to my Reno Sweeney, lifts me up in a big hug and spins me around before going off to find his girlfriend in the ensemble.

That was the final performance of my entire high school career. A tear joins the beads of sweat on my face.

And then my best friend's voice comes from behind the camera. "You did it, you did it!" Allie says. The final frame is a close-up of the beige sequins on my pantsuit. The video cuts out at the moment she gives me a bear hug.

There are matching tears in my eyes now, and I'm surprised to realize it's from a mix of emotions, not just nostalgia. I have a flash of a much more recent memory, when Alan gave some very pointed criticisms about my paddle turns in front of the whole class. I didn't let myself cry, but I wanted to. I didn't call my mom either, even though I wanted to do that too. I let a couple of tears slide down my cheeks now for that girl in the video who was the star of the show without having to feel like she had to prove it every minute of every day. And one for the girl whose parents knew exactly what she was doing and beamed at her like that.

But then I wipe them away. I'm about to head into the real deal, I remind my reflection in the bathroom mirror. And soon I'll be able to tell my parents everything—and make them prouder of me than they've ever been.

I take out my phone and make sure to add a new bullet point to the top of my List: I'm starring in a real web series!

That will clearly be the opening *and* closing statement of my monologue. Once I finally tell them.

CHAPTER 6

No Time at All

✫

Maybe my first sign of trouble is that the first day of shooting for *Small Town Dreams* falls on the exact day I'm supposed to meet with Clara to figure out this economics double-major thing.

"Can't you reschedule?" Beckett asks when I tell him.

"I guess I'm going to have to." The show obviously isn't going to rejigger an entire shoot because of one secondary actor's calendar. The double major is, in fact, *major* to my List, so its delay isn't ideal. But then again, the web series might ultimately be just as important of a bullet point.

Clara emails me that she doesn't officially have availability for a meeting until the end of the month, but when I tell her why I can't make it, she kindly lets me stop by her classroom fifteen minutes before one of her classes begins.

"Well, first of all, congratulations on the show!" she says. "This is very exciting"—I'm about to say thank you before I realize she hasn't completed her sentence—"and a lot to take on. Even with just one major, and Drama at that, here at Tisch. Are you really sure you want to be looking at a *double* major?"

"Oh. Uh..." I don't think I can come out and say, *Not really, but I probably need it as a make-good to my parents for spending the past six months lying to them.* So instead I go with "I'm just trying to weigh my options. See if it's doable."

"Well, anything is doable if you want it badly enough," she says in her magnificent voice. "I did go ahead and print out the economics major requirements for you so that you can look them over." She hands me a sheet of paper. "You don't have to officially declare a CAS major until the end of your sophomore year, but it might be in your best interest to decide even sooner, probably by the end of this year, so that you can start taking your prerequisites. And I'd be remiss if I didn't tell you that given the rigors of Tisch alone, I doubt it'd be possible to complete requirements for both majors in less than five years."

"Oh," I reply in a small voice as I take the paper. Five years? That's an extra year of school to pay for, which isn't the news I intended to break to my parents. It was supposed to be: *Surprise! I'm double-majoring in business and drama! We both get what we want!* Not: *Surprise! I'm double-majoring in drama and economics—which neither one of us particularly wants. Oh, and this will now cost you another full year of tuition. Yay.*

"My class is starting soon, and I take it you have to run to your shoot, so I'll just say congratulations again." Clara gives me a warm smile.

"Thank you. And thank you for this," I say, waving the sheet of paper. But once I've left the classroom and gotten a chance to glance at it, my head swims from the course titles alone. If courses called Introduction to Macroeconomics and Introduction to Microeconomics make me break out in hives, what's going to happen when we've already been introduced and have to, like, go out on a full-blown date?

Beckett is waiting for me outside of Tisch as he insisted on wishing me luck in person before my first day on set. I show him the course list and watch his eyes bug out too. But he composes himself before he says, "On the bright side, you're already taking Statistics."

"Which I'm likely to fail," I reply. I take the paper back from him and check the time. "I'm going to have to pencil in a nervous breakdown about this later, because right now I'm scheduled to have a nervous breakdown about my first real acting gig."

Beckett beams at me. "Yeah, you are! Tell me everything, 'kay? Livestream it!"

I laugh. "You want me to pirate the show I'm in while it's shooting?"

"Mentally livestream it. And then report back to me with all the details," Beckett amends.

"I'll do my best," I reply, and then give him a quick hug before I dash away.

Petie and his crew are renting out a small studio space

downtown, which, luckily, is only a few avenues over from the main Tisch building. This at least makes it easier to go from class to shoot. But as soon as I walk in, I'm overwhelmed by the sheer amount of *stuff* in the small space. Cameras, cables, and monitors seem to be everywhere. There's a rack packed with clothes and shoes thrown haphazardly underneath it. Next to it is a small vanity table teeming with all sorts of glosses, powders, brushes, and various other makeup paraphernalia. And there are at least fifteen people running around, shouting directions, their voices blending into a cacophony within the cramped space. I honestly wouldn't know what details to give to Beckett because I'm having a hard enough time absorbing everything myself.

I look around for anyone I recognize and finally see Petie, who is reading from a clipboard and giving instructions to at least five people standing in front of him. I waffle about whether to approach him, but seeing as how he's my director, I swallow down my nerves and sidle up to the edge of the group surrounding him. One by one they thin out as Petie gives them directions like "Light for the bedroom scene" or "Can someone punch this joke up? Don't we have an intern from the NYU dramatic writing program here?" When I'm finally the last person standing in front of him, he asks, without looking up from his papers, "Okay, what do you need?"

"Um, I'm Nasrin," I say.

"Who?" he asks.

"The actress . . . who got the part of Leila?" I say hesitantly.

"Oh, right. Great! Leila's here, everybody!" Petie shouts enthusiastically to the room at large, though no one stops anything they're doing to acknowledge my presence. "Get yourself in hair and makeup," he says, pointing to the corner with the wardrobe rack and vanity table. "It's the home scene so just wear something casual, like you just got back from school. And come show me when you're done."

"Uh, okay," I say as I go to the rack and look it over. A wide array of totally unrelated outfits in different sizes stares back at me. I thumb a pair of red-sequined booty shorts, unclear on what sort of scene they would be used for.

"Hey, need some help?" I turn around to see Tru, the pianist from my audition.

"Oh, hi! Um..." I stare back at the wardrobe. "I've been told I need a just-got-home-from-school outfit?"

"Ah," Tru says as she looks over the rack. "How about..." She goes over to a small basket that seems to house accessories and takes out a scrunchie. "Put your hair up in this," she directs, and after I do, she takes a step back and looks at me. "Perfect. Go show Petie."

I look down at my own outfit: jeans, a tie-dyed sweatshirt, and my staple rainbow-checkered Vans. They're rehearsal clothes, not shooting clothes. "Really?" I ask.

"Trust me," she says.

And, sure enough, when I pop up in front of Petie, he looks me up and down only once before he says, "Great. Shooting Leila's scene in five, everyone. Get the bedroom ready."

"Are we going to rehearse the song?" I ask.

"Tru sent you the track already, right?" Petie raises an eyebrow at Tru.

"Yeah…" I say.

"We'll just roll," Petie says. "If there's a problem, we'll do another take. No, don't put that mirror there!" he yells to someone moving a skinny full-length mirror into what, I guess, is my character's bedroom set. "It'll reflect the camera."

I take out my script and give it one last glance. I have it memorized, of course, but—still—this is my first professional take.

Before I've had time to finish rereading even one page, Petie is yelling. "Leila! Position!" He points to a spot in front of the bed.

It's a little unclear whether Petie is using my character's name to help me get into the part or because he doesn't remember mine. But I pull my ponytail a little higher in its scrunchie and choose to believe it's the former.

"We're going to start with the line 'They want me to be a doctor. But I just want to sing!' And then you, you know, sing."

"Okay. Is the actress who plays Fen here?" Fen is Leila's best friend, and the person Leila is speaking to in this scene.

"Nah, you guys had different availability. We'll cut in her part later. But Tru will stand in for her so you have your sight line," Petie says as he motions for Tru to stand to the right of the camera.

"Tru will?" Tru asks, but still walks over to the spot Petie pointed out.

"I hope I don't butcher your beautiful song," I tell her nervously. The dialogue in the script leaves a little something to be desired, but the two songs of Tru's I've heard so far are stunning. This one almost made me cry.

"You'll do great," Tru encourages me.

"Okay, everyone ready? Camera," Petie yells.

"Rolling," Jeff, the twentysomething cinematographer, says. He's rigged a large iPhone fitted with some enormous lenses up on a stand.

"And...action."

"They want me to be a doctor, but I want to sing!" I say, and then the piano track starts and I do, in fact, sing:

"If wishes were pennies, my world would shine

Copper as good as gold, if my dreams were mine—"

"Cut!" Petie yells. "This lighting is all wrong. It's throwing this weird shadow across her face. We need to reset. Tru, is the orchestration of this song finalized?" He turns to me. "Take five."

"I think so," Tru replies calmly. "Why, were you thinking of something different?"

While they discuss the song, I take a seat in a folding chair in the corner. The "they" in "they want me to be a doctor" are Leila's parents, of course. And while Maman and Baba never asked me for anything as clichéd as becoming a doctor, something about it is a little too on the nose.

Because I'd never seen Baba so happy as when I decided to join my high school's business club in eleventh grade. I mostly did DECA on my guidance counselor's advice to "diversify my extracurriculars," and as an excuse to hang out with a few of my friends, including Allie. But Baba took it as a sign that I was finally showing interest in something he thought could shape the rest of my life. And then, when our group placed in a competition for business presentations, my dad was beside himself. His mustache practically reached his ears, he was grinning so hard, and he bought me the largest bouquet of flowers I'd ever seen. It was at least three times as large as the *Anything Goes* bouquet and it came with a little card: *For my future CEO.*

Seeing that card was the moment I realized that what Baba told me after the *Chorus Line* audition was stuck in his head, no matter how many lead parts I got or how happy I seemed. My parents would support my love of theater as long as it was strictly a hobby—something to pass the time while I was growing up—and nothing more. They'd cheer as hard as they did while I was performing in high school, but they never intended to be doing that once I became an adult. They could never support this as a real career.

Tru's lyrics make me remember the quote I so carefully stitched for Baba:

Great minds have purpose, others have wishes.

I know, deep in my heart, that my parents see my love of theater as a wish, not a purpose. And as Tru so poignantly wrote, "If wishes were pennies..."

But then I look around at the set. My wishes *have* turned to pennies. I'm getting paid to be here: to act and sing and dance (the first episode ends with a dance-off, naturally). I mean, it's *literal* pennies right now, but if I can eventually show Maman and Baba real paystubs from this job, maybe that'll be what they need to accept that theater can be just as viable a way to make a living as business. A purpose for me, one that would mean as much as the DECA competition. And I can finally stop lying and see them cheering me on from the audience again in real life and not just in a memory.

That's it: Here's a paycheck from an acting job! mentally makes its way to the top of my List.

There's a smile on my face by the time Petie barks for me to get back into position again, and as I deliver my line, I can feel how it's infused with more hope and meaning than in the last take. "They want me to be a doctor, but I want to sing!"

"And you shot two scenes in two hours?" Beckett asks me in Acting the next day. "That seems fast."

"It felt fast," I admit. "Petie doesn't seem big on giving notes. But Liz did also warn us that the low budget and quick turnaround was going to make it go, go, go."

"Well, I can't wait to see it."

"Beckett and Nasrin, your turn," Clara says.

We spring up from our seats and make our way to the front of the classroom while Clara sets the timer for two minutes.

"And go," she says.

"I saw you with that bitch!" Beckett screams.

"I can explain," I reply.

"No, you can't," Beckett says. "There is no explanation...."

His voice starts to falter, and there are tears already forming in his eyes. Damn, he's good. The exercise is to improvise a scene in which we each have to scream, laugh, and cry—logically—in two minutes. Beckett has managed to get two of the emotions in within fifteen seconds.

"Yes, I can!" I yell. "I was just walking her. It meant nothing. You know you're my only pooch, my widdle wet-nose muffin."

Immediately, Beckett catches my drift and goes on all fours, his tongue hanging out. The class laughs.

We finish out the absurdist scene and, afterward, get some notes from Clara and some of our classmates—a couple of them even complimentary about our comedic timing, while the rest are more pointed and focused on making our extreme emotions more believably grounded. It is a little strange that I'm getting notes from an improv game and not the real, professional shoot that I just came from. I also can't help but wonder how I'd ever be able to use an exercise like this in a real gig. Does it have a purpose?

Ugh, no. That stupid little sampler is haunting me.

I can't think that way. If I'm learning and growing on my path to becoming a better actress, then of course that's a purpose. I focus on my two classmates who are up next, determined to give them the most helpful notes possible.

CHAPTER 7

Oliver!

✫

"Hey, do you want to come to dinner at my parents' house this weekend? There's someone special I'd like you to meet," Beckett says later, while we're in line for paninis at Weinstein's dining hall.

"Your parents?" I ask. I've already met them a couple of times, but briefly when they've come by to drop off care packages for Beckett—which mostly contain the British Cadbury bars that are only available in their Upper East Side deli.

"My boyfriend!" Beckett exclaims.

"Oliver's here?"

Beckett nods. "Took the train in for the long Veterans Day weekend. Yes, hi." He turns his attention to the chef as he gets to the front of the line. "I'll have the Reuben, please."

"That's awesome!" I say.

Beckett's smile falters slightly. "Yeah," he says.

"It's . . . not awesome?" I ask.

"No, it is. I can't wait to see him. It's just . . . the reason he came in was sort of an emergency."

"Next." The chef looks at me.

"A Caprese, please," I say, and step aside with my tray before turning my attention back to Beckett. "Are you okay?"

"Not that kind of emergency. A love emergency."

I laugh. "What's a love emergency?"

"It's when two people who know they love each other seem to be heading for trouble anyway."

I wipe the smile off my face. "Oh no. What happened?" The panini guy hands both of us our foil-wrapped sandwiches, and we step to the salad bar.

"That's just it," Beckett says. "Nothing specific happened. I almost wish it had, because it'd be better than all these little things that are hard to pinpoint but just make me feel like crap." Beckett shakes his head as if to clear it, and a small smile is back on his face when he says, "But he's coming. And I'm excited."

"Well, I can't wait to meet him," I reply as I place some cherry tomatoes on top of my arugula.

"And have some biryani?" Beckett asks with a twinkle in his eye, clearly remembering our first dinner together. When I ordered the biryani at the Indian restaurant, it was because it was one of the few items that didn't sport a little chili pepper next to it on the menu. Unfortunately, when the waiter saw two brown kids sitting together, he automatically assumed that "no spice" really meant "low-level spice." Which, for me, was *high*-level spice. Beckett watched with a mixture of horror and amusement as I nearly choked on the first bite and downed my whole glass of water.

"Here," he said to me, pushing a small dish of raita toward me. "This will help. Have some, and then mix it in with the rice to eat the rest."

I spooned the yogurt into my mouth and followed it up with a chunk of delicious, warm naan for good measure. Then I mixed it in with the rice like he said, and he was right— the result was a lot kinder to my sensitive palate. Didn't stop Beckett from laughing through the rest of the meal, though.

Or continuing to tease me about it to this day. "Don't worry," he says. "I'll have my mom tell the restaurant she's ordering it for a white girl."

"You know Persian food isn't spicy!" I protest. Even though both Indian and Iranian food traditionally involve a lot of rice, stews, and bread, the spices that each culture uses are very different, and Persian food usually doesn't have any heat.

"I know," he says. "But teasing you about it is still fun."

Beckett's family's apartment is stunning. It's on Fifth Avenue, overlooking Central Park, and it's either been styled by a professional decorator or Mr. and Mrs. Banerjee have talents that go beyond their academic and medical ones.

The dining room is almost as gorgeous as the beautiful couple sitting across the table from me. Oliver is every bit as delightful as Beckett has led me to believe: funny, charming, and handsome. He's currently embroiled in a deep discussion with Mr. Banerjee about dissecting cadavers, which, even if it's not appropriate dinner conversation, still manages to show Oliver, his dimples, and his genuine enthusiasm for the subject in the best light.

Beckett catches my eye from across the table. "What do you think?" he mouths.

"Dreamboat," I mouth back, and Beckett nods as he places his chin in his hands and gazes moonily at his boyfriend.

I wonder if anyone will bring out the heart eyes in me in real life, instead of just on a stage. For years, I've told myself I'm too busy to date, or even develop a serious crush. Between school, all my dance and voice classes, and community theater on the side, a love life always seemed like something I could think about once I got to college. But now that I'm *in* college, I feel even busier than before. And then I think about how Beckett is having all this turmoil because he and Oliver are too busy....

Uppercase-D Drama might have to take precedence over the lowercase variety, I decide. At least for this year.

"How's your food?" Mrs. Banerjee asks me.

"Delicious," I reply. And it's true. I don't know what Mrs. Banerjee told the restaurant, but there's no heat at all in my vegetable biryani. Just the delicate flavors of spices like cardamom and cumin. I help myself to seconds from the white boxes in the middle of the table, plopping more yellow rice onto the fine china we're using for the takeout.

"Beckett, how are your classes going?" Mr. Banerjee turns his attention back to his own son.

"Well, I'm not saving lives or anything..."

"I'm not saving lives yet either," Oliver cuts in.

"...but I am getting better equipped to play a doctor on TV," Beckett finishes with a grin.

"Season twenty-seven of *Grey's Anatomy* won't know what hit it," Oliver says.

"Exactly." They've been like that all night, talking so quickly over one another, it's like they're in an Aaron Sorkin movie. Or an episode of *Gilmore Girls*.

"Are you enjoying your classes, Nasrin?" Mr. Banerjee says to me.

"Yes," I say. "They're challenging but pretty incredible." The combination of both helpful and positive feedback from Clara's class a few days ago is making this feel particularly true.

"I feel like all the college-set media did not prepare us well for higher education," Oliver says. "I was positive it'd be all frat parties and romantic drama in between, like, an hour of classes a week?"

"You expected that in *pre-med*?" Beckett asks him skeptically.

Oliver laughs. "You're right. Maybe I should've paid more attention to the shows actually depicting my major. But who would've guessed *your* major would keep you so busy?"

I see Beckett open his mouth and then shut it until it forms a straight slash across his face. I catch his eye, and when I do, he takes a deep breath and opens his mouth again. "Did I tell you that Nasrin just snagged her first big role? A part in a new musical web series," he says.

I blink. That's not what I was expecting him to say, and it takes me a second to recalibrate to all the compliments and cheers being directed my way.

"That's wonderful!" Mrs. Banerjee replies. "Congratulations!"

"Thank you," I say, trying to catch Beckett's eye again, but he's too busy stuffing his face with samosas.

"What's the show?" Oliver asks.

"It's a show called *Small Town Dreams*. It's about a group of kids who secretly get together to stage musicals because their town has banned them," I reply.

"So like . . . *Footloose*?" Oliver asks, and Beckett elbows him in the side.

But it's okay. He's not the only one who's made that connection. "Kinda," I say with a shrug. "I think it's still finding its voice. But the music is amazing. The composer-slash-lyricist is another Tischie named Tru Davis, and she's incredibly talented."

"That's so exciting," Mr. Banerjee says. "I think we need to order dessert to celebrate."

"And champagne?" Beckett asks.

Mr. Banerjee eyes him warily. "Fine. But one glass only."

Mrs. Banerjee has already whipped out her phone and navigated to Grubhub. "Chocolate Nutella cake okay? This bakery around the corner makes one that is divine."

"Sounds amazing," I say with a smile, getting up to help clear the table—and snag a moment alone with Beckett in the kitchen. "Hey, you okay?"

"Sure," Beckett says as he clears space in the fridge for leftovers. "Why wouldn't I be?"

"It just looked like what Oliver said may have bothered you. About him being surprised your classes were keeping you busy."

I see the flash of irritation appear in Beckett's eyes again, but then it's gone in a heartbeat. "Nah," he says. "He didn't mean it like that."

I nod. "Sure, but did it? Bother you?"

Beckett sits down heavily on one of his kitchen stools. "I mean, it's annoying to have your life's work dismissed like that, I guess. And also ... I'm the one who keeps trying to set a consistent FaceTime schedule, because we're *both* busy. And he's the one who keeps blowing them off."

"Sooo ... it does bother you."

"Of course not. Why do you ask?" Beckett deadpans.

I give him a small smile. "It looked like you were about to call Oliver out on it, but then you didn't."

"I mean, we get so little time together. I don't want to start arguing during the *one* weekend we've seen each other in two months. You know?"

"Yeah," I say slowly. "But ..."

"It's fine," Beckett says. "Really. He didn't mean it like that, I promise. It was just a stupid joke. And *you* are going to loooove this cake. Trust me." He shuts the fridge with a definitive bang, and I get the feeling it's not the only thing he wants to close. So I do the same with the subject as I help him carry the champagne glasses into the dining room.

Twenty minutes later, I find myself surrounded by a family that's not mine, all celebrating my achievement. The last, and only, time I had champagne was when my family toasted to my NYU acceptance—except they were toasting to something that wasn't real. As I raise my champagne flute in the Banerjees' apartment, I feel a pang realizing how much I wish Mrs. Banerjee's smiling face was Maman's.

That night, back in my dorm room, I ready The List on my Notes app and press the FaceTime button to call my parents. Maybe it's time to come clean, even without a big paycheck or the show premiering.

"How has your week been, Baba jaan?" Baba asks, his face framed in a corner of my screen, right next to my top I'm now starring in a real web series! bullet point.

"Good," I say. "I just had dinner at my friend Beckett's house. Delicious Indian food. Actually, I think they ordered from a restaurant that might not be on your app yet." Am I stalling while I gather my courage? Maybe.

"Really?" Maman asks, grabbing a pen from their coffee table. "What's the name? Where is it?"

I give her the information I dutifully collected from Mrs. Banerjee.

"I'm glad you're making friends," Baba says. "And what about classes? How are they?"

Classes. Right. This is it. My opening.

Should I start with Acting I or Music Theory or Sight Singing? Maybe Acting, since Clara is also my adviser and I can segue it into my double-major plan.

My double-major plan that is still not even close to solidified...

"Statistics is giving me a hard time," I hear my voice intone. Which isn't exactly what I was planning to start with, but definitely the truth, and a tiny bit closer to what I really need to tell them.

"Really?" Baba replies. "I'm surprised to hear that. You were always pretty good at math."

I was pretty good at high school math, but I've come to realize there's a whole world of difference between that and college-level courses. "Yeah," I say. "I don't know why, but it's been difficult to wrap my head around it."

"Maybe you should get a tutor," Baba suggests. "After all, if you fall too far behind in these initial courses, it's only going to get harder later on."

I open my mouth. Should I tell him that these courses are too hard because I just don't care about them like I ought to?

"That's a good idea," I say instead, blinking at my List. Because it *is* a good idea.

"Statistics is a terrific foundation for a lot of what's coming," Baba says, reminding me that it's a literal foundation for my double major. Really, I should have that buttoned up *before* confessing. Why rush into it when the double major, the premiere, and the paycheck are all imminent? If there's one thing that DECA competition taught me, it's the persuasive power of a well-thought-out presentation *with* real-world examples. So I agree with my dad and let the conversation come to its natural close.

After we hang up, I log on to the NYU boards and search for listings for local tutors. There are a few options, but one sounds particularly good, like they're specifically focused on the class I'm taking. Plus, their rates are very reasonable and they have excellent reviews. I start composing an email.

CHAPTER 8

The Rain in Spain

✫

When I duck into Korner Koffee on a rainy Monday and see who's sitting at a two-top in the corner, I nearly reopen my umbrella and walk back out again.

Unfortunately, he's facing the door, so he sees me come in and waves me over.

Max.

Like, really? Of all the tutors, in all the world...

His email address was a generic Gmail one, but mine was my NYU email, so he must have known exactly who he was taking on when he accepted me as a client. This is probably just one more way for him to lord my cluelessness over me. Great.

I sigh and trudge over to the table, standing above him with my bag held in front of me like a shield. "Okay, your little joke is hilarious. Thanks a lot," I say.

"What joke?" Max asks, looking as serene as the wallpaper of my meditation app.

I roll my eyes. "The fact that you knew it was me who needed the help, and yet you didn't bother to tell me you were StatsTutorNYU-at-Gmail."

"You didn't ask," Max says.

"Right. Well, whatever. See you," I say as I turn on my heel.

"Wait," Max says, standing up. "Don't you need my help?"

"Not really," I lie.

"Um, okay. But I think you're going to fail if you don't get it."

Fail Statistics and say goodbye to double-majoring in anything less than *six* years. I turn around, exasperated. "I do need help. Just not *your* help."

Max shrugs. "But seeing as how I'm already here. And you've already paid the thirty dollars for an hourlong session...."

Ugh. It's so infuriating that he's right. Maybe I can piss him off just as much if I stay. "Fine," I say, marching back to the table and throwing myself into the seat across from him. "What do you got?"

"Do you want a coffee or anything?" he asks, indicating the tall thermos sitting in front of him. It has *Fletcher Ranch* emblazoned across it in a white font, and I recognize it as the one he was sipping from when he almost told on me to my mom.

"No," I reply. "Let's just get this over with."

"So what do you need help with?" Max asks.

I narrow my eyes. "You know exactly what I need help with, since the professor you're assisting assigned it!"

"Okay, fine," Max says calmly. "So the descriptive-statistics-versus-the-inferential worksheet. Do you have it?"

I reluctantly take the two pieces of paper out of my backpack. "I'm okay with most of the descriptive stats questions. But the inferential..."

Max nods. "A lot of people have problems with that. It's a little more abstract than the descriptive. See, the whole thing is that you're taking the data you know, the ones in the descriptive, and you're applying it to a larger data set. An inferential one."

I raise my eyebrows. "So you're telling me that inferential stats are...inferential."

"An example is, say, a medical trial for a vaccine," Max continues as if I haven't spoken. "The trial is done with a specific group of people, let's say ten thousand people. Once they figure out how many of those people were fully immune from the disease, how many had adverse reactions, et cetera, then they can take that data and apply it to the whole population. That's where something like saying *This vaccine has ninety-four percent efficacy* would come in."

"Oh," I say, staring down at the sheet again.

"That makes sense?"

I'm loath to tell him so, but: "Yes."

For the next forty-five minutes, Max goes over the rest of the worksheet, explaining each problem with a patience, and clarity, that surprises me.

As we finish up the last problem, he asks, "So, are you feeling better about this?"

"Yes," I reply, looking in wonder at the worksheet that about an hour ago might as well have been written in gibberish.

"Good," he says, nodding.

"Just one question."

"Okay."

"How come you aren't this helpful during your office hours?" I lean back in my chair.

"I, uh . . . I was having a really bad day when you came in that day. Sorry," he mumbles.

"I didn't quite catch that," I say, cupping my ear with my hand.

"I'm sorry," Max says louder. "I *was* rude."

"Well, hallelujah for that," I say, lifting my hands into the air as I gather up the worksheets and stuff them into my backpack.

"Can I ask *you* a question?" Max says.

"Yeah," I say as I zip up my bag.

"Why are you taking this class? You're a drama major, right? I think you can take a lot of other classes to fulfill your science and math requirement if this one is giving you so much trouble."

I stop mid-zip and eye Max through my lashes. Despite his

apology, I definitely don't trust him enough to come clean. But I think I can tell a half-truth. "This class is really important to my parents," I finally say. "Even if it's not to me."

"Ah," Max says, clicking his pen closed. "*That* I can relate to."

"You can?" I blink.

"Yeah," Max says, staring for a second at his thermos before his attention snaps back to me. "Still, like I said, I think you're going to fail if you don't give it more of your time and attention." I narrow my eyes slightly and take him in, but it doesn't seem like he's trying to be mean. Just truthful.

I sigh. "Do you think...we can do this again?"

He nods. "Sure. We can set up weekly sessions for now. Do Mondays work for you?"

"Not always," I reply, thinking of *STD*'s erratic shooting schedule. This week, I'm booked on Wednesday and Thursday night. Next week, I'm on Tuesday and Sunday afternoon. "But I can do next Monday at the same time, for now. Does that work?"

Max nods. "Sure. We can meet here again."

"All right," I say, picking up my damp umbrella and slipping my bag over my shoulder. "Then see you, I guess."

"See you," he says as he stands up as well. For a minute, I think we're about to walk awkwardly out of the coffee shop together, but thankfully he goes up to the counter to refill his thermos and I'm left to continue the rest of my day Max-free.

✧

Coffee seems to be the theme of my week. Wednesday's shoot seems like it might never wrap up. Right before the nearest Starbucks closes at 9:00 p.m., Tru sneaks out to get herself a Red Eye and asks if I want one too.

"Please!" I say, taking out my wallet to give her some cash. "And make it a double shot."

"Ooh, you're a genius," she says. Twenty minutes later, she's back with four double-shot Red Eyes. "These two are for later," she adds as she hands me a warm cup.

Thank God she had the foresight to get them. I find myself microwaving the second drink at around 11:30—when we haven't even started shooting the musical number Tru and I have been hanging around for.

"I'm going to be a mess at my classes tomorrow," I confide to Tru as I park my butt against the wall by the wardrobe rack that she and I have been occupying for hours now.

"Me too," she says. "My first one is at eight fifteen."

I groan on her behalf. Tru is in NYU's musical theater writing grad program. She has a semester and a half to go before she graduates, but she's already told me she might have to extend her stay if the schedule for *Small Town Dreams* continues to be this demanding.

"Okay, everyone who's in the 'Sing Like You Mean It' number, you're up," Petie says.

"Finally!" Tru says as we both stand on legs that feel numb from disuse. All five main cast members are a part of this group number. We shot our intros to it earlier—each of us singing a couple of solo bars in our "bedrooms"—and now

72

we have to finish it up in the "alleyway" where our characters always meet to sing their banned musical hearts out. Because what better way to keep your parents in the dark than to belt out high Cs every night in the center of town? But as Petie told me the first and last time I asked about a particularly nonsensical line of Leila's, "Let the writers deal with the writing, and the actors deal with the acting. 'Kay?"

"Everyone ready?" Petie asks. "We're gonna roll on this one."

I would've loved to rehearse the choreography one more time before shooting, but alas, "We're gonna roll on this one" pretty much applies to every scene with Petie.

"Do you ever think about the days when everything was shot on actual film?" Tru whispers to me, practically reading my mind. "Which was expensive to process and therefore required much more forethought about what actually got shot?"

"Every day." I talk through my teeth. "Or at least every day that I'm here."

"Places, everyone!" Petie calls, glaring at me even though I am in my place. But I shut my mouth, put my arms up in fifth position, and get ready to "sing my heart out." *Or at least the part of my heart that's awake*, I think, as I barely stifle a yawn.

CHAPTER 9

Turkey Lurkey Time

✭

The Tuesday before Thanksgiving break, I wake up to an Instagram DM from my cousin Minu.

Guess what?! it says, followed by a million emojis of eyes and hearts and detectives with magnifying glasses.

What? I write back. But I don't get a response.

I've only ever met Minu in person once, when my parents took me on a long-delayed trip to Iran. We got along pretty well as ten-year-olds, but most of our communication since then has tapered off to social media likes and comments, so I don't really know what she could be referring to now. And my last class before break makes me forget about it almost instantly.

"Your assignment today, should you choose to accept it," says our Ballet instructor, Aleksander, "is to create your own one-minute routine to any part of this song."

He hits play on his phone and a very intense piano chord blares through, followed by a tinkling melody.

I wasn't too familiar with Celine Dion's "It's All Coming Back to Me Now" before this. But after spending an hour in the hallway with Beckett, insta-choreographing a melodramatic pas de deux to it, and two hours watching my classmates perform their own interpretations of the lyrics, I'm pretty sure it will never *have* to come back—because it's never going to leave my brain.

The lesson is a little reprieve before we go away for break, and we each get a chance to perform it twice, incorporating some of Aleksander's mild feedback—which is mostly enthusiastic declarations of "There's no such thing as too dramatic when it comes to Celine." I'm still humming the bombastic chorus afterward, feeling buoyed by the fun class. Beckett even re-creates our fish dive in Washington Square Park in farewell; he's going to visit his grandparents in California over the break.

As I'm on the way back to my dorm, I get a text from my parents asking me to FaceTime them. I wait until I'm recaffeinated and equipped with a yogurt parfait from the street cart in front of my building before I do it.

"How are you?" I ask when I see both their faces squished onto my screen.

"We're good, jigar talah," Baba says. "How are your classes going?"

"I'm pretty exhausted," I answer truthfully, biting my tongue before I can say that it's *physical* exhaustion, due to three hours of pliés, jetés, and perfect posture. Fun or not, my muscles still had to *work* to emote the intensity of Celine's delivery. "I'm really glad there's a few days' break coming up."

"We're going to miss you," Maman says.

"Me too," I respond. With the exorbitant ticket prices and the fact that it's such a short break, we decided that it wouldn't make sense for me to fly home for Thanksgiving. "But I'll be seeing you in a month," I say.

"Yes, you will," Maman replies.

"And you'll also be seeing someone else!" Baba adds.

"Who?" I ask, taking a spoonful of yogurt.

"Minu!" Baba says.

"What? Really?"

Maman nods. "She was accepted to Barnard and approved for a student visa. So she'll be in New York by the end of the year!"

"She's really excited that she'll already have family there," Baba says. "You'll show her the ropes, right?"

"Of course," I say. I immediately flash back to the one summer we spent together, when we were both equally obsessed with hunting down Easter eggs in Taylor Swift songs. There was a lot of late-night giggling, not to mention the vital question of which Taylor red-carpet outfit would suit our personalities best. Minu was particularly gifted at photoshopping them onto our pictures. Our in-person interaction was short-lived, but it was also the closest I ever felt to any family outside of my parents. "I'll write her and let her know that I'm thrilled."

"Good," Baba says. "It's tough being alone in a whole new country." He doesn't elaborate further, but I know that's a sentiment that comes from experience.

When I get off the phone with my parents, I DM Minu **again:** Never mind! My parents just told me the great news! Congratulations! I can't wait to hang out again! We have so many new Taylor eras to go through.

There's something strange and yet oddly peaceful about an empty NYU "campus." The school famously has no *real* campus, of course, but Washington Square Park—which is normally teeming with students—now feels like a different place, its natural inhabitants coming out of the woodwork. I notice multiple babies in strollers and old men playing chess on my way to Korner Koffee. The only other two customers in the café are middle-aged tourists speaking a different language and poring over a guidebook. At dinner, I can even take my time perusing the salad bar in the dining hall, since there isn't a long line snaking behind me.

The school has put together a Thanksgiving meal for the holidays, so I load my tray with Tofurkey, stuffing, and three bowls of assorted vegetables and plop it down at an empty table. My body is craving greenery after weeks of craft-service junk food at the shoots and hastily slurped-up smoothies in between my classes.

Greenery, and solitude.

Except the latter is short-lived. Just as I'm spooning a bite of stuffing into my mouth, I hear a throat clear and someone say, "Hey."

I look up to see Max with his own tray of Tofurkey and sides. "Hi," I reply a moment later, after I've swallowed.

"Mind if I sit here?" he asks.

"No," I reply, though I can't imagine why he'd want to. Our second tutoring session earlier this week went pretty smoothly, but I still don't get the sense that we should be anything other than academically involved. Heaven forbid we actually become... friends.

"Thanks. I feel like us Tofurkiers should stick together," Max says.

"Imitation birds of a feather?" I ask.

"Exactly," he says, and then flashes a smile. He looks like a completely different person when he smiles: open and friendly. It gives me time to take in his features in a way I haven't been able to when he's mid-scowl or donning his serious lecture face. His skin is fair, making the sprinkling of freckles on his nose stand out. His strawberry-blond hair is cut short, a small flop of it parted to the side, but mostly out of his face so that his sea-blue eyes are more prominent.

"So," he says as he unrolls his silverware. "You didn't tell me you were going to hang around campus over Thanksgiving too."

"You didn't ask," I say with a shrug, but give him a small smile so that he knows it's official: I'm calling a truce.

"True," he replies, nodding. "How come you didn't go

home?" He scoops some peas onto his spoon and shovels them into his mouth.

"The plane ticket was too expensive, and the holiday was too short to make it worthwhile," I respond as I take a forkful of mashed potatoes. "And I figured I'd see my parents soon enough over winter break. Even though I miss them," I add quickly, feeling guilty for making it sound like I don't want to see them.

"Makes sense," Max says. We sit in silence for a few seconds, both eating.

Finally, I break some bread (literally, I tear apart a dinner roll) and the silence with it. "What about you? How come you're staying?"

"I always stay for the holidays," he replies. "If I can find a job for the summer, I try to stay then too."

"Oh," I reply, surprised. "Your family..." But then I trail off, not exactly sure what I'm going to ask or whether it'd be appropriate given that we're near strangers.

But he gives me an answer anyway. "We don't exactly get along. It's really better for everyone when I'm not around." He gives me a tight smile, so different from the one minutes ago.

"I'm sorry" is all I can think of to say.

He shrugs. "Why? You don't have anything to do with them being convinced I've become an 'East Coast elitist.'" He makes air quotes before using his fork to stab his Tofurkey, possibly a little harder than necessary. His face and voice remain calm and measured, though, just as they always have outside the single tiff we had in his office. He shrugs. "Sorry. I just got that text message five minutes ago. I'll shake it off in a couple of minutes."

"Will you? Seems like a tough thing to get over in a couple of minutes."

"A couple of minutes and years of therapy," he amends.

"That sounds more like it," I reply, matching his slightly playful tone. If he doesn't want to talk about it, I certainly shouldn't pry—even though I'm now curious about what sounds like a complex relationship.

"What about you? Any childhood trauma you care to share over a dining-hall Thanksgiving meal? It might make it feel more like Thanksgiving, to be honest."

"No, no childhood trauma," I reply. "My parents are pretty awesome and supportive. Well...most of the time."

Max looks up at me. "Go on."

"What?" I ask.

"You can't just drop a tidbit like that and not expand upon it," he says.

"I could say the same thing about you!" I retort.

"Touché," he replies, and takes a sip of his water. I take the momentary gap in conversation to make a decision.

"They don't know I'm a drama major. They think I'm going to Stern. In fact...that's why I have to take Stats. So I have something to talk about with them."

Max puts down his glass. "Wow," he says. "That sounds intense." But he says it in a way that's somehow judgment-free, compelling me to go on.

"I stupidly thought I could just double-major once I got here, but it turns out, I can't. Not with Tisch and Stern, anyway. I can try for economics at CAS, though I have to make a decision about that sooner rather than later..." I ramble. "Anyway, sorry. This is all very boring."

"Uh...this is the opposite of boring," Max says.

"You're right. This would probably be entertaining if it wasn't my life." I focus on cutting up my Tofurkey, taking my time so that I can compose myself before I change the subject.

But Max doesn't let me steer the conversation away quite yet. "It doesn't sound entertaining either," he says gently. "It sounds...complex." Funny, since that's what I was just thinking about his family. "My parents know I'm studying at Stern. They just wish I wasn't. In fact, that day when I was so snippy in my office, it was because I had just broached the subject of them maybe coming up for graduation. They were already making excuses as to why they couldn't."

I blink at him. "What sort of parents wouldn't want their kid to attend one of the best business schools in the country?"

He snorts. "The kind who think business schools are for snobs. My dad was convinced I'd be taking over his ranch with my brother." I remember the *Fletcher Ranch* thermos he's always carrying around and realize it's not a coincidence that his last name is on a your-logo-here marketing product. "Dad was none too pleased that cattle never seemed to interest me that much." He indicates his Tofurkey. "Not even enough to eat them."

"Well, hey, at least we have something in common," I say, gesturing to my own plate. "Who would've thunk?"

"Maybe we have more in common than you realize," Max says.

"Really?" I ask. "What were you into as a kid?"

"Uh...math workbooks," he says. "I was a real nerd, even as a toddler."

"*That* I can believe," I say, grinning. "But I guess I was a nerd too. Just a theater nerd. I used to watch the PBS *Les Misérables in Concert* specials every chance I got. Both versions on a loop."

"We're practically twins," Max says.

"Identical," I agree, slathering my Tofurkey with cranberry sauce. "So your parents are paying for you to come here, though?"

"Nah. The only way I could do it was to get a full scholarship. I try to make up for my living expenses with work-study."

Ah. Now the TA thing and the on-the-side tutoring make a lot more sense. Still... "Full scholarship?" I ask. "You must have had an impressive high school GPA."

"Getting the hell out of Dodge is a great motivator." Max shrugs. "Anyway, you must've also had some impressive high school career to get into Tisch Drama. Were you the star of all your school plays?"

"Uh..." Is it hubristic to say yes? Or just the truth? "Yeah, mostly. After freshman year anyway." I don't add that it's because I was like an auditioner possessed after not making the freshman musical and felt like I had to prove to everyone—especially myself—that I still had what it took. "I just really love it, you know?"

He nods. "Yeah, I know."

"Like you love Stats," I tease.

"There is something very comforting about Stats," he replies. "Data can always be quantified."

"Huh," I say. "I never thought of it that way."

"So how did your siblings deal with you being such a superstar? Or were they all gifted too?"

"Easy," I reply. "Only child."

"Lucky," he says wistfully.

I laugh. "I never particularly thought so growing up. I mean, all the best characters in kids' books and movies have siblings. I felt left out."

"Trust me, you can feel left out if you have a sibling too. Especially if you're nothing alike," Max says as he loads up his fork with his last chunk of baked potato and sour cream.

"Fair," I say. "Actually my cousin from Iran is coming to New York at the end of next month. We're the same age, and she's pretty much the closest thing I've ever had to a sister, even though we've only met in person once. My parents want me to show her around."

Max nods. "That's nice of you."

"Persian hospitality is kinda legendary," I reply. "And my mom extended it to her by proxy. Which is also classic."

Max laughs.

"So what do you think?" I say, eyeing our mostly empty plates. "Dessert?"

"Hell yeah," Max says. "There are at least seven differ-ent kinds of pie. We can use the number of remaining pieces and types to draw some statistical conclusions if you'd like."

"I would not like," I reply firmly as I get up from my seat. "This is strictly dessert. No business."

Max laughs as he stands up too. "You're no fun."

"Oooh, boy, are we going to have to take a deeper dive into your definition of fun," I reply.

Max chuckles all the way over to the dessert bar.

CHAPTER 10

Razzle Dazzle

✫

The following week, I'm at Petie's tiny Brooklyn apartment, crammed in with the entire cast and crew of *Small Town Dreams* like Rockettes on a Macy's Thanksgiving Day Parade float. We've been invited to watch *STD*'s YouTube premiere together. I'm sitting on an apple crate that Petie must've stolen from the set, sharing a bowl of chips and salsa with my castmate Morris and drinking some local IPA Petie got from the brewery down the street. Though I return to soda after only a couple of sips of the bitter beer.

Petie casts the video to his TV, and we all hoot and holler as each one of us makes our small-screen debut. When Morris's character, Nathaniel, gets the brilliant idea to stage a clandestine musical in the town square at night—which, naturally, turns into a group musical number—we all get even more hyped than our characters, acting like this is the first time we've heard this epic idea. Then Morris starts singing along with his part and we all join in, my heart swelling with every note that we belt out. It feels almost like my beloved cast parties of yore—except those were always after our final performances, and this is at the beginning of this journey.

That's one difference between live theater and film that I hadn't considered. Another is the occasionally wonky lighting and camera angles. It seems those parts of filming are only invisible if they're done well. If the camera suddenly and inexplicably cuts to an extreme close-up, cutting off an actor's chin and forehead, you definitely notice.

But it's our premiere episode. There's gotta be some growing pains. And if Petie doesn't look like he's taking notes on stuff to fix while at the party, I'm sure he's taking mental stock.

The episode ends with the "If Dreams Were Wishes" number, and we all cheer for five minutes, right through the credits, two ads, and a clip of an old *Glee* cover (thanks, YouTube algorithm). On the subway ride home, I remember that two salient points of my trifecta of persuasion have now been checked off: the show has premiered and I got my first paycheck. I still need to pick my classes for next semester, but since Clara said I have a whole year and a half to formally declare the double major—and since my Tisch freshman classes continue to look extra intense—I'm leaning toward opting out of the requirements on her list for the time being. But I can still at least show Maman and Baba the list of courses, proving my intention to take them. My presentation is pretty close to perfect, and now that I'm so close to seeing them for Christmas break,

I've decided it makes sense to deliver my whole spiel in person. Baba himself has often waxed poetic about the importance of being physically in the room during a business pitch—and as a live performer, I couldn't agree more.

The following few weeks fly by like a montage thrown together to save valuable running time. My first semester of college is ending in a flurry of final exams, final projects, and the shoot, though I miraculously manage to squeeze in a few more tutoring sessions with Max before my Stats final.

He catches me outside the classroom after it's over. "So?" he asks, looking anxious. "How did it go?"

"I actually think I did okay," I reply. "I understood everything."

He smiles. "That's a pretty good sign. I'll text you when I have your grade?"

"That would be great," I say, and then reconsider. "Actually, how about you text me only if it's good news? If it's bad news, I might need an in-person delivery with a side of dining hall pie."

"You got it. So . . . have a good winter break?"

"Yeah. You too," I reply. "You're not going home, right?"

He shakes his head. "Not until the summer, for my little brother's graduation. You are?"

"Yup. Though my parents haven't sent me my ticket yet, which is weird. Sometimes they get super distracted with work stuff, though." I shrug.

"Have a safe trip. I'm sure I'll be texting you." He waves his phone at me.

"I hope you're right."

"Happy holidays."

"Happy holidays," I reply. He turns to walk away before I remember to say, "Oh, and thank you! For everything. You really helped me out."

He gives me one of his secret radiant smiles. "It was my pleasure."

"See you around."

"See you." I feel like he hesitates for a moment, but when he turns around and walks away, I decide I imagined it. It's only then I realize that I might not be seeing him, since Stats is over—and so, therefore, are our tutoring sessions. Huh. He's become such a staple of my life over the past six weeks.

I don't have time to linger on it, though. Forty-five minutes after my Stats final, I'm in the overheated studio shooting a new scene for *STD*.

The set has gotten more intense in the three weeks since the show premiered. Every week, our viewer numbers have gone up exponentially—but so have the reviews and comments.

I've read a few praising my performance and my singing, and a few . . . less praiseworthy. But I know from my experience helping out with my parents' site not to wade too deep into the world of internet commentary. Petie, on the other hand, seems to know no such thing. I guess he wasn't taking notes during the premiere because he was expecting the internet to do it for him.

He starts giving us directions to make our performances subtler, since JazzUnicorn25 thought we were all too "theatery" for their taste. Then he changes course and tells us to act out bolder since Thirty4BWay complained that there wasn't enough energy. The costume rack has gotten three overhauls in the past two weeks, and Petie hired someone to do professional hair and makeup (after a back-and-forth thread where commenters tried to one-up each other with clever puns and memes about why our looks, apparently, sucked so hard).

Now, in this newly frazzled set, Petie is waving a piece of sheet music at Tru. "The thing is, do we need a key change in here?"

Tru arches an eyebrow. "Tell you what. If you can point out where exactly the key change is, on that piece of paper you're holding, then I'll rearrange the piece."

Petie stops waving the paper and looks at it. He tilts his head as he tries to decipher the musical notation.

"Petie," Tru says gently but firmly. "I know what I'm doing."

"I mean, she *has* gotten the best reviews of anybody," Morris says casually as Anouk the makeup artist pats some concealer under his eye.

It's true. While reviews have been generally mixed, the one thing that almost everyone has agreed on is how catchy the music is. Well, everyone except Beav4Trees apparently.

Petie takes one more look at the sheet music, as if he might be able to suddenly glean magic powers enough to read it, but then he thrusts it back at Tru. "Okay, fine. Leila..." he says, turning to me. "And Anouk. Can we talk a little about these hairstyles we're doing on her? The ponytails are a little too high, apparently...."

Petie's obsession with the comments makes every aspect of filming take twice as long. Which is okay, now that the semester is over, but I sincerely hope he cools it down by the end of January, when I have to juggle the shoots with school again. Though the breakneck speed of his shoots was jarring at first, I've come to rely on it now, and I don't think my schedule can handle any more time on the set. Petie has thankfully, though begrudgingly, agreed to give us a couple of weeks off around the holidays, but I suspect that's because several cast members threatened to revolt if he didn't.

I book it back to my dorm at around eight p.m., my stomach screaming at me for not feeding it a real meal when I expect the rest of my body to be constantly exerting energy. I have to try to hit the dining hall before it closes. Beckett has already left for the break—on vacation to Playa del Carmen with his family, which he had mixed feelings about on account of missing more in-person time with Oliver—so I'll be dining solo for the foreseeable future. Or at least until I fly home. I'm just about to scan my ID to get into my building when a call comes through from Maman.

"Salaam," I say as soon as I pick it up. "How are you?"

"Fine, azizam, how are you?" Maman says, her voice echoing in the way it does when she's on speakerphone.

"Good. About to grab dinner. Salaam, Baba."

"Salaam," my dad says. "It's a little late for dinner, no? Aren't your classes over for the semester?"

"Today was the last day," I say. "I was just hanging out with some friends to celebrate surviving our first college semester." I try not to think about how the lies are coming out much more smoothly now, especially since I'm *so close* to telling them the truth.

"Ah. Very good," Baba says. "So you're all set to meet Minu at the airport tomorrow?"

"Yup," I say. "Flight comes in at one thirty, right?"

"That's right," Maman says.

"By the way, do you have our tickets home? I don't think I ever got an email." The plan is for Minu and me to have a week together in New York before I take her back to Indiana for part of the monthlong break in between semesters.

"Oh," Maman says. "Yes...I mean no. There's, um... there's a sale tomorrow, so we're going to wait to get them then. We'll send them to you before this weekend is over. Promise."

"Okay," I say. Do airlines have sales a week before Christmas? I shrug it off. There's no reason my parents would lie to me about that.

"You enjoy your dinner, and we'll see you soon," Maman says.

"Okay. Bye. Love you."

Our dance teachers told us in no uncertain terms that we'd need to keep our muscles loose and limber over the break, so I spend my rare morning off taking a jog around Washington

Square Park while listening to the *Spring Awakening* cast recording.

After a quick shower, I set off on the long subway ride to JFK. When I get to the airport, I check the arrivals board for Minu's flight. It just landed, so I settle on a bench, remembering from my own trip to Iran that it's going to take her a while to get through customs, especially since she's not a citizen. The terminal is bustling with the jubilant hugs of families reunited, fresh flowers being thrust into open arms, and celebratory balloons dotting the air. It's a joyful place, the international arrivals gate.

I quickly make up my mind that Minu should at least be greeted by a bouquet, and I brave the long line at the flower kiosk to buy a colorful bunch of daisies and carnations. When I've finally paid and stepped back out into the terminal, I spot Minu, recognizing the grown-up version of her instantly from her many Instagram selfies. She has long, dark, curly hair with a pair of gold sunglasses perched on top. Her thick eyebrows look like an ad for microblading, even though I know they're natural, and she's dressed in a chic patterned jumpsuit; in short, she's every bit as beautiful without a filter. She seems to be searching the faces in the crowd.

"Minu!" I call to her.

She spots me and smiles before walking over. "Salaam, salaam!" she says, kissing me on both cheeks. Then she switches over to English when she sees the bouquet. "Aw, for me? You shouldn't have!"

Her English is practically flawless, with just the tiniest

hint of an accent—nowhere near as pronounced as my parents', though they've been living here for twenty years. It sounds even better than when she practiced with me throughout that summer in Iran.

"How was your flight? You . . . don't look like you just spent twenty hours traveling." I take in her linen outfit—did she manage to find an iron on the plane?

"I changed in the bathroom here," she replies. "The flight was good. I—"

But she doesn't get to finish because, just then, we hear another shout of "Minu!"

I turn around, confused at who else in New York would know my cousin.

And then my jaw drops.

Because standing there with identical grins on their faces, their arms outstretched . . . are my parents.

"Amoo Nader, Khaleh Samineh," Minu says, walking over to them and hugging my dad first.

It takes me a minute to unstick my jaw, and then the soles of my Vans, from the floor. I stare cluelessly at my mom's open arms before I remember what she expects me to do with them.

"Hi . . ." I say breathlessly as I embrace her. "What's going on? Is everything okay?"

Maman laughs. "Everything's fine. This was meant to be a surprise. A good surprise, we hope. You're happy to see us?" She crinkles her eyes as she looks at my expression.

"Of course! It's great to see you," I say, as feeling slowly starts to return to my cheeks. "I'm just confused because I was expecting to see you in a week at home. But...yeah. This is great. Are we all flying back to Indiana together?"

"We are not," Baba says. "We're staying here."

"Really?" I ask, taken by surprise again. "For the holidays?"

"For...ever!" Baba gives a wild sort of cackle that makes me all the more certain that I'm experiencing some sort of fever dream.

"I think I'm missing the joke here," I say to Maman, still smiling, because it *is* good to see them, despite my confusion.

She smiles and shrugs. "It was your father's idea to surprise you. I thought we should keep you in the loop from the start."

Baba isn't paying attention to us, though, as he asks Minu about her flight. "In the loop about what?" I ask.

"Well, since Rate the Plate has always been a remote operation, we thought...why *can't* we move the whole thing to New York? So that we can be near our only daughter."

I never knew before this moment that words could tumble out of someone's mouth in slow motion; it feels like Maman's statement has to fight through molasses before it reaches my ears and gets processed through my brain.

My smile feels plastered on as I try to clarify what I think I just heard. "So, uh...you're moving to New York? Permanently?"

"We sure are!" Baba says, tuning back in now that Minu has assured him that her flight was comfortable. "Best part is: I can help you out with your schoolwork in person! In case you still need it."

I know I don't need help with my *real* schoolwork, because the amount of acting I'm doing right now—with the smiling and the twinkly eyes—is Tony-worthy. Especially since on the inside the only line running on a loop is *ohshit-ohshit-ohshit.*

CHAPTER 11

Out Tonight

✿

My inner monologue is running express to Panicville as Maman and Baba come back with us to my dorm. Luckily I'd cleaned my room up because I was expecting Minu to be staying with me for the week. Also luckily, I am not actually living an episode of *Small Town Dreams*, or I'd have a flyer for my secret web series lying around for my parents to find. I obviously can't tell them right this minute, not with the cousin I barely know standing here and not while my brain feels like a malfunctioning subway train, trying to reroute in light of this new information.

Perched on my bed, I listen numbly as my parents tell us the rest of their plans. They're staying in an Airbnb for now while they look for an apartment. They still expect Minu to stay the week with me.

"You two have fun; explore the city," Maman says.

"I'm so excited to!" Minu says. "I bet Nasrin knows all the best places to go." I'm not sure how accurate that is, since I've been spending all my time in New York running from class to shoots. And something tells me that Minu is not going to be too impressed with the smoothies at the Tisch café.

My suspicions are confirmed the next night, after Minu has apparently gotten over her jet lag and put on a full face of makeup by seven thirty.

"So, where are we going out tonight?" she asks me as she sits down on Beatrix's bed to put on her thigh-high boots. My roommate signed off on letting my cousin use her bed while she was gone for the break—literally; I still haven't erased her "Sure —Bx" from the whiteboard. "And is there a good place to grab dinner beforehand?" Minu continues.

"Uh..." I look down at my own outfit: I'm wearing the tie-dye sweatshirt again. I've spent most of the day in a haze, still trying to comprehend the utterly mind-bending reality that my parents are going to be living on the same tiny island as me for the rest of my college career—the fake or real version of it. That hasn't left much room to think about entertaining my cousin or even attending to my wardrobe. I try to collect myself now. "Depends where you want to go. Like a café or a park or something?"

Minu looks at me through the mirror, crinkling her nose. "Dancing. Drinking." She sweeps her hand from her shoulders to her thighs, indicating her tiny black dress.

"Okay. Dancing. I don't... Maybe I can Yelp something," I say as I take out my phone and add, "We can't go drinking, though, since we're not twenty-one." I sense Minu's blank stare before I look up and see it. "Sorry, the drinking age here..."

"Yeah, I know," she says, waving her hand dismissively. "But you have a fake ID. Don't you?"

"Actually, I don't," I say. "I'm not that interested in drinking, to be honest. And I'm so busy with school, there really isn't much time." *School and the show,* my treacherous mind corrects me.

"But...school is out," Minu says.

"Sure. Right now."

"Okay," Minu says, regrouping. "Do you at least know where we can get an ID?"

I shake my head. "No idea."

Minu takes out her phone. "I'm on it." Forty-five minutes later, she tells me, "There's a guy operating out of Bleecker Street. He can see us tonight. You ready?"

"Uh..." I don't particularly want to go get a fake ID, but I also don't want to rain on Minu's American parade. So I say, "Just give me a minute to get changed."

A half an hour later, I'm sitting outside a small walk-up on Bleecker Street, waiting for a printout of a Maine driver's license. Minu is inside, still talking to Eddie the ID Guy (his trademarked name and Instagram handle apparently). I think she's trying to finagle a discount by flirting with him.

In no time, she bounces down the stairs and hands me a shiny, laminated license with my face on it. My birthday is now four years earlier.

I look at it. "Wow, looks legit. I mean, I don't really know what a Maine license looks like." I rub my hand over the smooth surface. "But it feels like a real license."

"This guy has great reviews. Plus I got him to knock twenty bucks off." She looks pleased with herself. "So, where to?"

I'd braced myself for this inevitability, and I already texted Beckett begging him for a bar recommendation. He suggested an Irish pub on Irving Place that he claimed is lax with IDs.

When we get there, the bouncer takes our brand-new IDs and shines a light on them. My heart pounds a little as he does, but he waves us in with hardly a glance.

The place is busy. Most of the seats by the bar are taken, and all four pool tables in the back are being used. I spot a couple just getting up from a small booth in the corner and point it out to Minu.

"You sit down and I'll get us a drink?" she says.

"Sure," I reply as I head over to the worn green leather seats. I slip in and look around me, realizing it's my first time in a bar. It smells like a combination of wood and beer in here, though it's not exactly unpleasant. I notice two clipboards on the wall with a pen dangling from each—the sign-ups for pool and darts. Names are crossed out near the top, but there's a long list of groups waiting for their turn at the bottom.

Minu comes back and thrusts a pink drink in a martini glass in front of me. "It's cheesy, but I had to do it."

I look at the drink. "Do what?"

"A cosmo!" she squeals. "You know...like *Sex and the City*? Since we're young and in New York?"

"Ah," I say. "I've actually never seen it."

She stares at me blankly. "You've never seen *Sex and the City*?"

"It's a little before our time."

"Oh. Things come a little later in Iran..." Minu says, and I realize she looks embarrassed.

I quickly try to rectify. "But I'm hopeless with most pop culture unless it has a musical number. Ask me anything about Fred Astaire and I will dork out."

"I think I know who that is...maybe," she says.

"We should do a pop culture exchange program. You show me *Sex and the City* and I'll show you *Funny Face* and *Easter Parade*. Taylor as a palate cleanser in between." I take a sip of the drink and nearly cough it right back out as it burns down my throat. My very occasional tastes of beer and champagne have done nothing to prepare me for this searing combination of sickly sweet and fire.

"Okay, that sounds cool," Minu says, smiling as she smoothly sips her own drink. "So...I assume there's no dancing in here?" She eyes the wood-paneled walls, the middle-aged men playing pool, and the Springsteen-blasting jukebox skeptically.

"Er, no," I say. "I don't think so."

"No worries. Maybe tomorrow we can go to a club."

"Um, tomorrow I have something...." My voice fades. The something is a last-minute pickup shoot that Petie just scheduled. He wants to reshoot an entire Leila-and-her-parents scene from scratch.

"What is it?" Minu asks me, her big, doe-like eyes staring into mine. "Can I come?"

"Not really," I say.

"Oh," she replies. "Okay. I get it if you don't want me to hang out with your friends." Her glossy lips push out into a small pout.

"It's not that...." I waver. Should I tell her? I think about how I told Max I wanted Minu to feel like a sister—and, if I had a sister, I'm sure I would tell her this. Besides, it won't be a secret for much longer anyway. "Okay. I'll tell you. But you can't say anything to my parents yet."

Minu's eyes light up as she leans into the table with both arms. "Ooooh. Yes."

"So, the thing is, I'm in a show. A musical web series."

"Okay. And your parents can't know about it because... it's too sexy?" she asks.

"Oh, no!" I say. "Nothing like that. They just... don't really know I've continued doing musicals in college. They think I'm in business school here." I start playing with the stem of the maraschino cherry in my drink.

Minu leans back, looking confused. "Ooookay..."

"But I'm not," I say. "I'm in school for musical theater. And then I got this gig. And my schedule has been insane, to be honest, and then they show up here unexpectedly and..." I look up at Minu. "It's fine, though. It's the perfect way to tell them in person. Right?"

"Right," she says. "I mean, if you want to tell them."

"Oh, I do. I really do," I say. "In fact, I'm doing it next time we have dinner with them."

"All righty," Minu says, shrugging as if it's no big deal. And maybe it really isn't. Maybe my parents will have a similar reaction.

"Hey, you want to put our name down for darts?" I ask, feeling suddenly optimistic.

Her eyes flick over to the clipboard dismissively. "Maybe later. Let's finish our drinks here and then figure out what we want to do."

"Sure." I take another tiny sip, even though the taste is really not better the second time. Somehow, I feel like I owe it to Minu to finish, so I grin and bear it.

I decline a second drink, though, since I have to be in relatively good shape for the shoot tomorrow.

"I get it. The camera forgives nothing," Minu says. "So do you just want to go home, then?"

"If you don't mind . . ." I say.

"No problem," Minu says, popping up from her seat.

As we're leaving the bar, my phone rings. I look at the number: Max.

"Uh-oh . . ." He promised he would text if it was good news. I hit accept with trepidation. "How many different pies am I going to need to get through this?" I ask.

Max laughs. "Zero. You passed. B-plus, actually."

"Max!" I yell. "You were supposed to *text* if it was good news. You nearly gave me a heart attack."

"I'm sorry," he says. "I just wanted to hear your reaction."

"My reaction is relieved," I say. "And also...grateful. Thank you."

"You did all the hard work," Max says. "So congratulations."

"Thanks."

"Sorry for scaring you."

"It's okay. And thanks again." I realize I've thanked him approximately one billion times in the span of a one-minute phone call. There's a few seconds of awkward silence.

"You're welcome again. I guess I should let you go. Bye. Happy holidays. Uh, again."

"Happy holidays," I say as I hang up the phone.

"Who was that?" Minu asks me, eyebrows raised.

"Max. My Stats TA."

"Ooh, is he cute?" She grabs the phone from me and navigates over to his contact page. "There's no picture."

"Uh, yeah. I don't have a picture of him." *Is* he cute? I mean, I guess. "I think he's pretty cute?"

"You think?" Minu says. "Does he have an Insta? I can tell you yes or no for sure."

"I don't know." Somehow, I don't think so, but when I take my phone back and search for his name on the app, I'm surprised to see his profile pop up.

There aren't a lot of posts, and most of them seem to be of various coffee drinks and his dog from back home. But then there is one selfie of him *with* his dog, both their mugs sharing 50 percent of the frame.

Minu looks at the picture. "What's wrong with you? Of course he's cute," she says as she zooms in on his face. And then, before I can stop her, she's pressed the heart button under the picture.

"Minu!" I say, grabbing my phone back. "This picture is months old! Now he'll know that I was looking at his Instagram and stalking his backlog!"

Minu shrugs. "So what if he knows you're interested?"

"But I'm not!" I protest. "Not like that. He's my tutor... or he was."

"Okay." Minu takes one more look at the photo and then hits the heart again, unliking it, which might even be worse than liking it in the first place.

"Can I have that?" I say, taking my phone back before she can do any more damage.

"Sure, but next time someone asks, you can confidently say: *Yes, my hot Stats TA is hot.*"

"I'll keep that in mind," I mutter as I walk us back to our dorm.

That night, while I wait for Minu to finish using the bathroom, a notification pops up: MaxFletcher03 is now following me. I hesitate for just a second before hitting follow back. Because the alternative would only make this weirder than it already is.

CHAPTER 12

America

✦

The shoot the next day starts at 10:00 a.m. and will end whenever Petie thinks we've created material that will be universally beloved—so, basically, never.

I ask Minu if she's going to be okay by herself. "I take back what I said yesterday. I can ask the director if you can come to the set with me," I offer. "It's a long day. And a little cramped. But he'd probably be cool with it."

"Don't worry about me," Minu says. "I'll find some people to hang out with."

I take her at her word, mostly because I don't have time to worry about it—not when I'm so busy worrying about myself. It doesn't help that the scene we're shooting today is with Leila and her parents. All day long, I'm acting opposite Chaya and Ahmet—who play my parents on the show—and thinking about my real parents and the conversation that's ticking ever closer. And while yesterday it seemed like a great thing that I could tell them in person, I'm suddenly realizing the downside to my plan if they do, in fact, freak out. Eventually, Chaya notices my plaintive staring in her direction.

"You okay?" she asks.

"Oh, yes. Sorry," I say when I realize what I've been doing. "Family drama," I explain with a sheepish shrug.

"Ah," she says. "Well, at least you can use it for the scene, right?"

She's not wrong. Clara has spent a lot of class time talking about making connections between our character's feelings and our own. For example, if Leila is feeling anxious, a good way for me to channel that would be to think about what makes me anxious in real life. Usually the connection isn't quite as much of a 1:1 parallel, though, as it is in this scenario.

Leila's anxious because she's lying to her parents. And, uh, yeah. Same.

By the time I come home from the shoot a little before midnight, all I want to do is fall headfirst into my bed. When I open the door to my room, it takes me a second to realize that it shouldn't be empty—and that's only after I hear a familiar laugh from down the hall. I turn around at the exact moment that Minu comes out of room 4D with a bunch of girls I've never even said hello to.

"Oh, hi! You know Nasrin, right?" she asks my neighbors.

"Actually, no. Never been formally introduced," one of the girls replies.

"Let me do the honors. This is my cousin Nasrin. Nasrin,

this is Monique, Michelle, and Marin. Or 3M." The girls laugh. "I just came up with that," Minu says as she winks at me.

"Um, hi," I say, and almost follow it up with "Nice to meet you" before I realize how weird it is that my just-arrived-in-this-country cousin is introducing me to my own neighbors.

"You want to go out?" Minu asks. It's only then that I notice all the girls are dressed up in short skirts and heels.

"Uh...I'm really tired," I say. "Also, it's pretty cold outside, Minu. December here is no joke." I feel about eighty years old even as I say it, and Minu's pitying laugh sort of confirms it.

"We're pretty warm," one of the 3Ms says, holding up a bottle of Patrón. "Do you want a shot?"

"No, thank you. I think I need to go to bed."

"Okay," Minu says. "But if you change your mind, just text me and I'll let you know what club we're at."

"Will do. Thanks."

I, of course, do not text Minu that night. And I barely see her over the next few days. She's usually sleeping in Beatrix's bed during the afternoons when I'm home, or out with the 3Ms. (Now called the 4Ms since she's officially joined their crew.)

On Wednesday morning, I wake her up before I head out for a jog. She opens one eye, the previous night's eyeliner caked under it.

"What?" she asks grouchily.

"Sorry. It's just...I didn't want you to forget about dinner with my parents tonight." I've been obsessing over it for the past twenty-four hours, reading and rereading my List of

Reasons I Belong in Drama School and Will Be Fine Choosing This as My Career. (I retitled it the other day.) But I doubt Minu has the dinner on her radar in quite the same way.

"Oh, right," she says as she puts her face back into her pillow. "What time is that?"

"Six thirty."

"Okay." Her voice is muffled by the pillow. "You'll come back here and we'll go together?"

"Yup."

"See you," she says.

"We can have lunch together too, if you want. . . ." But I'm met by just a soft snore.

I go for a jog and run an errand at Duane Reade, the whole time psyching myself up for tonight's conversation. If I can do a Shakespearean monologue or, better yet, an entire dramatic scene in complete gibberish as we did during our last week of Acting I, surely I can talk to my own parents about something that genuinely means this much to me. Off-book, I remind myself, because reading directly from my Notes will make me seem less confident than I need to be.

When I get back to my dorm around lunchtime, I half expect Minu to still be asleep, but I find her perched on my bed instead, her phone to her ear and finishing up a conversation in Farsi.

"Baba," she mouths to me.

"Tell Amoo I say hi," I tell her.

She relays the message and after a few minutes is off the phone.

"So, lunch?" she asks.

I was sure she was asleep for that suggestion but am pleasantly surprised that I was wrong.

"Sure. Is soup okay? There's a great little place around the corner."

"Great."

We head over there and have both ordered—carrot ginger for me and French onion for her—when she brings up dinner. "So, tonight's the night, huh? That you're going to tell Amoo Nader and Khaleh Samineh about the show?"

I wasn't sure she remembered, but I nod. "The show and school."

"Cool," she says as she takes a sip of her water. "I saw an episode, by the way. It's cute."

"Thanks," I say, and then, before I can help myself, "You think my parents will like it?"

"Um, I think so?" Minu says with a shrug. "I mean, you know them better than I do...."

"Right. Of course," I reply. The waitress comes over with our soups, and I wait for her to leave before I say confidently, "I think they will. I'm visualizing that they will."

"Great," Minu says as she takes a spoonful of her Gruyère. "Yum. Melty cheese is life."

"Truth," I say.

My parents' Airbnb apartment is in Hell's Kitchen. I'm a little jealous of its proximity to all the Broadway theaters (and its place in the musical pantheon as the setting of *West Side Story*), even though I know Midtown isn't exactly the coolest part of the city to live in. But maybe all that theatrical history in the air will make it that much easier for my parents to understand why I need to be a part of it.

The apartment is a second-floor walk-up above a burrito place that smells divine. The heavenly aroma of black beans, rice, and cumin is only outmatched by the glorious scent of barberries, rice, and saffron that explodes from my mom's kitchen when she opens the door.

"Salaam, salaam!" she says, giving us each a kiss on both cheeks. "Welcome!"

She opens the door farther, and we walk into a stranger's apartment. It looks like it was decorated straight out of the blandest page in a Pottery Barn catalog. Everything from the walls to the furniture is in shades of gray and white except for the subtle accents of untreated wood. It's nice but also . . .

"Does anyone actually ever live here?" I ask.

"I don't think so," Baba says as he emerges from the bedroom and kisses our cheeks as well. "Solid investment, though. The owner is making a thousand dollars per week renting it out!"

He looks over at Maman, who nods.

Huh. Suddenly, me telling them I'm making fifty dollars a week on my web series seems less impressive. "Dinner smells amazing," I say, changing the subject.

"It's almost ready," Maman says. "I was just about to set the table."

"We can do that." I indicate myself and Minu.

"Oh, yes, of course," Minu says.

We head to the kitchen, and I busy my mind and hands by haphazardly opening cabinets until I find the plates and silverware we need. Maman is already bringing out the heaping pile of white and yellow rice while my dad is setting down two glass dishes: one piled with golden chicken, and a smaller one holding seitan for me.

"How are you liking New York?" Baba asks Minu once we've all settled down and helped ourselves to some food.

"I love it!" Minu says. "Just as exciting as I've always imagined."

"Nasrin has been showing you the ropes?" Baba asks.

"Yup," Minu says without missing a beat. Baba seems to be pleased with the answer, though I'm sure he'd be less so if he knew Minu's idea of "the ropes" was going clubbing with fake IDs. Oh well.

Baba turns his attention over to me. "So, Nasrin. Do you want to pull up your schedule for next semester? I'd love to see what classes you have and where I might be of help." His eyes sparkle, reflecting the shiny fork he's holding like a trident.

Okay, this is it. This is the perfect opportunity.

I clear my throat and take out my phone, but instead of pulling up my schedule, I pull up my List.

I'm off-book, but it never hurts to have a little backup.

I'm nervous, I realize, taking note of my quickened pulse and tapping foot. I haven't been nervous about speaking or performing in years, so these feel like foreign sensations. The last time I felt like this was my audition sophomore year, the one after the *Chorus Line* disaster. I had to spend months convincing my parents to let me try out again. But that turned out well, I remind myself, because not only did I make the play, but I nabbed the role of Rizzo.

I can do this.

"So my schedule," I say as I tap my curtain necklace twice, "is...different." There's a frog in my throat. I take a sip of water to clear it.

"Different how?" Baba asks. "More advanced mathematics, I assume."

"Mmmmm," I say noncommittally, because I can't seem to stop drinking this glass of water. Once I do, I have to tell them.

My dad opens his mouth again, but Minu jumps in. "I have my schedule, Amoo Nader. In case you want to see it."

"Of course, of course," he says as he takes Minu's phone. I shoot her a grateful look, and she shrugs as she pops a dried barberry into her mouth.

"Very interesting," Baba says. "So your major is Middle Eastern Cultures?"

"Yup," Minu says. "Should be easy to be cultured in my own culture, right?" She grins but then, seeing my dad's more serious face, stops. "Just kidding, of course."

"And what's your ultimate career path, you think?" Baba asks. "Diplomat? Professor?"

"One of those. Maybe," Minu responds, unbothered.

My first thought is that at least Maman and Baba's deep desire for purpose extends to everyone, and not just me. But my second thought is one of sheer panic. I glance down at my List and realize it's not enough. I'm not officially double-majoring yet. The show doesn't pay me enough. I don't have the concrete bullet points—*with* examples—that I need to win my audience over. Baba's faint look of disapproval over Minu's blasé answers will be a thousand times more potent when it's directed at me.

Maman halts my internal spiral by changing the subject. "By the way, we've nearly closed on an apartment."

"Already?" I ask, my voice scratchy.

"We found a good deal. It's in Washington Heights, so near your school," Baba says, looking at Minu. "A three-bedroom. I spoke to your dad, and he's very happy."

For the first time, I see Minu look a little unsure. "Why is that?"

"He was hoping to save some money on your dorming. And now he can. You'll be staying with us! Isn't that great?"

Baba is too focused on finishing up the last bits of rice on his plate to see Minu's face fall. But I do. And so, apparently, does Maman.

"Don't worry," she says gently. "You'll still get a good college experience, even without staying in a dorm."

Minu plasters on a smile and nods. "Of course."

Talking about the new apartment and my parents' deep dive into New York City neighborhoods (and restaurant districts) keeps the subject away from my schooling for the rest of dinner—until, that is, we're saying goodbye at the door. "Don't forget to show me your schedule as soon as you have it!" Baba says as he kisses my cheek. "I can't wait to see what we'll be discussing together."

Now it's my turn to fake a smile and nod.

That night, Minu and I *both* have something to complain about in my dorm room.

"I choked," I say miserably. "I *was* going to tell them. I was."

"It's okay," Minu says, patting me absentmindedly on my shoulder. "You need to build up to it."

"I need more concrete arguments," I reply.

"Right," Minu says before flopping down dramatically on Beatrix's bed. "And I need a body double. If I'm living with your parents, I'll never be able to go out again!" She drapes one arm across her eyes. "I should seriously get in all my clubbing now."

"And how am I going to discuss nonexistent classes with my dad?" I reply.

Despite the fact that neither of us seems to have a solution for the other, something about the commiseration feels nice. I've never really had anyone to complain about my parents with before, at least not like this.

Twenty minutes later, Minu has gone in search of the 3Ms and I'm back on the NYU website, looking at my spring schedule. It's absolutely packed with requirements for my major, except for one fun elective dissecting the music of the Beatles. I look around now to see if there's anything "business-y" I can swap in instead. I'll need it for my dad—and the eventual double major, I remind myself.

And there, fitting perfectly into my schedule, is Stats II.

I hesitate for only a moment before I start pressing the keys to make the switch. If nothing else, at least I already have a good tutor lined up.

CHAPTER 13

Some People

✦

Thankfully, Beckett returns to the city a couple of weeks before our second semester starts. This means that not only can I hang out with my friend again but I can invite him over for dinner—creating more of a buffer between my parents and my lies.

While we're waiting for the 2 train, I dig for the scoop on his break. He's already told me everything about his week on the beach in Mexico, but he's been pretty quiet about what it's been like since he got back to New York. "Have you been spending a lot of time with Oliver?" I ask.

"Oh. Yeah." Beckett looks toward the tunnel to see if he can spot the train's headlights yet.

I wait to see if he's going to go on. When it doesn't seem like it, I probe. "So . . . how's that been?"

"Fine," he says.

I wait again. When he finally looks over and sees my inquisitive expression, he gives a small laugh. "No, really. It's been fine. It's just...it *has* been a lot of time together. And also not enough time. I don't know. I can't quite explain it."

"Did you guys talk? About how hard it's been during the semester?"

"Not really," Beckett says. "It's hard to bring up such a downer when we have so little face-to-face time, you know what I mean?"

"Yeah," I say slowly, thinking that's the same excuse he gave when Oliver came home for the long weekend. I'm just about to voice that opinion when Beckett changes the subject.

"So...where are we at with the Great White Lie? They still don't know, right?"

"Um. Right," I say. "But they will. As soon as I can get a meeting with Clara and make the double major official. And also, as soon as the show hits a hundred thousand subscribers."

Beckett raises an eyebrow at me. "Why a hundred thousand?"

"It just seems like a good, round, *high* number," I say as we get on the train. "We're close, though. Probably another week."

"Okay, got it," Beckett says as he grabs on to a pole. "And how do they think we met? I'm not supposed to be a Sternie too, am I?"

"Nope, you can just be your glitzy musical theater self," I say as the train lurches into motion. "They think we met in the dining hall."

117

"Which we do. Practically every day," Beckett corroborates loyally. "And you said your cousin knows everything, right? About the show and Tisch?"

I nod. "Right."

"And we trust her?"

"Yeah," I say. "I mean, she hasn't given me a reason not to."

"Cool," he says. "I'm looking forward to meeting her. She sounds like Party Girl Nasrin." He starts singing an old theme song about identical cousins.

I laugh. "Yeah, no. Not quite identical."

But he still hums the tune once he meets Minu for real. The two of them seem to hit it off immediately. Unsurprising, I guess, given that they both seem to be blessed with an ungodly amount of natural charm.

My parents are not immune to it either. Beckett and Baba are quickly engaged in a spirited conversation about Beckett's classes. I try really hard not to be jealous that Baba is discussing Acting and Sight Singing and Broadway Dance Styles with Beckett so enthusiastically.

"Nasrin used to be into all those things too," Baba says. "She was very talented." The past tense? Really?

"I'm still into it, Baba," I can't help but say.

"Are you?" Baba asks, looking at me curiously.

And then I think, *What's the difference between 83,000 subscribers and 100,000?* And I will be double-majoring very soon. "Yes. As a matter of fact..."

I look around at Beckett's and Minu's expectant faces. Beckett gives me a slight nod and an encouraging smile.

"Right," I say, putting down my fork. "You know how sometimes I can have dinner on Mondays and sometimes on Fridays?" I'll start with the show and work my way up to school.

"Oh, are you doing community theater again?" Maman asks me.

"Not exactly," I say. "It's a little bigger than that...."

Maman gets a buzz on her phone, and she looks over at it.

"Nader," she says. "It's the CNBC producer."

"Pick it up," Baba says.

"Sorry, azizam. Be right back," Maman says as she accepts the call and leaves the room.

"We might be on a segment on *Mad Money*," Baba says to me, eyes shining.

"Wow," I say. "That would be amazing."

"Yes, but anyway. You were saying? You're still acting.... Where?"

I look at Maman's empty chair and think of *Mad Money*'s millions of viewers. 83,000? That's what I was going to lead with, really?

"Um...just this improv troupe. Nothing that exciting."

I focus on my plate of celery stew, trying to avert my eyes from Beckett's and Minu's raised eyebrows. I think I see them exchanging a look, blurry as they are in my peripheral vision.

"Oh," Baba says. "Well, that's great that you're able to keep up with your schoolwork and your hobbies. I'm proud of you."

"Uh-huh," I say, pushing around a piece of celery. The word "hobbies" settles around me like a hot, stifling mantle.

Maman comes back into the room, a huge grin on her face. "We're in!"

"Aha!" Baba says, getting out of his chair and going to give her a hug.

Congratulations abound from everyone at the table, including me. But I can't help but wonder why Baba can be so excited for Beckett and his major, so thrilled to be getting on TV himself... and not understand why I'd want the same thing.

I suddenly have a sagging feeling that maybe I'm never going to be able to tell them the truth.

A couple of weeks later, Liz comes onto the set of *STD* to deliver some good news.

"Our streaming numbers are doing great. And, consequently, so is our ad revenue. So..." She takes a dramatic pause. "Everyone is getting raises!" There's a collective cheer.

"Scale?" Morris asks hopefully.

"Uh, not quite," Liz says. "We're still not big enough to be a SAG/AFTRA production. But I can tell you that everyone is getting at least double." Another cheer goes up. "Come see me sometime today to get your new rate."

Mine turns out to be $124 per week, which is a substantial improvement. And our subscriber numbers are inching closer to 200,000 now. But I still haven't told my parents, because I haven't found the time to meet up with Clara and start the official paperwork to declare a double major. It turns out that, unfortunately, the one thing money can't buy is more hours in the day. Between my second semester starting, STD, and weekly dinner with my parents, I feel like I'm hanging on by a very fine thread—and increasingly less sleep.

Now it's Friday night at eleven p.m., and maybe I should be out with friends or clubbing with Minu (who has managed to find a way to sneak out of the apartment just fine) or even getting in beauty sleep (my definition of beauty is less pronounced under-eye circles at this point), but instead I'm sitting cross-legged on the concrete floor of the studio, waiting for the two-line scene I have to shoot. I've been waiting for it for over three hours now.

"Here," Tru says as she thrusts a Starbucks cup in front of me. "You look like you might need this even more than I do."

"Thanks," I say, hesitating for a minute, since this would easily be my eighth cup of the day and my stomach is already pretty churny. But then I grab it. I have to stay awake for at least a couple more hours, seeing as how Petie has spent the last two trying to perfect Morris and Juliet's first-kiss scene.

Petie is incredibly concerned about this scene because it seems the budding love story between Nathaniel and Susie—Morris's and Juliet's parts—has proven one of the more popular aspects of the show.

"Give me romance. Give me longing," Petie is telling them

both. "Linger. Lingering is sexy. Actually, yeah, Jeff..." He turns to his cameraman. "Can you linger too? I might want to make this a longer shot."

"Dear lord," Tru mutters from next to me. "How much *longer* is this going to be?"

"Right?" I say. "And my scene is literally two lines."

"Why don't you go ask him if you can shoot it first?" Tru asks. "This seriously looks like it's going to take all night."

"You think?"

"Why not? It won't hurt to ask."

"You're right." I stand up, Tru's confidence bolstering me as I walk over to Petie. Only, it falters as I wait and wait for him to notice me standing to the side. Finally, once Jeff is taking a few minutes to move a light, I get the courage to say, "Excuse me. Petie?"

"Oh, hey, Leila. What's up?"

"It's just..." Tru is within my eyeline and gives me a quick, confident nod. I stand up a little straighter. "Do you think we could shoot Leila's scene while you're relighting this one? I've been waiting around for over three hours. And I have a *really* early class tomorrow."

"Uh... let me see." He flips his script until he finds my scene. "Oh, yeah. We can probably knock this out quickly."

"Really?" I ask hopefully.

"Yeah." He steps into the middle of the room. "Quick change of plans. Nathaniel and Susie"—he points to Morris and Juliet and I'm a little relieved to hear him use their character names too—"take ten. Jeff, just swing that light over this way. Okay, let me see." He walks over and looks at Jeff's frame. "Great." He turns to me. "Whenever you're ready, Leila."

"Um, okay. Great," I say as I walk over to the alley set, take a deep breath, and nod at Petie.

"Camera," Petie says.

"Rolling," Jeff replies.

"Action," he says.

"Math test or rehearsal?" I say, then lean against the brick wall and softly sing, "Algebra or arpeggios?"

I sigh, then walk off outside of the frame.

"Great!" Petie says. "You're wrapped."

"Wait," I say. "Really? You don't want another take just in case?"

"Nah," Petie says. "You were perfect. Thanks." He turns to Morris and Juliet. "Okay, Morris and Juliet. Let's talk motivation." Huh. Their real names this time.

I trudge over to Tru, grumpier than I expected, since Petie just gave me exactly what I've wanted for the past few hours: permission to leave. Tru hands me my backpack, taking a look at my face. "Let me guess," she says. "You never talk about Leila's 'motivations,' do you?"

"Uh..." I look over at where Petie is actually directing his two lead actors, who both happen to be white. "Yeah, not so much. Sometimes I feel like..." I hesitate.

"What?" Tru says.

"Nothing."

"You can say it," Tru encourages me.

"Like...I don't know. Like all the characters of color are

just...sidekicks. I mean, I know I sound like an embittered supporting actress."

"No, you don't. You sound like someone who's observing the truth," Tru replies. "I've actually brought this up to both Petie and Liz, and every time they promise me they're working on juicier storylines for you and Yui and Calvin. But then I just get more directives to write love songs for those two...." She sighs. "I know I should feel grateful for this platform. That I'm getting *paid* to write songs, which is what I've been working toward practically my whole life." *But*...She doesn't say it, and yet it hangs there in the air between us.

The thing is, I don't say it either. "It is amazing that we're getting paid to do what we love. Right?"

"Right," Tru says. "Most people would kill..."

"To be in our shoes. Yes. Okay, I need to go before I pass out. I'll see you on Saturday."

"See you," Tru says.

We both smile, but there's a large part of me that wonders if we're trying so hard to validate each other's gratitude because we really need to believe it for ourselves.

CHAPTER 14

I'm Not That Smart

✦

I know I must look like death when I walk into my first Stats II class on Wednesday. After all, four hours of sleep has never done anyone's face any favors. But you'd never guess it by the enormous smile that Max gives me when he notices me sliding into a seat in the back of the room. I give him a friendly wave, but since I'm one of the last to arrive, we don't get a chance to talk.

Fifty minutes later, after my head is swimming with even more complicated stats terminology than last semester's, he walks over to me as I'm packing up.

"Hey. Didn't think I'd see you in this classroom again," he says with a grin.

"Hey," I say, hoisting my bag onto my shoulder. From the corner of my eye, I see Beckett peeking his head into the room, and I give him a tiny nod of acknowledgment; he had a class at CAS this morning too, and now we're supposed to head to Acting II together. "It's a long story." I focus my attention back on Max. "I'd tell you, but..."

"Then you'd have to kill me?" Max teases.

I give a little snort. "No, but I do literally have to run to make it to my next class."

I vaguely indicate Beckett at the door, and he gives Max a friendly wave. Max reciprocates before turning to me again. "Maybe you can tell me some other time. Over coffee or something? Or food?"

"Sounds good," I say. "I'm sure I'll be needing your tutoring services again." A quick glance at my watch tells me I need to get out of here—no pun intended but—*stat*. "See you, Max!" I say as I run out the door.

"Bye," I hear Max call out as I'm speed-walking down the hall with Beckett by my side.

"Uh," Beckett says. "You want to talk about that?"

"Talk about what?"

"How your super-cute Stats TA just totally asked you out?"

"What? He didn't ask me out," I say as we emerge from the CAS building, into the weak January sunshine. "He was talking about tutoring."

"Really? That's not the vibes he was putting out." He glances over his shoulder at me as we cross the street. "He's hot, by the way. How come you never told me?"

I laugh. "Yeah, that seems to be the consensus. That's what Minu said too."

Beckett raises an eyebrow at me. "You needed Minu to tell you he's hot? Are you okay?"

I roll my eyes. "I just never saw him that way. First he was a jerk. And then he was my tutor."

"And now..."

"He'll be my tutor again?" I say, shrugging. "Honestly, I think I'm way too overwhelmed to think about dating, you know what I mean?"

"If you say so," Beckett says skeptically as we step into the Tisch building.

It's our first day of Acting II, with Clara again, but she dives right in like we all just haven't had six weeks off. It's an intense three hours, though the difference between this class and Stats II is that I at least feel like I have *some* natural acumen and interest to draw from in here.

At the very end of class, Clara makes an announcement. "Just to remind you, this semester you'll have to volunteer at least ten hours at our black box theater. Sign-ups begin next week in the lobby." Oh, crud. Somewhere in the back of my mind, I already knew about the requirement, but that fact was crowded out by the ten billion other things vying for my attention. Ten hours throughout the whole semester doesn't seem too bad, though; surely, I can find a way to squeeze it in.

"And one more thing," Clara continues. "I know there are lots of flyers for student-run shows and auditions around here, so I wanted to make sure you saw this one." She takes out a blue sheet that touts the specifics for a new play called *The Walk-Up*. "Lucia is a student of mine and a singular talent.

I've read this play, and I think it's an incredible opportunity for anyone who's lucky enough to be cast. I'm leaving these here for those of you who are interested."

Beckett's face is radiating enthusiasm as he waits a polite half second before leaping to grab a flyer. I know why, of course. Lucia is the writer of *Birds of a Feather*, the Off-Broadway play we saw in the fall. And if the buzz about her is even halfway true, then she's poised to be the next Phoebe Waller-Bridge, Kenneth Lonergan, and Katori Hall all rolled into one.

Beckett thrusts a flyer into my hand as well.

I stare a bit longingly at Lucia's name. "You'll have to tell me how it is when you get the audition sides."

"Naturally."

From the corner of my eye, I see Clara heading to the door. "I gotta go ask her when her office hours are so I can set an advisory meeting. I'll see you later?"

"See ya," Beckett says, still absorbed in his flyer. It takes all my courage to fold up my own and *fly* after Clara instead so that I can set this double-major thing in motion once and for all.

"Ah, memories," Baba says, misty-eyed.

He is, unfortunately, not misremembering lyrics from *Cats*, but rather looking fondly at my Stats II worksheet and reminiscing about his business-school glory days. I don't respond, but I also don't think he's really expecting me to.

It's just as well since I seem to have come down with a small head cold, and I feel like I'm listening to the conversation through a fishbowl.

Maman and Baba's new apartment looks a lot more like them, and like home, than the rental. They've had most of their furniture and art and Persian rugs moved over from our house in Indiana. The sampler I sewed for Baba has a place of honor in the dining room so I can see it smirking at me from the wall above Baba's head—I never knew that embroidery floss could smirk, but now I can add it to the list of things that life as a new adult has taught me.

"And how are your classes?" Maman asks Minu.

I look across the dinner table at my cousin, who's cutting into a green pepper dolmeh. "They're good. Just really busy," she says.

"They must be," Baba says casually as he continues looking over the worksheet. "You never seem to be home."

"I know, right?" Minu replies smoothly. "If it's not a class, it's a study session. American college is no joke." She's looking over her food at me, grinning in a way that makes me realize "class" is code. I concentrate on the bowl of soup that Maman whipped up for me as soon as she heard me sneeze. It's really none of my business what Minu's doing with her time. And also, who am I to judge anyone for misleading my parents?

"Iranian college was no joke either," Baba says lightly, but then he seems to let it go, instead turning his attention back on me. "Did Maman tell you that I might be teaching some classes?"

"Classes?" I ask through my stuffed nose. "No. What sort of classes?"

"Continuing education courses on entrepreneurship." He taps the worksheet. "Doing all this with you has reminded me how much I miss the academics of business. I'd love to pass on some of my experience. Maybe even inspire a new generation of rebels."

You love rebels? Then you'll love this little anecdote about a rebellious musical theater major . . . is what I want to say. But my meeting with Clara is in just a few days. I'm *so* close to having a concrete business-esque major to show them. Plus, I'm definitely too run-down to broach the subject right this minute. So I go with "That sounds great, Baba. Do you think you have the time?"

"I think so. I mean, Rate the Plate is kind of running itself."

"I didn't know you anglicized my name to 'itself,'" Maman says, with a raised eyebrow.

Baba laughs. "Okay, fine. Your mother doesn't need me." He turns to Maman. "Is that what you want me to say?"

Maman nods. "The truth is generally the path of least resistance."

"But maybe there *are* some people who need me. Young people like you," he says, looking to me. "What do you think?"

"I think that would be really fun for you," I agree. *I wonder how fun it'll be for Minu, though*, I think as I glance her way. They live so close to Columbia that I imagine that's the school he's talking about.

"I was thinking maybe it'd be fun for *us*," Baba continues, leaning back. "I spoke with someone at NYU...."

I involuntarily drop my spoon into my soup, splashing a little onto my sleeve. What? NYU? Oh God. I've always heard the island of Manhattan is small, but it's amazing how my parents have managed to make it feel almost *claustrophobic*....

I dab at my sleeve with a napkin before picking my spoon back up. Breathe. It's okay. Because surely he wouldn't get a job before the summer semester. And I certainly will have told them by then. *Before* then. In fact, yes. By the end of February. That's a perfect deadline. I'll have squared away the double major, and who knows how big our subscriber numbers will be. Maybe I'll even be getting paid scale, or at least the SAG day rate, which is $125. There could be so many excellent facts and figures to share.

I tune back in just in time to hear Baba say, "He suggested I develop a curriculum before I start interviewing. And I thought, what better way to spend time with my daughter and help us both out, eh?" He grins at me.

"What do you mean?" I ask.

"I was thinking we could come up with some business plans together. A different proposal every week!" The joy radiating from my dad's face can only possibly be matched by the horror on mine.

"Business proposals?" I repeat stupidly.

"Yes! It'll be just like that DECA competition you liked so much. And it'll help me develop a more robust curriculum. Win-win."

The rice in my soup feels like wet cement as I swallow it down. *With what time?* I want to yell. And who knew that goddamn DECA competition would still be haunting me *years* later? Maybe if I had followed my mom's mantra about the truth...I mean, why couldn't I have stitched up that platitude as a sampler?

"So do you want to think of one for our next dinner?" Baba says. "It can be anything! A store. An app. Anything at all."

End of February, end of February, I repeat in my mind, timing my breaths along with it.

"Nader, the poor girl is sick," Maman butts in. "Can't you talk about this later?"

I shoot a grateful look over at Maman and am simultaneously hit with a strong urge to tell her everything. Maybe then I could get some homemade soup for my conscience too.

"Of course!" Baba says. "Hopefully you'll be feeling better by next week and then we can dig into your idea, hmm?"

"Sure," I say out loud, because what else can I say?

CHAPTER 15

It's a Hard-Knock Life

✦

It turns out Baba gets his wish, and my cold is cleared up by Monday. But somehow, I don't feel any better.

"On top of everything else, I now have to come up with a new business idea?" I sputter to Beckett during our smoothie break. "EVERY. WEEK?!"

"It's like he thinks you're a business major or something," Beckett quips.

I scowl. "Very funny." I'm in no mood to joke about this right now. "And all this so he can get a job teaching here." I look around the Tisch lobby. "Or not here. Stern. The school he thinks I'm going to." I groan.

"Okay, but as you said, it's not like he's going to get this job immediately. And you'll have told him about the Tisch thing by the end of February, right?"

"End of February," I intone. "Yes. Definitely."

"Okay, so that's one problem taken care of. And regarding the business proposal," Beckett continues measuredly, "how advanced do you think this idea has to be? Can you just come up with a new restaurant or something?"

"Sure," I say unconvincingly, tapping the plastic cup of my blueberry-strawberry-banana concoction. "Maybe a smoothie shop."

"That sounds good." Beckett tries to sound appropriately encouraging. "And then use what you're actually learning in school for the rest."

I shoot him a quizzical look.

"Improv," Beckett explains as he brings up his cup in a toast. "That's what you're supposed to be doing with your free time anyway, right?"

I hit my cup against his. The muted sound of two plastic cups bumping into each other perfectly mimics how artificial my life has suddenly become—or, at least, the version I'm presenting to my parents.

End of February.

Twenty minutes later, we walk the few feet over from the Tisch café to the entrance of the small black box theater that's in the lobby. A tall student with a goatee and a stylus behind his ear is manning an iPad.

"Here for crew sign-up or the audition?" he asks.

"Crew," I say at the same time that Beckett says, "Both."

I look over at him. "Well, I'll be auditioning tomorrow," Beckett clarifies. "Okay if I take a peek at the competition?" he asks the goateed student.

"I mean, no one's ever explicitly told me otherwise, so be my guest." He gestures to the auditorium door.

"Thanks, man," Beckett says, and they exchange a drama school nod of camaraderie. "We'll do the crew sign-up first, though."

"Here you go." He hands us the iPad.

Beckett looks it over. "Seems like we can pick tracks. Lighting, costuming, or set design. What do you think?"

"You want my opinion?" Goatee asks. Beckett's question was clearly directed at me, but we both go along with it.

"Sure," I say.

"Lighting is the dopest. I know two kids who actually switched their majors from drama to stage management after trying it out."

"That sounds like a pretty ringing endorsement," Beckett says. "What do you think?"

"Uh...well, I already have the most experience with costuming. So I was thinking that would be the lowest time commitment, if I already know what I'm doing...."

From the corner of my eye, I see Goatee's expression turn dubious. It's probably not often this program sees a slacker.

"Oh," Beckett says as he looks a little wistfully at the iPad.

"We can do different tracks..." I begin.

"No," Beckett says after the slightest pause. "I don't really have any experience with costumes myself, so I'd be happy to learn more."

"So you'd *want* to try something new," Goatee states pointedly as he pulls the stylus from behind his ear and hands it to Beckett. I notice he steps a little bit closer to Beckett as we sign up; maybe he's concerned my lackadaisical attitude is contagious.

True to his word, Goatee doesn't stop us from taking a peek inside the theater. The place is packed, which is not the norm for the student-run productions that seem to pop up every week. Clearly, Lucia's reputation is a huge draw, and not just for us.

I see her in the front. She's a tiny thing, her highlighted rich brown spirals put up in a poofy ponytail. But when she climbs up on the stage, she commands it. Without a microphone—and with hardly a word—she gets the entire auditorium to quiet down and listen.

"Thank you all so much for coming out to audition for *The Walk-Up*. As you may or may not know, this will be my directorial debut." There's a round of applause, which Lucia puts a hand up to stop. "Let's save that for when we know if my performance is applause-worthy." She smiles. "I'm going to be calling people in pairs to audition. And I might switch up the pairings, so please stick around until the end of the auditions."

"Oh, so that's why the sign-up sheet asked if we had a partner preference," Beckett whispers to me.

"It did?" I ask.

Beckett nods, and when he turns to me with his mouth softened and the soulful look in his brown eyes dialed up to eleven, I know exactly what he's going to ask.

"Come on, Nasrin. Let's go in together. You know we play off each other like nobody else. We could be the next Chenoweth and Menzel. Or Michele and Groff."

"Beck," I say with a small laugh. "Seriously? With what time would I do this?"

Beckett points to the flyer on the wall. "There are three audition times. None of those work for you?"

I look at the three dates spread over the next week. Magically, two of them actually don't coincide with any classes or the shoot. "Well..." I say.

"I knew it," Beckett says, grinning. "Which one?"

"But that just happens to work out this week. There's no way it'll work in future weeks," I protest.

"It's just an audition," Beckett says. "Think of it as a chance to get a Lucia preview. Plus, you can never have too much practice auditioning. Even web series end, you know...."

I mean, he's not wrong: I definitely do need more practice auditioning. If I'm lucky, I'll be doing it for the rest of my life. I take one more glance at the flyer; Beckett keeps tapping it lightly with his fingers. "Well... I think I can do Wednesday."

"Great! I'm free then too," Beckett says, his potential energy turning kinetic as he swings into action, takes out his phone, and manages to send me an event reminder for next Wednesday within seconds. I blink at my calendar app, wondering if he had somehow preprogrammed that in. "And I'll email for the sides. On both our behalves."

"Uh, okay. Cool," I reply, still not entirely sure what just happened.

"It'll be fun," Beckett says, grinning at me. "Our first audition together."

"I nod because even my exhaustion isn't immune to Beckett's infectious enthusiasm. "Yeah," I say, allowing myself to be swept away for just a moment. "It will."

CHAPTER 16

Ya Got Trouble

✦

On Tuesday, I finally, officially meet up with Clara for a true advising session. She sends me the link for the forms to fill out to declare my double major and tells me she'll sign off as soon as I submit them. Though she doesn't voice any doubts about my commitment to economics, she does give me one understated warning. "Since you already have two semesters under your belt without most of the economics requirements, you should be aware that next year, in particular, will be a lot to juggle."

"But anything is doable if you want it badly enough, right?" I volley her words back to her.

Clara smiles. "Right."

I wish I were actually as confident as I sound, but the idea of having more to juggle, and more head-swirling classes like

Statistics to boot, makes me feel hot and itchy. I need to set that problem aside for future Nasrin. Present Nasrin needs to book it to a family dinner and show her dad a half-page proposal for a smoothie bar that "innovatively" incorporates a couple of staple Persian syrups: sour cherry, and mint and vinegar.

I get a text from Minu right before I buzz up to my parents' apartment.

Hey, I'm not going to make dinner tonight. Can you cover for me? Just say I have a study session.

I write back: Okay . . . but where are you really?

She sends me a beaming selfie, glitter eyeshadow artfully swept across her lids, dark burgundy velvet ropes swinging behind her. Blurrier in the background is a sea of equally hot twentysomethings. New club opening. Wanna come? I can send you a pin.

No, that's okay. Have fun.

I relay the message to my parents when I arrive, and it's promptly forgotten as Baba insists on looking over my proposal.

"This is a good idea," Baba says, glancing over his reading glasses at me. "These would be fresh tastes to most of the American market. Could be the next acai or pomegranate juice."

"Cool," I say, taking a bite of spinach lasagna, one of the three dishes my dad knows how to make.

"But we'd have to work out the logistics of these specialty

ingredients. It's an expensive proposal," Baba says, looking back down at the paper. "Let's figure out if it'd be cost effective. How much do you think you'd charge for each smoothie?"

I sigh, frustrated that Beckett's prophecy that I'd have to improv a longer conversation was coming to fruition. "Ten dollars?" I venture.

"A bit pricey, but not unheard of in New York. Let's see if we can get some bulk pricing for the sekanjebeen."

Before I know it, Baba has pulled up a distributor website on his phone, gotten rates, and brought his small Surface over to do some advanced mathematics in one of his business programs.

"Nader, can't this wait for after dinner?" Maman asks, and I internally pray for him to agree with her.

"It's a working dinner!" Baba says, smiling.

To my dismay, Maman just shrugs.

I don't even get to finish my lasagna before I feel the first pangs of a stomachache. I think longingly of the days when we could have normal dinner conversations about my dance recitals or play rehearsals or even actual math classes I was taking, boring as they were.

When dinner is finally over, Maman asks if I'd like to watch a movie with them, and the thought of zoning out on the couch—in the company of my loving parents but without having to actually talk to them—sounds too good to pass up. I wrap myself up in the cozy throw blanket that my parents have had for approximately forever and settle down on the cushions, hoping the warmth will ease away my stomach pains too.

"You want to pick the movie?" Baba asks.

"Really?" I ask.

"Sure," he says.

After a couple of minutes of searching, I opt for *Tick, Tick...Boom!* and allow myself to finally relax, soaking in the inspiring story of Jonathan Larson's quest for musical theater glory.

The film is only three-quarters of the way through when my mom asks me if I've heard from Minu. "She's not answering my calls. And it's almost midnight."

"Oh," I say. "I haven't, but...let me see if I can get in touch with her."

Where are you? I text her.

Eight minutes later, my phone buzzes.

"Is that her?" Maman asks, her voice tinged with worry.

Nobody thought a club opening was going to end before midnight, did they?

"Um, yeah," I tell Maman as I quickly type. "Let me just find out what's going on, exactly." No, but they certainly thought a study session would.

Cover for me, k?

I stare at the brazen text.

"Is she okay?" Maman asks. "Does she need us to pick her up from somewhere?"

What would I even say? I can't lie to my parents, I type.

Dots appear and disappear and as I look down at the words I just typed, I come to the same conclusion just as Minu spells it out for me.

I think we both know that you can.

CHAPTER 17

Ladies Who Lunch

✧

I'm taken aback by Minu's text, but luckily my formal training kicks in and lets me come up with a plausible lie. "Maman, I just remembered. Minu told me she was going to a movie with her friends after her study session. That must be why her phone is off." Spending so much of class time thinking up motivations or backstories for my characters has made me a better storyteller, I guess.

"But weren't you just texting her?" Maman asks.

"Right," I say, my mind shuffling through a deck of deceit. "She checked her phone when she went to the bathroom."

"Oh," Maman says. "Did she say when she'd be back?"

"Uh...I think she texted me about it." I take out my phone and pretend to scroll through my old texts while firing off a quick new one to Minu asking her what time she expects to be back.

144

"Oh, right. It was one thirty or two. Midnight screening," I explain further. "New movie."

"Okay," Maman says, seeming to be satisfied at last.

Meanwhile, for the first time, I can't help thinking that telling Minu my secret was a mistake.

The next morning, I get another text from my rogue cousin.

Thanks for covering for me last night. I'm gonna make it up to you.

I'm about to type an insincere that's not necessary when I get another text.

I'm in front of your dorm.

Sure enough, Minu is standing on the sidewalk, looking fresh as a daisy, her long, curly hair tumbling to her shoulders. If she's hungover or even remotely tired from being inside a packed, sweaty nightclub just hours before, you'd never know it.

"Hi," she says, giving me a hug and a kiss on both cheeks. "Can I take you out for coffee? Do you have plans?"

"Uh . . . just supposed to meet Beckett for breakfast in the dining hall," I reply.

"Bring him along too!" Minu says.

I text him, and twenty minutes later, we're all standing in front of Korner Koffee, waiting for a table during their busy brunch service.

"It's so nice to see you again," Minu gushes to Beckett as she goes in for a hug.

"You too!" Beckett says enthusiastically as he shoots a

glance at me over her head. I know what he's thinking: He's not actually going to get the full scoop on the story I teased over text last night: Meet me for breakfast at Rubin tomorrow? Have I got a doozy of a story to tell you about my cousin.

I shrug, indicating that it'll have to wait for another time.

"Minu for three?" The harried-looking hostess pops open the door of the café. "A table just cleared."

"Great," Minu says, stepping aside to let someone leave the café. Since I'm looking down, I recognize the yellow-and-white Air Jordans first.

"Max!" I say, looking up into his face.

He looks startled for a sec but then takes off his head-phones when he sees me. "Nasrin. Hey."

"Hi," I say. "Sorry, I've been meaning to text you about setting up more tutoring, but this week has been crazy."

"Tutoring. Right. Sure, no problem." He takes a look at Beckett and Minu. "Well, you know where to find me." He lifts his thermos in a quasi-toast. "I won't keep you. Have a good breakfast."

He pops his headphones on again and walks away.

I stare at his receding back for a second as Beckett holds the door open for Minu and then for me. "That was weird."

"What?" Minu asks.

"He was just . . . I don't know. More like the old Max than the new Max."

"Well," Beckett says as he sits down and takes a photo of the menu above the counter so that he can zoom in and read it without squinting. "Did you ever give him an answer?"

"An answer about what?" I ask.

"The date," Beckett says.

"Date?"

"The coffee/dinner/whatever thing he asked you about." Beckett is looking at me like I'm being obtuse.

"Oh," I say, remembering now. "No, I didn't."

"Cold-blooooooded," Beckett sings.

"No, I didn't mean...I just forgot. Besides, I told you I don't think it was a date."

"Uh-huh," Beckett says.

"Well, if you're not going to date Max," Minu says as she casually glances at the menu above my head, "I'm happy to give that a go."

"Uh...okay," I say, unsure how to react to this statement. Because it would be weird to have my cousin dating my... stats tutor? Friend? Max?

"Speaking of dating," Beckett says, still staring at the menu on his phone. "This seems like as good a segue as any to tell you that Oliver and I are officially on a break." His voice seems to hitch on the word "break."

"No!" I say, gasping.

"Oliver. Your boyfriend?" Minu asks.

Beckett nods.

"Pic, please?" Minu asks.

Beckett scrolls through his phone to find one. I notice Oliver's not the wallpaper anymore.

"Cute," Minu says. "Bummer."

I try to ignore the fact that Minu's determination about

whether Beckett's change in relationship status is sad or not comes down to whether she deems Oliver attractive. "What happened?" I ask.

"Just the same stuff that's been happening," Beckett says with a shrug. "Long distance is hard. He doesn't really make time for me. Blah, blah, blah. Anyway, I'm fine."

"Good," Minu says. "I'm sure we can get you hooked up with someone else in no time."

"Nah. I think I really do need a break," Beckett says, putting his phone facedown on the table as if to punctuate it. "Anyway, I'm going up to order. Can I put anything in for you two?"

"French toast and a black tea, please," Minu says as she hands over her wallet. "And remember it's my treat."

"You don't have to treat me too..." Beckett says.

"Consider it a breakup brunch," Minu says.

Beckett barks out a laugh as he takes her wallet. "Okay. Thank you."

"I'll come up with you," I say.

"Sure," Beckett says.

"Hey," I say quietly once we're at the counter together. "Are you sure you're okay?"

Beckett looks at me, and for a second, I think he might be about to spill something. But then he shrugs. "I'm fine. It's not like I couldn't see it coming. I'm getting a Spanish omelet, by the way. In case you need help deciding."

I eye him for a second. He does look okay. But then again...

Beckett is a really good actor. Still, if he doesn't want to talk about it, then all I can do is take him at his word. Especially since I feel too drained to stir up extra drama.

"Sounds good. Make that two." After Beckett orders, we walk back to the table to wait on our food.

"So, get this, Baba liked the smoothie shop idea," I say.

Beckett nods. "Makes sense that you spent fifteen minutes on it and hit it out of the park."

"Well, not quite," I say as I sit down and unroll my silverware from its napkin. "He says he wants me to think of something more 'out of the box' for next week. Just...why is this happening, you guys?" I groan.

"'Cause you're clearly not busy enough, Nasrin. The universe needs to throw more stuff at you," Beckett says.

"Can we brainstorm something right now?" I plead. "I literally have no other time this week to think about this."

"Do an app," Beckett says.

"A new filter," Minu offers.

"An app that you have to download for a specific filter."

"Great idea," Minu says.

I take out my phone and quickly type out some of the ideas they're throwing around. Maybe I can impress my dad again if I spend another fifteen minutes cobbling something together.

While I'm typing up my Note, I get an event notification for tomorrow: Dinner at Goshneh. I forgot that I made a reservation at that new Persian restaurant months ago like my mom suggested. It was for two, but I realize I haven't invited anyone to go with me. I'm about to open my mouth to ask Beckett, but then I have a better idea.

After breakfast, when I'm back at my dorm, I compose a new text.

CHAPTER 18

You're a Good Man, Charlie Brown

✧

Goshneh is bustling. The small curbside tables, each placed next to a heating lamp and adorned with a centerpiece of a bowl of pomegranates, are completely full. And despite the frigid February air, there's a line of people wrapped around the white brick building, hoping to snag a walk-in seat. I stand to the other side of the gleaming gold door.

"Whoa," Max says as he approaches me. "This place is hopping."

I nod. "It got written up in the *New York Times* last week, so now it's impossible to get a reservation."

"So how come you got one?" he asks.

"My mom predicted its success before it opened," I say with a smile.

"Wow," Max says. "Thanks for inviting me."

"Of course. Ready to head in?"

Max nods, and we walk in, braving looks of envy from the human Popsicles standing by the large picture window. I give my name to the maître d', who shows us to a table near the back.

"Complimentary coat check?" she asks me.

"Sure," I say, and I hand over my long down jacket.

Max takes off his navy peacoat and passes it to the maître d' before he glances my way. "You look . . . really nice." I'm wearing a long-sleeved white maxi dress patterned with bold red flowers and paired with brown ankle boots.

"Thanks," I say. "I thought it might be a dressier sort of place."

Max looks down at his jeans and button-down in alarm. "I'm sorry. I didn't know. . . ."

"You look fine," I assure him. "Look." I point out the rest of the dining room, where at least half the men are wearing the standard straight-guy uniform, just like Max.

Max looks relieved as he takes his seat and starts removing papers from his satchel. I catch a glimpse of numbers and data sets.

"What are you doing?" I ask.

"Oh, I'm sorry. Did you want to do the tutoring after food?" he asks.

I laugh. "I didn't want to do the tutoring at all."

Max looks confused for a second but then colors. "I'm so sorry. When you asked me here, I thought it was to work. . . ." He indicates the sheets.

"Just a friendly dinner. If that's okay?"

"Yes, definitely. That's definitely okay." He sweeps the papers off the table and back into his satchel.

I pick up the small laminated menu and look it over. I recognize a lot of the dishes as ones my mom makes, but with fancy names like Dried Lime and Herb Stew instead of ghormeh sabzi, and prices to match.

"My treat, okay?" I say without looking up.

"Oh, no," Max says. "That's not necessary...."

"I invited you to dinner; it's my treat," I reply firmly. "I just got a raise at work." I haven't forgotten what he told me about his financial situation, and besides, I get a little thrill from knowing that my acting job can, in fact, treat us to this dinner. This and a small necklace from Etsy have been my only splurges, since I'm mostly trying to put money away to prove to my parents that I can handle the difference in tuition between Tisch and Stern.

"Congratulations," Max says as he raises his glass of water to me. "The show's going well, huh?"

"Apparently. The subscriber numbers seem to be going up every week," I say as I pick up my own glass.

"I'm not surprised. It's good. And you're great in it."

I blink at him. "You've seen it?"

"Sure," Max says. "I'm one of the subscribers."

I guffaw.

"What's so funny?" Max asks.

"Nothing. I just...didn't picture you as a musical web series kinda guy."

Max glances down at his own menu and smiles. "So quick to judge."

After the waiter comes over and we order our appetizers and main courses, Max asks, "So you said your mom knew this restaurant would be a hit. How come?"

"She's the cofounder of RatethePlate.com. It's a site—"

"Um, yeah, I know what that is. Your mom cofounded that?!" Max blinks at me.

"Along with my dad."

"Wow. So business is in your blood."

I groan. "Don't say that. That's what they think, but I swear if you cut me open it'd be all tap solos and 'I Want' numbers."

"Sorry," Max says. "From one black sheep to another, I should know better."

"It's okay," I say. "It's just been stressful since they decided to move to the city. And now my dad wants us to try and come up with a new business plan every week. As a 'thought exercise.'"

Max leans forward in his seat. "Really?!"

I laugh. "Would you like to get into your Nasrin disguise and go to weekly dinner with them? I'm sure whatever you come up with will be way better than what I have. Which, so far, is..." I whip out my phone and read my note aloud: "'Some kind of app. Or maybe filter?'"

"Hmm. Depends on what exactly this cosplay would involve," Max says as the waiter brings over our strained yogurt and cucumber appetizers. "I'm not sure I can fit into

154

your dress. And I gotta tell you, I can only vaguely carry a tune."

"Luckily, they don't expect me to sing an aria every night," I quip.

"Whew." He breaks off a piece of barbari from the bread basket.

But as he dips it into the yogurt, an idea occurs to me. "Actually, if you really want to come, you're more than welcome. I'm sure my parents would love to talk business with someone who actually cares about it."

"You serious?" he asks, his eyes wide.

"Sure," I say. "I'll double-check with them, but they love entertaining. And I'm positive they'll adore you."

"Thank you. That's...thank you." Max looks a little choked up, and I feel a surprising pang of guilt knowing that I asked him, at least in part, to get myself off the hook. "This bread is amazing, by the way. And this yogurt..." he says as he dips another hunk of barbari into it. "I don't even like raisins. How are they magically delicious in this?"

I look at the creamy yogurt, dotted with sprigs of dill and mint along with the cucumbers and raisins. "The right herbs can make anything taste perfect," I say. "My mom is always saying that."

"Does your mom make this stuff?" Max asks.

"A version of it," I reply. "I think most of the menu here is like an elevated version of Persian home cooking."

"I don't even know the last time I had *any* home cooking," Max says.

"So now you *have* to come over." I smile at him.

While we're waiting for our main courses, Max looks around the restaurant, the walls of which are decorated with elegant gold Persian calligraphy.

"Can you read that?" he asks.

"No," I say ruefully. "I wish I could. My parents put me in Farsi school for a couple of years, but then all my other dance classes and voice classes and everything else got too crazy. So I never got so far as to learn how to properly read it. And this is like cursive Farsi."

"AP Reading?"

"Exactly," I say.

"Well, it's beautiful," he says, taking it in.

"It is," I agree. We both glance around at the fine, inter-locked letters, and I'm suddenly hit with a flashback of Maman's and Baba's faces when I told them Advanced Contemporary Dance was only offered on Saturdays, at the same time as Farsi school. It was the first time I could remember seeing them look disappointed in something I'd said—though they never voiced it. I clear my throat. "So have your parents never visited you here? In New York?"

"No, not yet. The only time we've ever seriously talked about it was that once when I mentioned graduation...." He hesitates.

"Did you bring it up again?" I ask curiously.

Max shakes his head. "Reject me once, shame on you. Reject me twice..." He takes a sip of his water.

"But I think it might be worth trying," I say gently. "That day in your office was a while ago."

"Not much has changed since then," Max says, shifting in his seat before looking back up at my encouraging smile. "But maybe you're right. I mean, how often does your son graduate from college, right?"

"Graduate cum laude from one of the top business schools, you mean," I amend.

He raises an eyebrow. "How do you know I'll be cum laude?"

"Excuse me, but my schooling has taught me all about character studies," I say, taking a sip of my water. "So...am I right?"

"Uh, yeah. Probably," he says, hiding his smile with another piece of flatbread. "It's not official yet."

"Great," I say. "I'm going to tell my Acting professor. Maybe I'll get extra credit. Anyway, you were saying...you're going to invite your parents to graduation again?"

"That's not exactly what I was saying," Max replies, the smile still on his face.

"Let me ask you this: Who's hesitating more, you or them?"

His eyes squint a little as he thinks, the blue in them somehow bright even in the dim lighting. "A little bit of both. My mom claims she won't be comfortable in a room full of academics. But maybe it's more...me."

"Why?" I ask. "At least they know your major. That's a big win in my book."

Max gives a small laugh. "They do. But...I don't know. New York has felt like it's mine, without being tainted by memories of them being derisive or dismissive or..." He looks uncomfortable for a second as he glances around the room again.

"Or?" I prod gently.

"Offensive, I guess. Racist. I...don't even think I could take them someplace like this." He shakes his head as he looks around at the calligraphy on the wall. "I hate that about them. Feeling so embarrassed. It must be amazing to have parents you're proud of. Who've done something so cool."

"Yes..." I say, my stomach giving a little flip. "Although there's that other part of it, where I don't think they'd be proud of me if they knew what I've really been doing here these past few months." I let the words sit, heavy on top of the refreshing appetizer, and then follow them with ones that take me by surprise. "And there are times when I don't exactly feel proud of what I'm doing either."

"Really?" Max asks, eyebrows raised. "How come?"

Now that I've let myself think about it, it's like a floodgate's opened. The words that got bottled up with Tru come tumbling out. "Just some subtle things going on with the show. Nothing outwardly racist, of course, but things like the cultural ambiguity of my character. The way she doesn't seem to have much agency or story of her own but serves as a sidekick to the white characters..." I taper off, not having expected it to be Max that I'd tell all this to. Maybe it feels easier voicing it to someone removed from the work. I shake my head and laugh, trying to disperse the uncomfortable feeling that's settled in my chest. "Sorry! This is silly. No one complains about being a working actress. Especially during a fancy meal that's being paid for by said job." I take a sip of my icy water.

"It's not silly," Max says slowly. "Have you talked to the show creators about it?"

"Not really. My friend Tru, the composer, has. And I think the director said he's working on it." I shrug. "There isn't much time to harp on it, honestly. The shoots are constantly go, go, go."

"I've noticed you seem to always be running around."

"Yeah. But I'm also lucky to have this job. Especially at my age. I mean, people are really watching me, I guess. Even, would you believe it, my stats tutor!" My eyes twinkle at him from above my water glass.

"That guy?" Max says, his jaw dropping. "I thought he was just a numbers nerd."

"Me too," I say. "Me too."

CHAPTER 19

Whatever Lola Wants

✫

Baba seems less than impressed with my "business plan" for an app/filter that turns users' photos into headshots from different film and theater eras.

"Those one-off filters go viral for a minute but have no longevity," he says, glancing at the proposal I jotted down in my phone.

"Right," I say, realizing this might be the perfect opportunity to finagle an invitation for Max. "Well, I told a friend about the business proposals, and he looked at me like a puppy dog eyeing that." I point at the hamburger my dad just finished grilling on their rooftop barbecue. "He would really love to meet you and Maman. He thinks you're total celebrities."

"Who is this friend?" Maman asks, eyebrows raised.

"His name is Max. He's my Stats TA, and he's a huge

business geek. I'm sure you'd have lots to talk about." *Giving me an hour or so off from fudging my way through those same topics.*

"He's cute too," Minu says as she fiddles around with her phone at the table.

"Minu!"

"What?" she says. "It's the truth. And didn't you guys go out on a date this weekend?"

I blush. Both my parents' heads whip in my direction like they're watching a tennis match. I know why. They've been waiting at least a couple of years for me to tell them I have a boyfriend, or even someone I'm interested in. Maman has, anyway. "It wasn't a date," I say quickly. "He's a friend. And my stats tutor."

This seems to satisfy Baba. "Well, of course he's welcome to come over anytime. Can't disappoint a fan." He winks.

Maman is looking at me with a more knowing expression. "He's just a friend!" I repeat.

She raises her hands in surrender. "All right. You know any friend of yours is always welcome here."

"Thank you," I say. "I'll let you know when he can make it."

"By the way," she says, squinting at my neck, "is that a new necklace?"

My hand instinctively goes to the two chains around my neck: the short curtains pendant that I never take off, and the new, longer chain with two small silver charms on it.

"Yup," I say, hoping that'll be the end of the conversation.

But then she gets up and walks over to me, peering closely at the charms.

Shit.

One is a star, representing both the fact that I got a starring role on a show and my character's name, which means "night" in Arabic. But the other... is a clapboard. Like a movie clapboard.

My mom lifts it gently off my neck and looks closer at it. *She's going to ask what this means and... I don't know. Is this my opportunity to tell her?*

My stomach starts to tie itself into knots, practically wringing out the veggie burger I just ate.

But then Maman just says, "Pretty," and lifts a serving dish from the table to carry into the kitchen.

I let out a big breath, feeling my back lose its normal ballet-perfected posture in favor of folding in on itself in relief.

After dinner, Maman has left Minu and me to load the dishwasher when Minu pipes up. "So, I have another favor to ask," she says as she rinses some plates.

"Okay," I say, taking them from her and placing them in the dishwasher.

"Do you think you can sit in on my Medieval Persian Poetry class tomorrow? It's from three thirty to four thirty."

"What?" I laugh. Because surely she's joking.

"I got VIP tickets to Christian Siriano's Fashion Week runway show. But my professor told me my attendance is already a bit of a problem."

"Uh... it's, like, your third week of school."

"I know. What a party killer, right?"

I stop loading the dishwasher to look at her. "You're actually serious."

She nods and continues piling up silverware on the counter while I try to wrap my head around this crazy request. "Just take my Barnard ID. I'm sure you'll have no problem getting in. Who's going to notice a slightly different black-haired, olive-skinned girl? Besides, there's a family resemblance."

"Minu. I don't think whether we look alike is the problem."

"Then what?" Minu asks.

"How about . . . it's unethical? Also, I have my own classes."

"Right," Minu says. "And the shoot." She walks over to me and lifts the clapboard pendant off my neck. "This is pretty. Just like Khaleh Samineh said. But I guess she doesn't really know what it means, does she?" She says it so casually that it takes me a second to realize it's a threat.

"You *wouldn't*."

"It'd only be this one time," she says, and I can't help notice that she doesn't respond as to whether she *would* or *wouldn't*. "Please, Nasrin? This is such a once-in-a-lifetime thing. All that time in Tehran, I just watched the fashion shows online, hoping that maybe one day . . ." She shrugs, and I find my resolve softening, just a bit. "Besides, you owe me. Taking Max out on a date as soon as I said he was cute?" I'm about to protest, but her expression tells me that, this time at least, she's teasing.

But the way she looked before makes me uncertain that she's teasing about the other thing, the telling-my-parents

163

thing. And I can't tell them yet. Because surely, the way things are going, another raise is coming. And I can look Baba in the eye and vanquish his echoing words about never being able to make a living as an actress once and for all.

I numbly take out my phone and look at my schedule. I have Acting II tomorrow, and the audition for Lucia's play, but no shoot.

I can't believe I'm going to say this, but... "Just this one time?"

"Of course," Minu says, then gives me a big hug. "You're the best."

I honestly half expect the guard to stop me from getting into Barnard's campus. Then for somebody to stop me from entering the building. Or someone from Minu's class to recognize that I'm not her.

But none of those things happen. Minu has accurately predicted how easy it is to pose as her, plus her class is in a giant lecture hall with at least a hundred people in it. Not exactly the intimate salon of Acting II, where we all knew each other's names (and, thanks to an icebreaking exercise, biggest fears) from day one.

At least the subject matter is somewhat interesting. We're reading a section of Ferdowsi's epic poem, *The Shahnameh*. The text is translated into English but, for the second time this week, I find myself looking at the Farsi calligraphy and wishing I could read it. Maybe over the summer, when things are a little calmer, I could take some Farsi classes and surprise my parents by finally learning how to read and write it.

From Columbia's uptown campus, I take the subway back to the Tisch building. I've missed Acting, of course, but I should make the audition. I stayed up late last night to make sure I'd at least memorized the sides.

"How was Acting?" I ask as soon as I see Beckett waiting for me outside 721 Broadway.

"How was Impersonation?" he quips back. I'd indignantly texted him the absurd request from Minu the night before, so he knows the whole saga.

"Well, it worked just like Minu said it would." I shrug. "At least the class was interesting."

"Onetime thing, right?" Beckett asks.

"That's what she swears."

"Good," Beckett responds, nodding. "Because I really think you should only pursue one fake major at a time."

I playfully hit his arm. "Seriously, though, what happened in Acting?"

"Oh, you know. We all had to pretend we were prehistoric apes. A territory fight broke out between Massimo and Ezra within exactly three minutes. Sides were picked. Chests were pounded. I think somebody might have discovered fire, but I don't know for sure." I don't have to look at Beckett to know he's not kidding. Now I'm even sorrier to have missed it.

"Sounds like fun," I say ruefully.

We head to the black box theater downstairs, signing in at the front, and settle into a pair of auditorium seats that I soon realize are just a few rows ahead of Beatrix. I point her out to Beckett and whisper, "If she's auditioning, does that mean we might actually get to hear the sound of her voice?!"

Beckett gives me a faux jaw drop. "Imagine that!"

It turns out I don't have to, because Beatrix gets called up relatively quickly. And suddenly there it is: the elusive speech pattern of Beatrix Adamson. Her voice is lower and grittier than I expected. I had pegged her as a soprano, but now I'm pretty sure she has to be an alto. Though when Lucia asks her a question about a potential schedule conflict with another play, she's back to signature form: *I would give up my firstborn for this role*, her whiteboard proclaims.

Beckett and I are called up not long after. The play is a three-act about an apartment building in Long Island City, with each act focused on one of the three different apartments housing a pair of characters. It sounds like it would be complicated and disparate, especially since only two of the pairs ever interact with one another, a single instance when they both use the garbage chute at the same time. But Lucia somehow manages to tie all the threads together and tell a cohesive and gripping story.

In our audition scene, Beckett and I play bickering roommates who passive-aggressively try to one-up each other. We're in the "kitchen," and Beckett's character, Ali, is miming piling up uneaten leftovers that my character, Shauna, has apparently left to rot in the fridge. Meanwhile, after every line, Shauna is casually throwing a piece of garbage into the bin that is Ali's turn to empty. When I run out of things to throw from my side of the kitchen, I eye the invisible leftovers Beckett has been placing on the counter. Purposefully ignoring it, I casually walk over to an equally invisible notebook, mime tearing out a page and throw that out instead.

"That's a recyclable!" Beckett-as-Ali finally explodes.

"Oh, is it?" I say, and then toe the mimed piece of paper off the top of the trash bin. "I'll start a pile for those, then, shall I?"

We get huge laughs from the other actors in the audience, and my own face breaks out into a giant grin as soon as we've finished the scene.

"Great chemistry," I hear Lucia whisper to her producer just as we're getting offstage. The producer nods. Beckett and I beam at each other.

We wait around for Lucia to call auditioners up a second time in different pairings. But when Beckett and I get called up, it's together again. She hands us a few new pages and asks us if we'd mind reading from them even though we haven't rehearsed them. She gives us a minute to look over the lines, and when we perform them, we get more laughs. I see Lucia whispering to her producer again, but this time I don't hear what they say.

At seven, she wraps up the audition. I have to give her credit: The whole process took exactly the two hours that it said it would on the flyers. Maybe I need to introduce Petie to her for a lesson in directorial time management.

As we're leaving, Beckett turns to me and asks, "Not to jinx it, but... do you think that went as well as I do?"

"I mean...yeah. I didn't hear anyone else get some of those laughs."

Beckett nods. "Me too...Okay, okay. Let's not talk any more about it. Let's just see what happens."

"Yeah," I say hesitantly, realizing that Beckett's idea of jinxing it and mine might be quite different. As much as I enjoyed the afternoon, the last thing I need is yet another obligation. But then I relax, deciding I'm not going to worry about a nonexistent play schedule right now. There were so many people in that room, not to mention all the other audition times. What are the odds that I'll actually get the part?

CHAPTER 20

Popular

✮

"And five, six, seven, eight."

Juliet, in toe shoes, leaps into the air and lands in Morris's arms. They stare longingly at each other for a beat before breaking apart and floating to opposite sides of the set, Juliet's gauzy scarf—carefully chosen by costume designer Saul—creating gorgeous patterns in the air as she moves.

"And five, six, seven, eight," the new choreographer, Gigi, says again. This time it's my, Calvin's, and Yui's turn to step into the number. Quite literally, because we tap-dance as one unit in the background, doing a move that I can only describe as vaudevillian. It doesn't even remotely match the mood set by Juliet and Morris just moments before.

I can't really blame Gigi, because she's just following the directives from the script and Petie himself. But then again, she's also not stepping up to question the seemingly nonsensical change in tone.

I focus on my taps and try to get my head back into the routine; I've been more critical than usual today. Ever since I told Max about some of the things that have been bothering me about *Small Town Dreams*, it's like a portal has been opened in my brain, cataloging all the other things that the show could be doing better.

I also think I'm cranky and, quite frankly, in need of a nap.

But there's no rest for the wicked—or those who dream of starring in *Wicked.* Two hours later, my body is being put to the test with the intricate salsa routine that Beckett and I have been assigned in Contemporary Dance. By the end of it, I feel sore from head to toe; even my messy ballet bun is achy. But it's not the number that bears the brunt of my exhaustion.

"This routine makes more story sense than anything I did on set today," I grumble to Beckett as we're both changing back into our normal shoes. "And it's not part of a story!"

I expect some sort of reaction from Beckett, but when I don't hear anything, I look up from my feet to catch him staring in disbelief at his phone. "Beck?"

"We got the parts!" He looks up at me with wide eyes.

"The parts?" I ask dumbly.

"*The Walk-Up!* We're in."

I stare at him for long seconds before I find words, and when I finally do, what comes out is "You're kidding."

"When you're hot, you're hot, Nasrin," he says as he stands

up and offers a hand to help me off of the floor. "I'm just glad you're taking me along for the ride."

"Are you sure we *both* got the parts?" I ask as I put my sweaty hand in his.

"Yup. An email directly from Lucia, sent to the two of us." Beckett turns the phone so I can read the email, the subject line of which reads: *Congratulations to My Shauna and Ali!*

The text of the email reiterates that we had great chemistry, that she can't imagine anyone else for the roles, and that she's so excited for us to make her words come alive with our comedic chops.

"Ugh," I say, slapping my head.

"Um..." Beckett says off my look as he takes his phone back and quickly scans the email again. "We're reading the same thing, right? 'So funny and talented'..."

"Yes, I know. It's just...there's a rehearsal schedule too. Twice a week? Beck, most of my weeknights are booked with *STD*. They're already doing me a huge favor by working around my school schedule."

"Can't you give them this schedule to work around too? It's steady. It's only for two months, and one of the rehearsals is on Saturdays."

Beckett knows that we don't shoot on Saturdays on account of Petie using that day to work on the scripts with his cowriters.

"I don't think so," I say. "I feel like I'm stretched so thin as it is...."

"But weren't you *just* saying that the *STD* material leaves a lot to be desired? You know this play is brilliant, Nas."

"I know...." I shrug helplessly. "But what can I do? I can't add more hours to the day. I'd have to drop out of school or something...."

I shake my head at the absurdity, but Beckett looks unfazed. "It's not like you'd be the first. Plenty of people drop out of drama school when they get a real acting gig." He sees my open jaw and puts a calming hand on my shoulder. "I don't mean that you have to. I just mean, the one thing I know about this business is that when you get an opportunity, you kinda have to seize it. Like *STD*..."

"Which I increasingly suspect that I should have turned down." The words spill from my mouth without hesitation, and I realize it's because they've been like a splinter of truth, burrowing into my heart until they became impossible to ignore. It's so strange on set to feel both stressed out and overlooked at the same time. I can't even really explain it.

"It's a credit, Nasrin," Beckett says measuredly. "I know the material isn't exactly up to your standards. Or utilizing your talents in the best way. But it's going to lead to other things." Beckett is voicing every single inner response I've ever had to my misgivings about the show. "Isn't the whole point to show your parents you can 'make it'? That you can have a viable career doing this? I mean, you're not going to lie about acting to them for the rest of your life, are you?"

"Not even for the rest of the month," I immediately respond. "By the end of February. That's a hard deadline."

"Great. And when you do tell them, you can show them paystubs from your real acting gig. And an originating part in what is bound to become a real Broadway play someday," Beckett says. "*STD* is a way to prove to them that you can feed yourself. And this play is a way to prove that performing can still feed your soul."

I sigh. "I can't argue with that, Beck. But I wasn't joking about time being at a premium. If I do this, where would that leave school? I know people drop out, but I don't want to do that."

"So don't," Beckett says gently. "Talk to Petie and Lucia. See if they can work around your schedule. And if they can... yeah, it'll be a sleepless semester. But won't it all be worth it?"

I think about everything Beckett just said and realize he's right. If I don't seize every opportunity when I can, who knows if another one will ever come along? "I think so," I finally say, and smile a little at the thought of being able to perform some of Lucia's brilliant dialogue with one of my best friends—and for a real live audience.

It turns out Petie is in a really great mood at the next shoot. Some TikTok influencer did a spoof of one of our numbers, causing *STD* to trend for about an hour, and our subscriber count almost doubled.

173

So when I take the opportunity to ask him if I can skip shooting on Thursday nights, he gives me a hearty grin and a "Sure! Maybe we'll even be able to hire a body double for you by the end of the week."

I watch him walk giddily away to talk to Jeff and our new set designer, Puja, about their next setup.

"Do you think he was being sarcastic?" I ask Tru, who's been a few feet away reworking a melody on her portable keyboard.

"Not really," Tru says. "He probably *would* use the extra money to hire a body double."

"Well," I say, slightly amused. "I guess I already know of someone who'd be perfect for the part." Beckett would be so pleased if his "identical cousins" prophecy came to fruition.

"I have to give Petie credit," Tru continues. "He's for sure investing all the revenue back into the show itself."

I look around at Puja, Saul, and Gigi in various corners of the set. Tru's right; however ambivalent I sometimes feel about the show, there's no doubt about Petie's belief in it. And when the person steering the ship has that sort of confidence, it has a way of trickling down to even the lowliest of oarmen. Maybe all my recent doubts are owing to nothing more than a lack of sleep.

"Well, I hope you got another raise, Tru," I say, feeling more cheerful than I have in a while. "Since your song is the only reason the TikTok thing even happened."

Tru gives a sly grin. "As a matter of fact..."

"Excellent," I say and hold up my hand for a high five. She

slaps it. "It didn't bother you, did it? That they were basically making fun of it?"

"Nah," Tru says as she stops playing a chord and makes a notation on the sheet music in front of her. "No such thing as bad press, right? Besides... they weren't making fun of anything we didn't already know."

It's true. In the video, Melanie, the influencer, played all five of our parts, melodramatically delivering ridiculous lines that weren't actually from our show but easily could have been. It didn't really bother me either.

And the good news is that now I can do the play, the series, and school. Maybe what Beckett said is right, and it'll be worth it to have one sleepless semester in exchange for all my dreams coming true.

CHAPTER 21

Feed Me

✦

"Are you sure this is okay?" Max is standing by the front door of my parents' apartment building, dressed in a button-down with slacks this time—khakis, to be precise. He's holding a bouquet of irises.

"Yes!" I say for the third time since our subway ride up here. "Promise. And, also, the flowers are totally unnecessary, but my mom will love them."

"Hello?" my dad's voice comes through the intercom.

"Salaam, Baba," I reply.

"Salaam, Baba joon." A loud buzz opens the front door for us.

I see Max adjusting his collar on his way up the elevator. I'm not sure I've ever seen anyone this nervous to meet my sweet, benign parents.

Baba is waiting for us in the hallway when the elevator door springs open. "Salaam, salaam," he says, giving me a kiss on both cheeks. "Hello! You must be Max." He extends his hand, and Max shakes it.

"Mr. Mahdavi. It's such a pleasure to meet you. I'm sure Nasrin has told you that I'm a huge fan of yours. Your Rate the Plate business model was revolutionary."

"Well, I always say: Any fan of mine is a friend of mine," Baba says.

"Baba," I groan.

"What? I'm not allowed to have Baba jokes?" He grins at me, and despite his corniness, I can't help but smile.

"Hello! Welcome!" Maman is coming out of the kitchen as we walk into the apartment, holding a basket of glistening, just-washed fruit that she places on the coffee table. Max shakes her hand too before she indicates the couch. "Have a seat. Can I get you anything to drink? Water? Seltzer? Soda? Or are you over twenty-one?"

"I'm twenty-one, but seltzer is fine. Thank you so much, Mrs. Mahdavi," Max says as my mom bustles into the kitchen and my dad goes after her on the pretense of bringing out the good pistachios.

"Ooooh. The good pistachios," I whisper to Max. "See? They already love you."

"Damn, the good pistachios," a voice says from the doorway. "I brought those from Iran myself." Minu comes in, and while Max puts out his hand, she goes right up and hugs him.

"Nice to formally meet you. I've heard so much about you." She smiles at him, and I'm reminded that the one time they crossed paths was when Minu volunteered to date him.

"It's Minu, right?" Max asks her now.

She nods beaming. "That's me."

"Here, Max. You have to try these." Baba brings over a small silver dish shaped like a relief from Persepolis.

"The good pistachios in the authentic dish. Nice," Minu says.

Max picks a nut up.

"The trick, Max," Minu says as she picks one up too, "is you have to suck on them first, then crack them open." She proceeds to demonstrate, somehow making it look both elegant and a little...seductive.

"Uh..." Max asks, turning to me.

I shrug. "It's true. The shells are coated in lime and salt. It's what makes them so good." I take one and pop it in my mouth, knowing for a fact I don't look anywhere as appealing as Minu doing it.

Max follows suit. "Delicious," he says around the nut. "But how do I unshell it now?"

Minu laughs. "A true connoisseur would do it with her mouth." She takes a tissue and gingerly spits out the shell, chewing and swallowing the nut. "But you can just take it out and unshell it with your hands." She hands a tissue over to him.

I can tell Max is uncomfortable handling spat-out food in front of my family, so I try to change the subject.

"I've been telling Max about our weekly proposals, Baba. And he thinks it's a great idea." I refrain from saying that he's way more into it than I am.

"Oh, really?" Baba asks.

Max nods as he swallows his de-shelled pistachio. "It's such a pragmatic learning opportunity. Especially coming from you two."

Maman shakes her head. "This is strictly a Nader-and-Nasrin thing."

"Samineh is too busy running our actual business to putter around with hobbies," Baba explains. "But I'm really glad to hear you think so. I don't know if Nasrin told you, but I'm trying to come up with a draft of a curriculum for a possible teaching opportunity."

"She didn't," Max says. "But that's fantastic. I'm sure you'd have people clamoring to take a class from you. I know I'd be first in line."

I almost want to roll my eyes, but the thing is, I know Max is being genuine. He literally would clamor to do a weekly business proposal with my dad.

And maybe, given that these aren't conversations he can easily have with his own parents, the enthusiasm is warranted. I guess I know a little something about that. Though I have to remind myself the situation isn't exactly identical; my parents were at least supportive of my high school performing arts career, whereas Max's parents may never have understood him at all.

"Nasrin, are you busy Sunday at four?" Maman's words

pull me out of my thoughts. "We were thinking of hitting up the Chef Battle NYC event. It sounds as if it'll be like a live episode of *Top Chef!*"

Back at home, my mom and I could watch competition culinary shows for hours. But I don't even have to check my calendar to know that I have to spend Sunday afternoon shooting *STD.*

"I wish I could," I say. "There's, uh, an all-day freshman seminar at Stern, though. Kinda like this...." I indicate the lively discussion my dad and Max are immersed in. "But more expensive."

"Nasrin and I were going to try to do some more fine-tuned budgeting for her smoothie shop today," we hear Baba say during the break in my conversation with Maman.

"You were?" Minu mouths to me, and I shrug.

"Would you like to sit in on it too?" Baba asks Max.

"I'd love to!" Max says.

"Okay, boys," Maman says. "After dinner, okay? Which is ready. So if you'll all follow me."

I let Max and Baba walk ahead in front of me, twin looks of elation on their faces. While I didn't particularly want to spend my evening doing budgets, it's certainly going to be a lot more palatable having a buffer in the form of Max.

And, besides, it's nice to see them both smile.

"The looks on the two of your faces when you brought up long-range planning...I won't lie, it was a little obscene." It's

Sunday and the first time I've seen Max since he left my parents' house an hour or so before I did on Friday. I'm sitting across from him at a tiny Israeli café in Gramercy. Ever since I took him to Goshneh, he's been keen to venture out past Korner Koffee for our tutoring sessions.

He gets a faraway look in his eye now. "Yeah," he says dreamily. "That spreadsheet's division of direct materials versus production versus labor was a work of art."

I snort. "If you say so." I take a bite of my falafel. "Do you want to come to all my family meals? It was the least stressful one I've had since they moved here."

"Ha! I wish," Max says as he takes out some Stats papers from his satchel.

"Well, I'm sure you'd be more than welcome."

Max stops shuffling his papers around. "Are you serious?"

"Why wouldn't I be? You saw them gush over you. Trust that my acting skills are not hereditary."

"That was honestly one of the best nights I've had in a while. Maybe even since I started at NYU. The food. The company. The spreadsheets..."

"You are such a nerd," I say, throwing a napkin at him.

He raises an eyebrow. "Okay. But try to convince me that if your dad brought out the score to *Oklahoma!*, you wouldn't be geeking out just as hard."

"If only," I say, and it comes out sounding more sincere than I intended. If only that smile Baba had for what Max wanted to do with his life could transfer over to what I really wanted to do with my life.

"Well, if you ever want to go over the score of *Oklahoma!* with somebody, I did play Will Parker in my high school production," Max says casually, then starts talking stats at me like he didn't just drop a grenade.

"Hold up!" I say, lifting my hand to stop the numbers talk. "You played Will Parker? Can you tap-dance?!"

"Not really. But I can lasso. And do rope tricks," Max says. "You know, from growing up on an actual ranch."

"But you said you can't sing!" I say.

He shrugs. "I can vaguely carry a tune. Isn't that usually all a guy in the theater department needs?" His eyes twinkle with mirth.

"Touché," I say. "But you acted on a stage? And wore a cowboy hat? And chaps? Did you have chaps?"

Max laughs. "No idea. I had whatever was on the costume rack with the tag for 'Will Parker.'" He stares up at my shocked face and waggles his eyebrows. "This is really blowing your mind, huh? That I veered into your lane for a second?"

"It's not that it's my lane, it's just that . . . well, Will Parker is a fun role. *Oklahoma!* is a fun musical. . . . I mean, the Persian rep of Ali Hakim is problematic, but . . ."

"So what I'm gathering here is you think I have no interest in fun."

"It's a surprising layer of complexity to your character, sure," I say.

"I'm glad I can become a little more three-dimensional for you," he replies in a teasing voice. "Anyway. Do you want to do this?" He indicates the sheets in front of him.

"No," I say honestly. "But I guess we must."

Twenty minutes later, while we're in a deep discussion about something called a scatter plot (which, much to my dismay, does not include an actual story plot) I hear an all-too-familiar voice say, in confusion, "Nasrin? Max?"

I look up to see my parents standing above our table. "Hi. What are you doing here?"

"We read the review on City Eats. Figured we'd check it out."

"Oh. Duh," I say, smiling. Of course they would have read the review on the site they introduced me to.

"But what are you doing here?" Maman asks. "I thought the Stern freshman seminar was today?"

The smile slowly drips off my face. That *was* what I told them, wasn't it? About why I couldn't go to the Chef Battle Maman was excited about.

"Yes. It is," I say slowly, followed by an interminable pause as my mind goes completely blank.

"We're studying during her lunch break," Max's steady voice breaks in.

I look up at him, surprised. His face is calm and open. I guess he really is better at acting than I would've guessed.

"Ah," Baba says. "Well, I'm glad you're studying, but don't work too hard. You need time to refresh the well too."

I nod. "Right, of course."

"How much time do you have?" Maman asks.

"You gotta leave at three to make it for the rest of the seminar. Right, Nasrin?" Max looks at me.

I nod, grateful. That's when I told him I needed to ske-daddle to make today's shoot.

"Mind if we join you for the next half hour, then?" Maman asks.

Max looks at me for affirmation this time. "Of course," I say. "Let's see if we can borrow those two chairs."

Max gets up. "I'll get them."

Baba goes to help him, and before I know it, not only are they both sitting down, but they're already deep in conversa-tion about the imaginary plans for the imaginary smoothie shop.

"Two peas in a pod, right?" Maman asks me, nodding toward them.

"Yeah," I say. "You think Baba is gonna replace me?"

"His jigar talah? Never!" Maman says.

I smile. But deep down, something lodges in my gut like sand in a clamshell. It's obvious my dad would be a lot happier if I were really more like Max, sharing his genuine interests instead of just pretending like I do.

CHAPTER 22

My Shot

✪

I've spent the past two hours choreographing and rehearsing a solo routine to Billie Eilish—which probably sounds like a dream class to anyone, including high school me. Only it's been exhausting. And it ends with my professor remarking, "You spent too much time trying to showcase the perfect chassé and not enough time thinking through your intentions. The assignment was an *emotive* routine."

So now both my body and my ego feel bruised; even zipping up my jacket makes my upper arms scream.

"Hey, you have time to grab a coffee or something?" Beckett asks me, leaning against the wall of the class. His own routine got significantly more accolades than mine.

I check my watch. "I gotta be on set in forty-five minutes." I want to be on time so that I have some leverage when

I beg Petie to wrap my scenes before ten p.m. I've been putting off my Stats work all week, and I really need to review it before tomorrow's class. Plus I have to prepare a monologue for Acting.

"Oh. Okay. Never mind."

The tone of Beckett's voice makes me pause and look up at him. He's staring down at the floor and frowning.

I don't think I've ever seen Beckett frown.

"Forty-five minutes means I *definitely* have time for a coffee," I say as I link my arm into his. "Come on."

As soon as we've grabbed our cups and snagged a corner table, I wait for him to tell me what's bothering him. When he doesn't speak first, I nudge. "Hey, so what's wrong?" The clock on the café's brick wall informs me that I only have thirty minutes before I have to be on set.

"It's Oliver. We're over," Beckett says miserably.

"Oh," I say, trying to backtrack a bit in my mind. "Didn't you guys already break up?"

"We did, but...not really. At least, I thought it was not really. But he, apparently..." Beckett just sighs, takes out his phone, and navigates over to a new photo on Oliver's Instagram account. It's Oliver and another guy cheek-to-cheek, the camera so tight on their faces that their twin grins each reach one border of the photo. For his caption, Oliver has simply put the heart with a bow emoji.

"Oh," I say, frowning. "Wow. I'm sorry. Do you know who that guy is?"

"After some light internet stalking, I found out he's

another premed in one of Oliver's anatomy classes." He looks up from his phone. "They probably have so much in common."

"For, like, two weeks," I say supportively. "You can only discuss cadaver stitching techniques for so long, right?"

"Have you met my dad?" he says, and then sighs again, staring at the photo. "I miss him. Look how cute he is...."

"Give me that," I say, grabbing the phone and managing to peek at the time as I do. Twenty minutes until set. I quickly navigate over to Beckett's settings and put a screen-time limit on his social media. "You have ten more minutes to be on social media. After that, no more for today, okay? *This* doctor's orders."

Beckett takes the phone back. "Okay. You're right." He spends one more minute taking in Oliver's face. "But how could he move on so easily?"

"It's just Instagram," I say. "Not real life. That emoji says nothing about how he really feels."

"To Oliver, it means 'new love,'" Beckett replies. "I know because that's what he said when he used it for his first picture of us."

"Ugh. He can't even be original?"

Beckett's eyes flash up, looking hurt. "He's very original." Okay, so we're not at the disparaging-the-ex portion of his moving-on process. Unfortunately, I don't have time to figure out exactly what portion we *are* at, because it's getting to the point where I have to sprint over to the studio.

"Don't forget: a few more minutes and then no more social media for the day." I get up, putting my bag on my shoulder.

"Where are you...?" Beckett's eyes catch on the clock behind my head, and his mouth sets into a firm line. "Right. The set."

"Why don't you spend the rest of the day getting some fresh air? Or go to a museum. Do something out of the ordinary," I say as I slowly start to back toward the exit.

"Good ideas," he grumbles unenthusiastically.

"I'll talk to you later?" I say when I'm already at the door.

"Yes. Thanks."

I blow him a kiss and then turn on my heel and fly down the sidewalk.

When the elevator door opens onto the loft, the usual sight greets me: twenty people running in a million different directions. Petie is one of them, of course, though when he sees me, he screeches to a cartoon-style halt.

"Nasrin!" he says, clapping me on the shoulder. "Hello! Hi! It's going to be a great day." He shoots me an enormous grin before Jeff calls him away to check frame on something.

I walk over to Tru and her keyboard, pointing to Petie's spinning form. "Wow."

"I know. He's been like that all day. I think he might be coked up or something." She plunks out a few measures of "Flight of the Bumblebee" on her keys.

I snort as I throw my backpack in the corner with everyone else's stuff. "I didn't even think he knew my real name."

"Curiouser and curiouser," Tru says as I head over to Anouk and Saul at the wardrobe rack.

I quickly start to suspect that Tru's idea about Petie being on drugs might not be inaccurate. For the next couple of hours, Petie practically leaps from place to place as he directs us, complimenting almost every single line said or note sung. There are hardly any second or third takes. On the upside, my ego's feeling picked up and dusted off, *and* I should make it home in time to prep for my classes tomorrow.

Except Petie calls us all in for a meeting right after he yells "Cut!" on the final group scene.

"I know we still have a couple more scenes to shoot, but I wanted to make an announcement while everyone's still here." I think he means to pause dramatically, but he's bouncing on the balls of his feet—too energized to make it past one beat of silence. "We are close enough to finalizing a deal that I feel comfortable telling all of you: Hulu is about to pick up *STD*. We should be a part of their summer lineup!"

We all stare at him, stunned, until Morris lets out a huge whoop and everyone immediately joins in. Tru is clapping and laughing next to me.

I turn to her. "Is this for real? We're gonna be on a real streamer?"

Tru is breathless. "I guess? He hadn't told me either."

"Wow," I say, stunned.

"Wow," Tru whispers. "This is it: our big break."

"Yeah..." I say, and the elation on her face, in combination with the buzz of equally excited voices around me, grabs ahold of me. It's my freshman year of drama school and my big break could already be here? I'm finally understanding what Beckett was trying to tell me all along: This is such a huge opportunity.

I've just left the building in a joyous haze when I feel my phone vibrate. A FaceTime from Minu.

"Hey," I say when I answer.

"Hi!" she replies. "How are you doing?"

"I'm...great, actually," I say, feeling my face break out into a smile. "Just got some good news about the show."

"That's awesome," she says. "So you're in a good mood?"

The way she's batting her eyelashes at me makes me slightly suspicious. "Y-e-e-e-s...Why?"

She laughs her tinkly laugh, the one that sounds like bells. (I should get her to try her hand at singing; the timbre of her voice would probably make her a natural.) "I'm just happy you're happy!"

"Oh," I say.

"And..."

Here it comes. I patiently wait.

"Okay, I'll just ask. Is there any, any way you might be able to sit in on one more of my Persian Poetry classes? There's a midterm that day, but I can give you all my notes...."

"Wait? What?" I blink. All the chimey laughs in the world wouldn't make this okay. "Are you serious?"

"Just one last time. I was invited backstage at the Junk Mail concert...."

I hold up my hand. "Sorry, Minu. No. You said it was a onetime thing. And even if you hadn't, I'm not taking a test in your place. Even if I wanted to . . . I seriously, seriously don't have time."

Minu hesitates for one second, and I think she might be about to say something about the secret she's keeping for me again. But then she just smiles. "I gotcha. No problem."

I was preparing for more resistance, so I'm surprised by the sudden about-face. "Yeah?"

"Yup. So what's the good news? About the show?"

"Oh, um . . ." I hesitate. But it's not like this is a new secret—just building upon the one she already knows about. "It might be getting picked up by Hulu."

"Wow," Minu says, her eyes wide. "That's incredible. You're gonna be famous. For real."

I laugh. "Well, maybe. I'm still just a secondary character. And it's not definite. . . ."

But Minu pays no mind to my doubts. "You *will* invite me to the red-carpet premiere, right?"

"As long as it doesn't interfere with your Persian Poetry class . . . sure."

CHAPTER 23

Anything Goes

✪

Wednesday's Acting II class is tough, and Beckett has a doctor's appointment, so he's not even there to help me get through it. I hastily memorized a monologue the night before, and the critiques are *not* treating me kindly.

My classmates start in first. "It all felt a little too surface," Ricky says.

"I agree," says Emme. "It was almost like...I knew you were an actor playing a part?"

And then Clara goes in for the kill. "I don't feel like you're connecting to your character's emotions, Nasrin. Did you consider using the 'magic if' method to help determine how to believably react to the scope of Ophelia's problems?" She's referring to one of the first lessons we learned in Acting I. Stanislavski's "magic if" method involves asking yourself a few simple questions about your character's backstory and motivations—none of which I even thought about while I was hurriedly trying to make sure I knew my lines.

"Also think about what you can you use from your own life to convey Ophelia's devastation," Clara continues. "The line 'Woe is me' has become so ingrained in the vernacular that it almost feels clichéd. But it's our job as actors to breathe new life into even the most mundane or overwrought texts. And one way to do that is to find the part of you that feels that way. Because that's something the audience has never seen: *your* specific sorrows, *your* woes."

I nod, hiding my face as I take notes.

"And one more thing, class. When you're given open assignments like this, you can feel free to bring in pieces that are off the beaten path or more obscure. Okay, next..."

I don't hear who gets called, since the heat crawling up my cheeks seems to stretch its tendrils into my ears. Clara is implying that I chose this monologue haphazardly, without much thought or effort. It stings more knowing it's true.

I do a quick breathing exercise and try to focus my mind back on the present, determined to, at least, be a contributing member of the class.

That night, while I'm reviewing some Stats worksheets, I get a text from Cheryl, Petie's new assistant director. She tells me that *STD* is rescheduling a pickup shoot for the following evening—which *would* be okay if it weren't also the first night of rehearsal for *The Walk-Up*.

I call Petie to ask about it, reminding him that he said they wouldn't be shooting me on Thursday nights.

"That was before," Petie answers.

"Before?"

"Before we had a major streaming service about to pick us up!" Petie explains, exasperated. "We have a ton of executive notes to get through. I'm sorry, but this is gonna have to take priority over your student play."

I want to argue with him, to tell him he doesn't get to say what takes priority. But the thing is, I know he's right—and so was my gut instinct about doing the play in the first place. I simply don't have the bandwidth to keep burning the candle on three ends. I mean, candles don't even *have* three ends. And for good reason.

At least, given Beckett's feelings about what the show means for my future prospects, I know that he'll understand. I decide to call him before I email Lucia, but it goes straight to voice mail. I text him: Hey, you around? I got some news.

He doesn't respond right away, and I get distracted with trying to make sense of the worksheets again. I don't realize that my phone is on silent until I pick it up to look at the time, way past ten p.m. I have a missed call and several missed texts from Beckett, the final one indicating that he's worried and coming over to check on me.

I call him right away. "Hey. Sorry, my phone was accidentally on silent."

"I'm literally outside your dorm," Beckett replies. "You scared me half to death. You don't say something ominous like 'I've got news' and then go radio silent, you know?"

"It wasn't ominous. It was more like 'I got news, exclamation point.'"

"Then you should've put an exclamation point! Or a dancing Gene Kelly GIF. Or *something.*"

I laugh. "Sorry. Do you want me to come down to sign you in?"

"Can you just tell me the news first? This suspense is worse than a season-finale cliff-hanger."

"Okay, okay. So... cone of silence, but Hulu is in final talks to pick up *Small Town Dreams.*"

"Oh my God," Beckett says. "*Oh my God.* This is serious!"

"I know," I say.

"This is incredible, Nasrin. Who knows how many opportunities this will open up for you?"

"Exactly," I say. "Although, unfortunately, it's gonna *close* one opportunity for me too...."

"What's that?" he asks.

I sigh. "*The Walk-Up.* With everything going on, Petie's not cool with me missing the shoot for rehearsals anymore. So I was just about to email Lucia."

There's silence on the other end.

"Hello?" I ask. Did the call drop out or something?

"I'm here. They won't work around your schedule?"

I shake my head, even though Beckett can't see it. "I asked, but Petie said no. Luckily, Lucia has a list of auditioners a mile long and we haven't even started rehearsals yet. So she should hopefully be able to find a replacement really quickly."

There's another pause before Beckett says, "Only...she seemed so taken with our specific chemistry."

This hesitancy wasn't exactly the reaction I was expecting from Beckett. "That's only because she hasn't seen how great you are with anyone else. You can play off of anybody."

I think I hear Beckett give a faint *Mm-hmm*, or there could just be silence again.

"Beck? Are you okay?" I finally ask.

"Yeah. Yes. I'm fine." But he doesn't sound very convincing.

"You said yourself this is the opportunity of a lifetime, Beck. You know I already barely had time for the play, and the shoot schedule is only going to get more demanding...."

"Right," Beckett says curtly. "You're right. There's nothing else you can do."

After another pause, I ask, "So, now do you want to come up?"

"Actually, I'm pretty tired. I should be well rested for tomorrow's rehearsal. Especially now that I won't know who I'm playing opposite." He says the words matter-of-factly, not with a bite, but I can't tell which one is Beckett's true emotion and which one is a facade.

"Okay," I say.

"Congratulations, Nasrin. Let's talk more about it next time I see you, okay?"

"Okay. And you'll tell me all about the play rehearsal?"

"Will do. Good night." He doesn't wait for me to reply before hanging up.

I stare at the phone for a second, wondering why that

conversation took such a strange turn. But maybe it's just that I threw Beckett for a loop. I'm sure once he's settled in with his new scene partner, he'll be back to being his cheerful self.

Thursday night's shoot goes well past two a.m. The set's Hulu-inspired jubilation has turned into tension—or at least more anxiety on the part of Petie. While he's stopped turning to every comment for directorial advice, he does go over every note from the Hulu executives, which sound a hundred times more legitimate—and nerve-racking—than whatever BeaverDam40 had to say.

By the time I get to dinner at my parents' on Friday night, I'm exhausted. When Baba brings out his spreadsheets, I actually groan.

He looks at me, surprised. "You don't want to do this?"

The hurt in his eyes makes me backtrack. "I do. I've just had a really long week," I say. "Can we pick it up again next time?"

Baba takes one longing glance at the binder he's made up, with a title page slipped into the cover reading "Smoothie Operator" (Max's punny contribution to our efforts). But then he nods. "Of course."

At least once this Hulu thing becomes official, we'll *definitely* be a union show, and then I'll be armed with everything I need to come clean to my parents: a legitimate acting job, substantial paychecks, the double major . . . and maybe we can cool it on the fake proposals.

"If you're free, can I take you out for a meal and a mani-pedi tomorrow?" Minu asks, peering at my face. "You look like you could use the break."

I'm touched and a little surprised by Minu's friendly suggestion. "I'm free in the morning," I say, though I feel a little guilty knowing the only reason that's true is because I dropped out of the play.

"Great," she says, smiling. "I'll come by your dorm around... ten?"

"Sure," I say.

True to her word, Minu is waiting for me outside of Third North at ten a.m. "Korner Koffee okay? Or do you want to go somewhere else?"

"Korner sounds great," I reply. "I'd love a feta quiche."

"So tell me everything about the show," Minu says as we walk over. "When is it going to premiere on Hulu?"

"Well, it's not definite yet, so I don't know. But it seems like we'll find out in the next month whether it's green-lit or not."

"Do you think you're going to a bigger set somewhere? You'd have a lot more of a budget, right?"

"I..." Wow, I hadn't considered that. My first thought is that I *hope* not, because I can't afford for the set to be farther away from my classes. "I guess that would make sense, but I don't know."

"I bet you will. And I bet you'll have more amazing costumes and songs and stuff."

"Well, the songs are already amazing," I say, feeling defensive about Tru's work.

"Yeah, sure," Minu says. "But maybe they'll have, like, better production value. Oh, good, there's a table." She smiles at the hostess pointing us in the right direction.

We settle in, and Minu insists on ordering and paying for my quiche.

"Mmmm..." I say, taking a heaping forkful of feta, spinach, and cherry tomato.

"So are you pretty much shooting every day this next week?"

"Not every day," I say as I dig around for another cherry tomato. "Tonight, and then Tuesday and Thursday."

"Ah," she says, daintily slicing up her banana-walnut muffin and putting a small pat of butter on a piece before she takes a bite. "So you're free Wednesday."

"I mean, aside from my classes," I say, and then look up at her, the fatigue fog of my brain dissipating just long enough to let suspicion peek through. "Why?"

"No particular reason," she says. "I have my poetry midterm that afternoon, and I was wondering if you might be free to run some flash cards with me that morning."

"Oh," I say, frowning. "Can't you have someone else do that? Maybe Maman or Baba? Their grasp on Ferdowsi is a lot better than mine."

"Of course," she says, taking a sip of her cappuccino. "Oh, hey, there's your hot TA again. Is this his local haunt?" Minu waves, and I turn around to see Max walking over. I'm surprised she's still referring to him that way, given that they've now spent enough time together for her to use his name.

"Good morning," he says to both of us.

"Good morning," I reply.

"Morning, Max," Minu says. "Do you want us to find you a chair?"

"Thanks, but unfortunately, I have to grab my coffee to go this morning. I have office hours. Which I promise I'll be a lot more pleasant at if I'm caffeinated." He shrugs at me and smiles.

"No problem," Minu says. "Can I find you a chair another time, then? Maybe over dinner?"

Both Max and I stop looking at each other to stare at Minu, who's batting her mile-long lashes and smiling innocently up at Max. And did she have that burgundy lipstick on this whole time or did she just magically swipe it on in the last two seconds?

"Uh...dinner?" Max asks, blinking.

"Dinner *date*," Minu continues. Max turns to look at me, and Minu jumps in again. "Oh, good idea. Nasrin probably has the inside scoop on where to go. Got any restaurant recs, Nas?"

"Uh...yeah," I hear myself say. "There's this new Portuguese place. On University." In fact, it was the place I was going to suggest for our next tutoring session. That's why the sight of Max conjured it to mind so quickly, even though I was caught off-guard by Minu's question.

"Great. I've never had Portuguese food." Minu turns to Max. "What do you think? Are you free tonight? Or tomorrow night?"

Max stares at me for a few seconds longer, and I just smile

at him encouragingly, not knowing what else to do. "Okay," he finally says, turning to Minu. "Sure. I can do tonight."

"Eight o'clock?" Minu asks. "I'll meet you there?"

"Okay," Max says.

"Cool," Minu says. "Here, Nasrin, can you find the restaurant's address and I'll text it to Max?"

She hands me her phone, and I robotically put the restaurant's name in Google Maps. Minu takes the phone back and then politely asks Max for his number so she can text it to him.

When that whole bizarre exchange is done, Max takes his leave rather quickly. "I really do have to go."

"See you tonight!" Minu calls out after him.

"Yeah, see you." He takes one final quick glance at me before he pushes the door of the café open and leaves.

"He didn't even get his coffee," I say, feeling a little numb.

"Guess he's not going to be so pleasant for his students after all," Minu says as she shrugs and takes another sip of her cappuccino.

CHAPTER 24

A Boy Like That

✫

Another post-Hulu change is Petie's decision that being on set is more important than a day dedicated to scriptwriting, so we no longer have Saturday nights off. Not only that, but I have to be extra focused during tonight's shoot because I happen to have three back-to-back scenes and my very first solo number. It's a reprise of a song that Juliet sings earlier in the show, but still.

Petie has lots of directions for me, mostly where to go and where to look, but at least he hardly says a thing about my singing. I'm pleased with the satisfied look on both his and Tru's faces when I'm done.

Waiting for the set designer and cinematographer to set up my final scene for the day, however, gives me some downtime. And the first thing that pops into my head is: *I wonder how Minu and Max's date is going.*

I take out my phone and stare at it. I can't very well text either one of them in the middle of a date. Even if just the word "date" regarding the two of them makes me feel ... weird.

Luckily, Petie calls me up for my next scene, and I'm forced to put my phone away.

When we wrap, it's past one a.m. I look at my phone again, knowing the probability of Minu still being awake is high. Should I?

Before I can overanalyze it, I send her a quick text: Are you up? She would have put her phone on Do Not Disturb if she was sleeping—right?

But by the time I've made it back to my dorm, brushed my teeth, and put on my pj's, there's still no response from her. *Sleeping*, I think ... *probably.* I make myself go to bed before my mind can wander too far into what *probably* means if she—and maybe Max—*aren't* sleeping.

The next morning, there's still no text from Minu. But I'm not gonna sweat it. Instead, I'm gonna sweat, literally, by taking a jog around Washington Square Park. It's freezing, and after I've made just one loop of the small park, I decide to head back to my dorm. But just then, my music (the 1993 London West End cast recording of *Grease*, starring Debbie Gibson) is interrupted by ringing.

It's Minu calling. I hit accept on my phone. "Hi."

"Hey," she says. "What's up?"

"Nothing. Just going back home after an ill-advised jog. Did you know it's like twenty degrees outside?"

"I didn't, because I'm not outside."

"Smart," I say.

"Yeah," she says. There's silence.

"So…"

"So?"

"How did your date last night go?" I can't believe she's making me drag this out.

"Oh. That," she replies, like she's already forgotten about it. "It was fine."

"Just fine?" I guess that short jog still brought my heart rate up. That would explain the quick pounding in my ear.

"Yeah." I can practically hear the shrug in her voice. "I mean no doubt, the boy is attractive. But."

I wait and then, when it's clear she isn't going to tell me if I don't blatantly ask, I sigh and play along. "But…?"

"I mean, he's just a little…boring."

"He is not." The words come out immediately and without my express permission.

"Oh, no?" Minu asks, sounding amused.

"You just need to get to know him," I insist. "There's a lot more to him if you do." Three-dimensional, that's what he called it, right? I consider telling her about the Will Parker thing, but somehow I don't think she'd find it anywhere near as charming as I do.

"Okay," she says. "Maybe I'll give him another shot."

"Um." I pause. What else was I expecting out of talking him up? "Right. Good idea," I say stiffly.

"Anyway, have you given any more thought to whether or not you can make it Wednesday?"

"Make it?" I ask, genuinely confused. "To where?"

"Persian Poetry? The midterm?"

I stop abruptly, nearly causing a lady in a stroller to smash into me. "Sorry!" I call out as she manages to swerve around me in the nick of time, and then I lift up the little mic connected to my headphones to hiss into them. "You're still on that? I already said no."

"Yeah, you did," Minu says. "But I thought maybe you'd changed your mind."

"Why would I change my mind?"

"For one thing, this meet and greet is really important to me, Nasrin. I've been listening to Junk Mail since I was five, knowing they'd never come to Tehran and there was no way I'd ever get to meet them. And now I'm here. . . . it would mean *a lot* to me to be able to go. A lot."

"And what's the other thing?" I ask.

"Well . . ." There's a pause. "I mean, the other day I had to distract your mom while she was watching a cooking video on YouTube, and the algorithm somehow had *Small Town Dreams* in the bottom row of suggested videos."

I gasp. "It didn't."

"It did," Minu says. "And what's more . . . I saw that episode, Nas. Did your character really talk about her grandfather riding a camel to work. Like, for real?"

I wince. I hated that line—*hated* it. But it was shot at the end of the night when everyone was already exhausted, and I knew Petie wouldn't listen to me anyway. So I just said it, we cut and wrapped, and I put it out of my mind.

But now Minu says, "How would Amoo Nader and Khaleh Samineh feel if they not only found out you've been lying about the show itself, but that you've been making fun of us— your own culture?"

She says it like that's what she's really concerned about, and maybe it is. But then again, it also feels a lot like blackmail.

Before I can think of anything to respond with, she tells me she has to go. "Next Wednesday. Think about it," she says before ending the call.

By the time I make it up to my dorm room, I'm feeling out of breath and a little dizzy—none of which was caused by the exercise.

Obviously, the only way out of this is to tell my parents before Wednesday. *But I can't*, my inner monologue whines. The Hulu pickup isn't official, and I don't have time to fill out Clara's forms. Except . . . I know I've just been putting that off. It's not going to take long at all to fill the forms out and send them over to Clara.

With a lump in my throat, I click the link to the forms and start with the easy part. First name: Nasrin. Last name: Mahdavi.

A few hours later, I'm sitting at Korner Koffee again. When Max texted asking where I was going to take him for our tutoring session that day, I wasn't in the mood to add more to my plate. Too tired to scout a location. Korner Koffee okay?

Sure, he wrote back.

Now he's coming in, smiling somewhat shyly at me. "Hi," he says. "I brought you something."

"Oh, goody. Stats worksheets." I really am so exceptionally tired. Am I even going to be able to absorb anything from this tutoring session? Maybe I should've canceled.

"Nope," Max says. "Well, yes, those too. But...check it out."

He places a folded-up newspaper in front of me. I glance at the title: *Gilbert High Gazette.*

"Below the fold," he tells me.

So I open it up and look at the story right under the front page's crease. "*Oklahoma!* Thrills Oklahoma" the headline reads. And there, underneath it, is a picture of Max, one leg in the air, expertly lassoing a rope and... "You *did* wear chaps!"

"Apparently so." He grins as he settles down. "You'd think one would remember pants that constricting, but..."

"You were probably too focused on your big 'All Er Nothin'' number," I offer.

"Probably."

"This is most excellent," I say as I take out my phone and snap a picture of the article. "In case I need it for blackmail later." I wink.

"Your grades can't be bought, Mahdavi. Just don't forget that," he jokes, even though we both know he has no say whatsoever over my grades.

"I wouldn't use it for *that*," I reply. *Because I'm not Minu.*

"What else would you need to blackmail me for?" he says as he opens his satchel and takes out the dreaded worksheets.

"Maybe making sure you treat my cousin right." I look directly at him, trying to gauge his reaction.

He doesn't really have one, other than a shrug as he continues digging for the papers. "Minu is nice. And I get the sense she's good at looking out for herself."

I wasn't expecting that, but then again, I'm not sure what I *was* expecting. Nor can I fully explain what comes out of my mouth next, or whether it's not just a little bit intentional. "Yeah, she can. And speaking of blackmailing for grades..." I shake my head as I slide one of his worksheets over to my side of the table.

I've got Max's attention now. "What do you mean?"

"She just...She wants me to sit an exam for her. Because she has this"—I make air quotes—"'once in a lifetime' band meet and greet that just happens to be taking place at the same time as her Persian Poetry midterm. And since I did it once before..."

"Hold up," Max says, putting up his hand. "You sat an exam for her?"

"No, that's not what I meant. I just attended class for her one time."

Max is blinking at me. "Why?"

"Well, she had tickets to Fashion Week...and she was also helping to keep my show secret from my parents." It sounds worse hearing the words come out of my mouth.

"So she blackmailed you? To impersonate her in a class?!" The tips of Max's ears have turned red.

"I know, right?" I say. It feels good to have someone on my side.

"I think that's illegal," Max says, frowning.

"Ah, well...I wouldn't say it's exactly illegal," I start.

"I mean by university rules. She could definitely get expelled. In fact, she probably should—"

"You're not going to go call Barnard Police, are you?" I ask, half joking. But then I notice the little line on Max's forehead that I only ever saw that one time in his office at the beginning of the year.... "Wait, are you?" I ask, a little panicked. I don't totally agree with everything Minu has done, but I don't want to get her expelled.

"This is a really serious offense, Nasrin," he says.

I shake my head. "Look, it sounds worse than it is. I was being *dramatic*, as dictated by my major." I emphasize with jazz hands, trying to lighten the mood.

Max seems undeterred. "But you really did sit in on a class for her. And she really did ask you to take an exam in her place. Right?"

"It's not exactly like that. It's her first couple of months in America, and I think she's just overexcited by all the things she's allowed to do here, all the opportunities she has. She's very into fashion, and to sit front row at a fashion show..."

"But also to attend class at Barnard," Max butts in. "That's the real opportunity. What about all the people who *didn't* get into her school? I can only imagine how I'd feel if I hadn't gotten into Stern and I knew there were people who did who weren't even going to class."

"It's only a couple of times," I immediately say. Suddenly, I'm not so sure I like the idea of Max disparaging my cousin.

"And not everyone can go through college not making a single mistake." I mean it to sound light and friendly, but that's not how it comes off.

"Not everyone can afford to make mistakes," Max mutters, shaking his head.

"Look," I say, swallowing hard. "You really don't know anything about her life or where she's come from or what she's doing here. So maybe she's not as perfect as you or as you expect everyone to be." I wave my hands at the worksheets sprawled out in front of us.

"I don't expect perfection. Just basic morality."

"Ugh," I say, crumpling back into my seat, staring at his *Fletcher Ranch* thermos. "Are we back to holier-than-thou, early-first-semester Max? Because I don't think I can take that right now."

Max is silent, and when I look up at him, I see that he's just nodding, his eyes hard as aquamarines. "Nah. I'm just the same Max I've always been. Unrequited crushes and all." He gets up and starts putting the worksheets in his satchel.

"What?" I ask.

"Never mind. Okay if we reschedule this session? I suddenly have a splitting headache."

"Um..." I watch him snap the bag shut. "Max..." I say.

"I'll catch you later, Nasrin," he says, then gives me a wave and practically vanishes from the café.

CHAPTER 25

Have an Eggroll, Mr. Goldstone

✦

"Okay, so turns out you were right," I say as I plop down across from Beckett in the dining hall on Tuesday morning.

"Of course I was," Beckett says. "Though about what in particular this time?"

"Max. I guess he *was* asking me out on a date after all."

"Duh," Beckett says, but he seems extra absorbed in cutting up his waffle. I give him a minute to finish, but even after he does, he doesn't seem to have anything else to add to the conversation. Odd.

Oh well. I change the subject. "How was rehearsal on Thursday?" It's been such a busy weekend that I haven't had a chance to talk to Beckett since I told him I had to quit *The Walk-Up*.

Beckett shrugs. "Fine."

"Is Lucia as good of a director as she is a writer?" I probe.

"Hard to say," Beckett says. "It was only the first rehearsal. And most of my day was spent auditioning against other actresses to play Shauna." Do Beckett's words have some bite to them?

"How's that going?" I ask.

He shrugs again. "Going. I think it's between three people."

"Oh. She didn't pick yet?"

Beckett looks up at me now. "No. She was supposed to spend Thursday rehearsing, not auditioning. And now it's thrown the whole schedule off. For everybody." No ifs, ands, or buts about it: There's definitely bite now.

"I'm sorry," I say. "How was I to know this Hulu thing would happen?"

"You weren't," Beckett admits. "But you did make a commitment to something when you signed up for the play. And to someone." He could mean Lucia, but I'm pretty sure he means himself.

"Sorry," I repeat, not knowing what else I can say.

Beckett goes back to his food, and an awkward silence shrouds the table.

I try to think of something I can break it with and settle for some gossip. "Hey, did I tell you that Minu went out with Max this weekend?"

Beckett slams his fork down angrily. "Can we stop talking about you for one second?"

"Whoa," I say, taken aback. "Where is this coming from?"

"It's coming from you being so absorbed in everything

you're doing that you can't see when one of your best friends needs you." He glares at me.

"Look, I'm sorry about the play, but to be fair, I told you from the beginning I didn't think I could do it. Except you insisted I try out…"

"It's not just about the play," Beckett says.

"Then what?" I ask, exasperated.

"I'm going through a really bad breakup. And it hurts and I could use a friend to talk about it. Which you'd know if you'd take five minutes to ask, 'How are you doing, Beckett?' 'What's new with you, Beckett?' 'Beckett, are you okay?'"

I throw my hands in the air. "Or you could, I don't know, just tell me you're feeling shitty instead of waiting for me to read from some script I'm supposed to know."

"I tried to!" Beckett says. "But you 'had to run to the shoot'—"

"Well, if we're talking about commitment, then yes, I did!"

"Okay, fine, but you could've asked me about it later. You could've texted or called after the shoot to check on me."

"I'm sorry I'm not a mind reader, Beckett," I start, but Beckett is already getting up from the table.

"Do you think it takes a mind reader to know how to be a good friend?"

"No, but I'm starting to feel like it might take one to be *your* friend. Or boyfriend," I snap back. "You expected Oliver to just magically know how you were feeling all the time too, didn't you?"

We stare at each other across the cafeteria table, the air

as charged as a Tesla coil, while I wait for his retort. But then Beckett slides his tray off the table and dumps most of his uneaten breakfast into the trash before walking out of the dining hall.

I stare at the empty seat in front of me. I can't believe that just happened: a fight with calm, cool, collected Beckett? With my best friend at Tisch?

I numbly put a few more morsels of food in my mouth and then, for once, am thankful that I have to run to the shoot. *Small Town Dreams* seems to be the one aspect of my life that's headed uphill instead of down.

The set is chaos as usual, but I try to use the frenetic energy to reallocate my attention away from Beckett, Max, Minu, and my parents and into giving Leila her due.

It must work, because Petie gives me a rare direct compliment at the end of the scene. "Powerful delivery," he says. "Great work."

I try to buoy myself with those words for the rest of the afternoon. If I'm not a great friend or daughter or cousin... maybe, at least, I can be a great actress.

During our lunch break, when I'm sitting on the floor eating my vegetable fried rice with everyone else, Petie ends a phone call and then dramatically strolls up to the center of our makeshift dining table.

"Ladies and gentlemen of *Small Town Dreams*. I just got off the phone with Alison Goldstone, an executive at none other than Hulu. And..." He looks at us, stretching the moment out. "Drumroll, please..." This being a gathering of performers, three people volunteer to tap out a drumroll, with Morris adding an impressive impromptu beatbox.

"*STD* is officially on the Hulu slate! We did it!" The entire cast and crew seems to explode into a chorus of whoops as they jump to their feet, upending containers of rice and dumplings. I abandon my rice right along with them, especially when Tru pulls me into a hug.

"Can you believe it?" she asks. I shake my head. "We gotta remember this moment, cherish it, so we can recall it later in interviews. Our big break."

"You're right!" I say, smiling.

"Okay, okay, one more thing," Petie says once we've all settled down enough to hear him. "We owe a lot to this little studio here, and I'd like to think we really made the most of it. But as of the end of next month, we're going to have to bid it farewell, because we are relocating to..."

Oh no. Here it comes. Just as Minu predicted. *Please don't say uptown. Please don't say uptown.*

"Vancouver!" Petie says, followed by slightly more subdued cheers.

Vancouver. Vancouver?! "Canada?" I say stupidly, and as if the word has elemental powers, a chill settles into my skin, making the hair on my arms stand on end.

"I guess so," Tru replies. "Wow. Wow."

Neither of us speaks over the next ten minutes as we listen to everyone freaking out about the good news. In order to stop

215

my shuddering, I concentrate on helping to clean up all the spilled food. When the last dumpling has been thrown away, I slowly gather my belongings, including the character shoes I lugged from home for a tap number we didn't even get to shoot.

Tru is waiting for me at the door, since we're both headed to classes in the Tisch building. As we walk out, she says, "You're awfully quiet."

"I just…Vancouver," I say in a small voice. "And here I was hoping it wouldn't be uptown. Like, farther away from school." I indicate the street sign for Broadway up ahead.

Tru gives a faint laugh. "Yeah. I guess this is a little farther up."

"So we'd have to drop out," I say.

"Maybe. Or defer for a year. In case the show doesn't work out."

I bring my hands to my temples. "How can I tell my parents I'm dropping out of school? And moving to Vancouver? Especially when they uprooted their whole lives and moved to New York to be closer to me?"

"I guess you'd have to tell them about the show itself first," Tru says gently.

"Yeah," I say miserably, looking at her. "That was the plan, anyway, though. But now…what exactly am I going to say?" I suddenly realize that for all my lists and self-imposed deadlines, I've never fully thought out the actual conversation. Maybe because I've always considered it Future Nasrin's problem. *Wanted* it to be Future Nasrin's problem.

Tru tucks one of her locs behind her ear. "Well, I haven't

met your parents, but . . . won't they be happy that you're doing a job that you love? And getting paid for it? I mean, wasn't that the whole point of the deception? Now you can prove to them that they won't have to worry about you choosing this life. That you can make a living doing it."

"Yes. You're right," I say, because she is. But I have this nagging feeling that that's not exactly true, and taking this job would only further disappoint them. Because then I'd be leaving school completely. And none of us ever wanted *that*.

"I'm sure your parents will understand," Tru says. "Eventually."

"Understand what?" comes a voice that makes me whip around. Because appearing on the sidewalk like a bespectacled phantom, right in front of the building flying a purple Tisch flag, is my mother.

CHAPTER 26

Mama Who Bore Me

✦

"Maman. What are you doing here?" I ask, blinking at her.

"Fancy meeting you here," she replies. "I was just about to surprise you at your dorm and take you out for a late lunch!" She beams at me.

"Lunch?" I repeat, my half-eaten vegetable fried rice churning on cue.

"Yes, you're free the rest of the afternoon, right?" And then I remember that I'd haphazardly given her a copy of my "schedule," cribbed entirely from Max's, with some freshman-level courses subbed in for his advanced ones. It was a little over a month ago, though at this point that feels like eons.

I guess in that version of my schedule, I'm free. Whereas right now, I'm about to be late for Vocal Technique.

Maman turns to Tru while I suppress a mini internal meltdown. "Hi, I'm Samineh, Nasrin's mom."

"Tru Davis. Nasrin's friend," Tru says, without missing a beat, giving me an extra minute to collect my thoughts.

Okay, it's probably best if I just skip voice class in order to go out to lunch with Maman. I'm about to open my mouth to tell her so.

"What's this? You just carry those around with you?" Maman points to my hand, and it's only then that I realize that it's clutching the clear Ziploc . . . with my character shoes in it.

"Uhhh."

"Aren't they cute?" Tru chimes in. "Mary Janes are back in style."

Maman takes another look at the beige shoes. "With taps?" Clearly all those years of taking me to my classes, and watching all my recitals and plays, are coming back to haunt me now.

Tru glances at the metal plates screwed into the bottoms of my shoes and lets out a slight laugh. "No. I think you're going to have to take those off, Nasrin."

I nod blankly. "Yes. I do."

And then who should I see rounding the corner but Petie? I'm hoping he won't notice us, but let's face it, I don't have that kind of luck. "Hey, guys!" he says, waving at Tru and me.

"Hey." I wave back, mentally willing him to move along. But as my mom turns to look at him, he stops right in front of us. Where are Juliet and Morris to divert his attention when you need them?

"You must be Nasrin's mom. Or...her sister?" Petie says cheesily.

Maman gives him a slight smile. "You were right the first time. And you are...?"

"Petie," I butt in, hoping I can somehow divert this trainwreck. "This is Petie."

"Nice to meet you, Petie," Maman says, shaking his hand.

"Likewise," Petie says. "Has Nasrin told you the good news yet?"

Oh God. I feel like there's a vise around my lungs, slowly squeezing all the air out.

"I don't think so. Good news about what?" Maman answers pleasantly.

"The show being picked up by Hulu. Vancouver is going to be amazing."

No, not a vise. A straight-up anvil in the center of my chest. And since I'm not Wile E. Coyote, this is it for me. I'm dead.

Maman looks at me in confusion. "What show?"

Petie laughs, clearly thinking my mom is joking. But then she turns to him and asks again, "What show?"

Petie stops laughing and gives me a look. I can't speak because of the whole lack-of-oxygen thing. "Nasrin. Have you really not told your mom about the *hit show* you're on?"

Maman furrows her brow. "How do you have time to be on a show and go to school?"

"I mean, who needs drama school when she's going to have actual credits on the back of her headshots?" Petie responds. The anvil on my chest is now being joined by a whistling sound in my brain. Is this what happens when your body shuts down?

Maman blinks at him. "Nasrin isn't going to drama school. She's going to business school."

"Is that right?" Petie looks at me. "You little devil. Did you lie about Tisch on your CV?" He indicates the purple flag waving valiantly above us. And then his face breaks out into a wolfish grin. "Good for you. Everyone does it. I think you're going to do just fine in Hollywood."

Maman turns her whole body this time so that she's standing squarely in front of me. I can see in her eyes that everything is starting to come into focus for her at the same time that all my illusions are coming apart at the seams.

I close my eyes, but all I can think about is that I am so, so tired. It's too much: running around, having everyone mad at me, keeping up with all the lies. My stomach hurts all the time, and now I feel light-headed to boot.

"No," I finally say as I fling my eyes open and look into Maman's startled brown ones.

"I don't understand," she says.

"I didn't lie on my CV. But..." I take a deep breath, bracing myself for the point of no return. "But I have been lying to you."

"I can't believe it. I just can't believe it," Baba is saying over and over again as he stares at an ottoman in the corner of their apartment.

221

"Well, believe it, Nader. Because I saw her go into the drama school with my own eyes," Maman replies in clipped tones.

She let me go to class after our confrontation on the street, probably because she was too dumbfounded to protest. But she was waiting for me on the sidewalk when I got out, and she let me know in no uncertain terms that I was coming home with her.

That's where I got to watch Maman tell Baba the whole sordid story. He didn't say a word as she spoke, just looked more and more incredulous as she went on.

He turns to me now and is silent for what feels like a full minute before he speaks. "How come I've been paying Stern, then? The bill that comes says Stern on it."

"Um. I created a fake website," I say in a small voice. "Using Maman's YouTube tutorials."

They both stare at me, mouths hanging open. "Wow," Baba finally says.

"I'm sorry," I say hurriedly. "I didn't mean for any of this to happen."

"That can't possibly be true," Baba says. "You don't accidentally create a whole website. You don't just happen to give your mom a completely made-up schedule."

"It wasn't exactly made up. It was just Max's instead of mine." I don't know why I say it, except now that I've started telling the truth, I can't seem to stop until they know everything. It feels like my penance.

Neither of my parents seem amused. "If only you used all

of that energy you spent lying to us to *actually* go to business school," Baba says. "The things you could've learned..."

"You're right," I say, nodding furiously. "I lied. I shouldn't have. But you would never have let me go to Tisch...."

"Of course not!" Baba says, his voice finally rising in volume. "Why would we pay all that money just so you can be destitute one day?"

"But I'm not!" I say. "That's what I've been trying to tell you. I'm on a show that's paying me. It's going to be on Hulu."

"Something else you lied about," Maman interjects.

"Because I was waiting for it to be good enough for you before I told you," I say, my face feeling hot and itchy. "I wanted to present it in the right way. So you'd understand. I was going to officially have a double major squared away too. And make sure I had decent paystubs from the show. And that my classes were going well. And then...I was going to tell you."

"When?" Maman asks. "On our deathbeds?"

"See! You don't believe in me!" I say.

"Not believe *in* you, Nasrin. Just believe you. I mean, at this point..." Maman says.

"But you never believed that I could do this," I interject, my voice increasing in volume too. "You never believed I could pursue acting professionally." I turn to Baba. "I heard you telling Maman how upset you'd be if I was waiting tables after everything you sacrificed to move to America."

Baba blinks at me. "I *never* said that."

I nod emphatically. "Yes, you did. The night before the

Grease audition. I came downstairs for some Sleepytime Tea, and I heard you."

Baba looks at Maman for some corroboration, but she shrugs in an "It sounds like something you might have said" way.

"You don't even remember?" I ask incredulously, thinking how it could be that they have no recollection of the words that have been damning my life like a bad omen over these past four years.

"Are you really turning this around on us, Nasrin?" Baba asks.

"No," I say. "But I can't believe you don't remember."

"Okay, fine. But do you *remember* telling us you applied to Stern?" His voice is soft and dangerous now. I feel like I'm in open water and there's a predator just feet away, smelling blood.

"Yes, but...sometimes I feel like you don't listen to me, or to what I want. Just to what *you* think is best for me. I told you again and again that I was ready for that *Grease* audition, and you still barely let me go." I'd had to lie then too, I realize, by promising them I wouldn't take the audition too seriously.

"But you never gave us a chance to listen about this," Maman says. "You never even told us about Tisch."

"He just said he wouldn't have let me go." I point at Baba.

Maman raises an eyebrow. "But you never really gave him that opportunity, did you?"

It's like we're swimming in circles, and maybe I just want the shark to snap and get it over with. I look at my dad, almost willing him to yell at me. Instead, he turns away and sits heavily on a leather armchair. He won't even look me in the eye.

I turn away too, catching a glimpse of Minu on the couch. She's been sitting there this whole time, quietly watching the entire exchange. I can't help noticing the slight smirk on her face. "What the hell are you so happy about?" I spit at her. "You should be just as upset. Now you don't have anything to blackmail me with."

Minu's mouth drops open. "Blackmail?" she says.

My dad turns to her now. "You knew about this?"

Minu looks troubled. "Yes, Amoo. But I...I couldn't tell on her. I wanted Nasrin to be my friend."

I shake my head as I look at her wide eyes and the way she's biting her lip. "Maybe you're the one who should be in drama school," I mutter.

"I don't think anyone should be in drama school," Baba says. "But apparently no one cares about what I think." He gets up abruptly. "I can't talk any more about this right now. Nasrin, good night."

"Are you...kicking me out?" I gasp.

He turns to me, his eyes looking tired. "I would never kick you out of my house. But I will admit that I'm not sure I really know who you are."

This is so much worse than a shark attack. This is a slow poison that trickles from my ear through to my heart, made bitterer by the fact that neither of my parents has uttered a single untrue word this whole night.

CHAPTER 27

You'll Never Walk Alone

✪

That night, my mind feels like it's playing a retrospective of my life on a loop. Starting with that goddamn *Chorus Line* audition.

My first problem was that I went in with too much confidence. I know that seems like an oxymoron, because how can you audition without confidence? But all my years of voice lessons and dance lessons, of community theater over the summers, and of getting the lead parts in all three of my middle school plays hadn't prepared me for one cold, hard truth: Freshmen are the last ones picked for the high school musical.

Even though I knew that the chances of getting a lead were slim, I still belted "Nothing" in my room and let myself dream about being cast as Morales—all while telling myself that I'd be content with any speaking (or singing) role.

But I didn't get any speaking or singing role. I didn't get a role at all. When the cast list went up, I stared at it in a stupor for over five minutes, trying to will the words *Nasrin Mahdavi* to appear on the short twenty-name list under Ensemble. All kinds of ludicrous scenarios ran through my head, ranging from a transcription error to a prank involving invisible ink, before the truth finally sank in like an anchor scraping the depths of my stomach: I didn't make the play. All those years of lessons and rehearsals and deep dives into the best way to take care of my voice and body and...I didn't even make the *ensemble* of my high school play?

I was a wreck. It was no lie when I told Beckett that I cried for months—every single hour I should've been at rehearsal and every night until the closing night of the play. My parents were beside themselves. They eventually took me to a therapist.

Talking to her helped. A lot. And, in a weird way, I realized not making the play was a blessing in disguise. Once I got over the initial shock and grief, it only made me surer that theater was what I cared about most; the rejection fueled my determination for my next audition, and the one after that.

But Maman and Baba couldn't see that. That's when they started throwing the word "hobby" around constantly. And then one night I overheard my dad saying that thing about me waiting tables, and all I heard in his voice was shame: the shame he'd feel if his daughter ended up being an actress.

Maybe that's when the seed of this plan took root, without my even realizing it. *I'll ace every audition, and I'll watch them watch me succeed at this.* But when it came time to apply to Tisch, I couldn't imagine telling them I was doing it. *If I get in, it's a sign,* I told myself. But then . . . there was a part of me that was sure I wouldn't get in, wasn't there? Because I'd never be that fearless fourteen-year-old auditioner again, not when I'd experienced a rejection that went so bone deep. So I guess I thought I'd never have to tell them. And everything since then has been . . . an improv.

I toss and turn in my bed, watching Beatrix leave for a night out with her friends and wishing I could talk to someone about this. No, not just someone. There's only one person who would understand the full scope of the situation and still have some comforting words to say to me—if only Beckett hadn't taken his own Nasrin-specific vow of silence.

The next morning is the first in months that I've woken up and gone to my drama classes without the burden of being dishonest to my parents about it. But the pit in my stomach belies any relief I'd expect to feel.

I have Stats first, but Max isn't there. I take notes robotically, feeling as lost as in my first week of class.

In Acting, I come face-to-face with Beckett for the first time since our fight—or at least, face-to-profile. He's studying a script when I walk in. I waffle about approaching, but then I think about everything he said about my being self-absorbed, and I realize all I would be doing is going on and on—again—about what's happening to me. I eventually trudge over to a chair on the other side of the room.

It occurs to me that I've never felt so alone in my life.

Right before class, I get a text from Cheryl, the AD, telling me they've scheduled an *STD* pickup shoot for me for tonight. Fine, I text back without much enthusiasm, even though I should be glad for both the distraction and the paycheck. After all, it's the only concrete thing I have to lord over my parents to justify my poor decision-making.

"Okay, class. We're doing a repeat of an exercise we did in Acting I," Clara says as I quickly put my phone away. "The Meisner repetition exercise. Pair up, please."

I glance quickly in Beckett's direction, but he's already asking his seat neighbor if he wants to pair up. I decide to do the same and end up with Emme. Clara gives us a phrase: "My hair is turning gray."

We take turns repeating it to each other: angrily, comedically, dramatically. I'm relieved this is mostly a rote exercise, because that's all I feel capable of right now: going through the motions of class. How ironic since *this*—the privilege of being in one of the premiere drama schools in the country—is exactly why I was lying to my parents, and why my life has gone to shit. If I can't muster the strength to focus here, then what even was the point?

After ten minutes, Clara tells us it's time to switch partners. I end up with Ricky, repeating the phrase "I know you are, but what am I?" It's so silly that we're both laughing by the end of it, which feels almost foreign to me at this point.

"Switch again," Clara says.

This time, everyone has paired off by the time Beckett and I realize we're the last two left.

"Slightly different instructions this time," Clara says. "I want you to each choose your own phrase—different phrases—and repeat them to one another."

Beckett is across from me now, and I find myself staring into his dark brown eyes. They are inscrutable.

We look at each other for a solid thirty seconds. Finally, Beckett says, "You are such a liar."

I feel like I've gotten slapped. I want to respond with "I know you are, but what am I?" I want to respond with something cruel. But then something within me breaks, and all the unshed tears of the past twenty-four hours come bubbling to the surface. They fall freely, turning the light gray of the classroom's vinyl floor into slate. I simplify my phrase. "I know," I whisper.

Beckett hesitates, but then he says his phrase again, this time in a joking tone.

"I know," I repeat, not changing my somber tone. And I think that's when he realizes that I'm not acting.

He grabs my hand and waits for me to look him in the eye this time before he repeats "You are such a liar" so gently that I know that he's really saying, *Are you okay?*

"I know." *No.*

"You are such a liar." *What happened?*

I'm not a gifted enough actress to subtext this story in a two-word line. So I give a small, sob-infused laugh before I say, "I know." *I'll have to tell you later.*

And then, before he can say his line again, I look him in

the eye, grab him by the other hand, and say, "I know." *I'm sorry.*

He looks at me, and then the corner of his mouth goes up. "I know."

Beckett places a honey-banana-acai smoothie in front of me before settling across the table in the Tisch café.

"Okay," he says. "Spill."

"Well, first of all, I know I subtexted it in our acting exercise and all, but you deserve a proper apology: I'm sorry I wasn't there for you with the Oliver thing. Obviously, you were hurting. . . ."

"Well," Beckett says, waving his hands. "You were right too. I kept telling you I was fine. . . ."

"Yeah, but if I'd been paying attention, I'd have known you weren't," I say. "And maybe a part of me did know but felt too busy to push more out of you."

Beckett shrugs. "Maybe."

"I was a shitty friend," I say. "Let me own up to it."

"Okay," Beckett says. "Apology accepted. And I'm sorry I wasn't more transparent about needing you."

I smile, feeling a weight lift off of me. Though, I realize glumly, it's not enough to make me feel fully unburdened.

"But back to you," Beckett says as he sits up, looking more serious. "What's going on? What happened?"

I sigh. "Well, first of all, Max hates me."

"Because he lurves you?" Beckett asks, batting his eyelashes.

"Maybe," I admit. "Secondly, *STD* was officially picked up by Hulu—"

"Whoa!"

"—and is moving to Vancouver," I say before Beckett can get too invested in celebrating.

"Whoa," Beckett says again, his voice's timbre getting lower. "So you're leaving?"

"I don't know. And that's not even the biggest thing that happened over the past couple of days."

"What could be bigger than moving to Canada to star in your own TV show?"

"How about my parents finding out? About the show. About Tisch. About everything."

"Whoa," Beckett says for a third time, this time whispering it. It's like the Meisner exercise has seeped its way into our real life.

"Whoa, indeed," I say, swirling my smoothie with my straw.

"I take it they're ... not happy."

"Worse. They're 'disappointed' in me."

"Brown Kid Detention?!" Beckett responds. "Ouch."

I laugh despite everything, and it feels good to have someone to commiserate with. No, not just someone. Beckett. "I'm glad *you're* not mad at me anymore, at least."

"Me too."

"Anyway," I say. "How are you? Is Oliver still posting pics with that boy?"

Beckett sighs. "Yeah. Though I took your advice and set myself a daily Instragram limit. Now at least there's a clock running on my moping."

"Are you guys talking at all?"

"We were," Beckett says. "But then I put a limit on that too. I realized I was just fishing for information on the new guy. It wasn't good for my mental health. Obviously I still love him, and maybe one day we can be friends, but definitely not now."

I nod. "I'm sorry, Beck."

"The thing is," he says, taking a sip from his smoothie, "you were right. I told *you* that I felt like we were growing apart, but...I never really told him. I wanted so badly for our limited time together to be happy that I swept everything else under the rug. And it blew up in my face." He gives me a sad smile. "Lesson learned for next time, I guess."

"I mean, who am I to drag anyone for not having open communication, though?" I acknowledge. "But, yes, lesson learned for next time. For both of us. And either way, you don't deserve a broken heart."

"I'll use it for my art, right?" he says.

"Oh, have you decided to go Method?" I joke.

"Shhh..." Beckett says, looking around furtively. "Don't let the Strasberg kids know I'm cribbin' their style."

CHAPTER 28

A Wonderful Guy

✪

We're shooting all weekend, including Friday night, which means I have to tell my parents that I can't make dinner. The only good thing is that if they ask me why, I won't have to lie. But they don't. Maman just responds with: Okay, have a good weekend.

I'm a little sad at the icy response but relieved to eke out a few more days before I have to face them again. After all, my major hasn't changed since last week, so I doubt anyone's feelings about it have changed either.

The set is more frenzied than usual. Petie explains how he wants to wrap up some of the storylines for "this version of the show," because the Hulu version will start over with a newly shot pilot. And evidently—based on what I overhear Petie and his cowriters discussing—a revamped script. Though, for now, they seem to be as off the cuff about the script as they've always been.

"Let's write a few lines in this scene where they talk about graduation. That seems a good way to end it, right? Graduation?" Petie is asking.

"It's a classic way to end a show set in high school for a reason," Benjamin responds.

"Great," Petie says.

If I had to sum up this show's philosophy in one sentence, it would be: "If it's worked before, let's just do it again." Maybe I should gift Petie a sampler with that stitched on it.

"Hey," Tru says as she walks up to me during a rare lull from Petie asking something of her. "How did everything go with your mom?" She had a night off during Wednesday's pickup shoot, so I haven't seen her since she watched my world implode around me on the sidewalks of New York.

"About how you'd expect if, I don't know, Leila's parents found out their only daughter was lying to them." I indicate Chaya rehearsing with Ahmet in one corner of the room.

"Ah," Tru responds. "So...a musical number?"

I burst out laughing. "I wish. Especially if it had been written by you."

Tru smiles, but her eyes look genuinely worried for me. "I'm sorry. It was bad, huh?"

I nod. "It was bad. But I guess it could always be worse." I shrug. "I'll survive."

"Did you talk to your adviser yet?" she asks. "About deferring?"

I shake my head, thinking about how long it took me to finally send over that double-major form—which is all moot now anyway. "Did you?"

Tru nods. "There's a bunch of paperwork to fill out."

"Okay," I say. "I'll set up an appointment." It suddenly feels like there's a tiny caterpillar crawling just beneath my skin. I wonder if it's embarrassment that I'll basically be telling Clara *JK about the double major, in fact I'm leaving school altogether.* But then I realize that it's not that. It's more like heartache. I'll be telling her I'm leaving school and her classes for . . . this. *Woe is me,* I think ironically.

"Places, everyone," Petie yells, and points at Yui and me.

"Places where?" Yui asks him. "I thought you were shooting a Morris-and-Juliet scene."

"Nope, scene eight. High school set. Everybody's in," Petie replies, not acknowledging that this is the first time he's relayed this information.

He walks away before Yui turns to me and mutters, "Like anyone knows what scene eight is since we haven't had a physical script in weeks."

She's not wrong. Petie stopped handing out full-length scripts sometime in February, probably because that's around when he stopped writing them. Now it's all spontaneous on-set meetings with Benjamin and Alex where they figure out story arcs and lines on the go.

Yui walks over to the lockers, and Petie tells her where to stand. I take a deep breath and walk over too.

"Leila, lean against this locker," Petie directs. "Look pensive. Here."

He hands over his phone, and I see the line they just wrote for me.

I can't believe high school is almost over, I'm supposed to say.

I *pensively* think: *I can't believe college is either.*

On Wednesday, I walk into Stats II and immediately scan the room for Max. He's there, but he either genuinely doesn't see me or he's purposefully not looking at me. I start to suspect it's the latter, as he manages to avoid glancing my way for the entirety of class.

Afterward, he books it so fast out of the room that I haven't even had time to put away my laptop before he's gone. I hurriedly cram it into my bag and run out into the hallway. He's almost reached the end of it already.

"Max!" I call out, running to catch up to him.

He stops at the end of the hall, seeming to hesitate for just one moment before he turns around. "Oh, hey, Nasrin," he says. "Sorry, I'm running late."

"Okay," I say, nodding. "I just wanted to apologize. If I have to do it quickly, that's okay."

Max sighs as he shifts his bag from one shoulder to the other. "You have nothing to apologize for, really. I overreacted."

I shake my head. "You didn't. You weren't really wrong about Minu. Plus, Beckett's right. I've been too self-absorbed lately to notice things that are happening right in front of my face. Or other people's feelings."

Max gives me a tight smile. "You don't have to apologize for my feelings, Nasrin. Or yours. It's okay."

"So you think you can...?"

"Tutor you again?" Max asks. "Sure."

I shift my weight from one foot to the other. "I was going to say be my friend again. Do you think you can do that?"

He blinks once. "Of course," he says gently.

I beam at him. "Good. I feel like I could really use one right now."

Max looks concerned. "Why? What happened?"

"Oh, nothing," I say, waving it away. "I know you have to go. We can talk about it later."

"I, uh... don't really have to run. So what happened?"

I shrug. "My parents found out about me lying. The show's moving to Vancouver. Maybe I'm dropping out of school?"

"Oh," Max says. "Wow. Uh... do you want to go grab a coffee and talk about it?"

I smile. "I'd love to."

Max waits until we've settled at a table and I have my hands around a steaming cappuccino before he broaches the subject.

"Okay, so talk to me."

"I mean, I already told you the big-picture stuff," I say.

"Right. But what about the little-picture stuff? Are you okay? Are you really moving to Vancouver?"

"I mean... how can I not? How can I turn down this opportunity to be a cast member on a Hulu show? A *musical* Hulu show."

"It's pretty huge for a musical theater performer," Max says measuredly.

"Yeah," I say slowly. "And I want to perform. And to have the opportunity to do it on a global scale like that? And get paid for it?"

"School can't hold a candle to that, right?" Max's voice remains steady, but he's looking at me like he might be expecting me to refute that.

I look down into my lap. I'd be leaving behind Meisner exercises, student-run productions, and grueling dance classes for the real thing. It seems like a no-brainer.

"And your parents?" Max continues. "How did they react?"

I snort. "To which part? The part where their daughter has been lying to them for the past ten months, or the part where said daughter might be dropping out of the school she's been lying to them *about*?"

"Both," Max replies.

"I guess a pretty typical reaction. I can't blame them for being mad or disappointed." My shoulders hunch, and my voice is smaller when I add, "Not when I feel all those same things about myself."

Max nods. "I've felt that a lot too. Disappointed and ashamed at myself for being so different from my family. For not having the same priorities or beliefs. But at some point I realized that I also had to be true to myself, or I'd spend my life regretting everything."

I take that in. Some of it sounds like things I've felt, but so much of it is different too. "That's what I thought this was," I finally say. "Being true to myself."

"It's not?"

"It is, but... I don't think they deserved the lying, you know?"

"Maybe not," Max says. "But Nader and Samineh also seem like pretty reasonable people. Maybe once the initial shock wears off, you can talk to them."

Hearing Max call my parents by their first names makes me remember how much he seems to worship them. I smile wanly. "They seem reasonable to you because you want to do what they want to do. But I just... don't."

Max leans back. "Fair. I shouldn't judge your relationship by what I see. Pretty much everyone at home thinks I'm ungrateful for walking away from my perfect parents."

"But they're not perfect," I say. "Not if they can't appreciate how hard you work to become what you're going to become."

"I could say those words right back at you."

"I'm working hard for something 'foolish and unstable,'" I say with a snort.

"Now that's your parents talking," Max states.

"Yeah," I say. "And the show proves them wrong. But the show also takes me away from school... I don't know. It's all such a mess. The thing is, I don't want to disappoint my parents. Not really. But I'm guessing you didn't either."

Max shrugs. "No. But it seemed like there was no other

way. If they couldn't accept my choices, even after I tried to explain it to them then—disappointing them seemed like my only option."

"I guess the difference here is you never lied to them," I say. I think for a minute. "My parents didn't deserve that. But maybe they do deserve an explanation of my choices. Like you said."

Max nods. "I think so. And from the little time I've spent with them, I think they'll ultimately be a lot more willing to listen than my folks were."

"Speaking of which," I say as I dump a packet of sugar into my cappuccino. "How are things going with them? Are they going to come to your graduation?"

Max shifts uncomfortably in his seat. "I don't know. I only mentioned it to them that once and . . . I haven't brought it up again. It's a few months away, anyway."

"Well," I say gently. "I know you think they won't listen, but maybe it's worth asking again. Don't you think?"

Max looks up at me. "Maybe."

I stir my drink and suddenly hit upon an idea. "Hey, in the meantime, do you want to come to our next family dinner? It's on Friday. You can get some parental practice."

"You sure you want me to?" Max asks.

"Yes," I say, thinking that Max deserves some familial support, even if it's not from his own. And maybe spending more time in that environment will give him the courage to reach out to his parents. But out loud, I explain, "I haven't seen them in person since the night they found out. I could use the moral support."

"All right," Max says. "How can I say no?"

I beam at him. "Thanks, Max."

The right side of his mouth has gone up. Not quite his full-voltage smile, but not so far off either.

CHAPTER 29

There's No Business Like Show Business

✧

Maman looks extremely surprised when she opens the door and sees Max towering behind me, though she quickly rearranges her face.

"Hello," she says, a little stiffly. "Welcome." In retrospect, I probably should've told them Max was coming, but I was afraid they'd ask him not to. And I really need him to be here.

"Hello, Samineh," Max says, and then lifts up a white box. "I brought some cookies from Veniero's."

Maman smiles as she takes the box from him. "Thank you. That's very sweet of you." She gives me a look but doesn't say anything else. "Nader, Max is here too," she yells into the dining room, giving my dad a little extra time to recalibrate his expression as he walks into the foyer.

"Ah, Max," he says, shaking his hand. "My favorite theoretical business partner." All three of us realize the implication that his own daughter is not his favorite person of the pair of us. Baba glances furtively over at me, but then he turns to the dining room without apology. "Come in. We just set the table."

Max touches my elbow lightly and bends down to whisper, "You okay?"

I nod and lead him into the dining room. We've taken our seats when Minu walks in, staring at her phone. "Salaam," she says without looking up.

"Salaam," I say.

"Hi," Max says.

She looks up from her screen then, surprised. "Oh. Hi. I didn't expect you to be here."

Max shrugs. So much has happened in the past week that I practically forgot about the one date they went on. Ah well. If it's awkward between them, it's nothing compared to how it's going to be between me and my parents for the rest of the night. Or, possibly, the rest of my life.

Maman and Baba come in then, carrying dishes of rice, fake smiles plastered on both of their faces. Baba runs back into the kitchen to grab an extra place setting for Max. Over dinner, he seems to relax a tiny bit, politeness dictating that he make conversation with our guest. They eventually get around to talking about the business plan of their pretend smoothie shop—which I guess I've now been cut out of. I sigh as I spoon a heap of rice, carrots, and barberries into my mouth. Baba is so passionate about this, and yet he can't seem to understand why my passions are so important to me.

I'm left in relative peace during dinner because my

parents wouldn't dare display their ire in front of a guest. I realize a large part of me already knew that. Isn't that why I asked Max to come in the first place? So does that mean I'm using Max? Is Beckett's assessment of me as selfish and self-absorbed just who I am, and not the result of my being "busy"? The rice grains turn heavy in my mouth and I have a hard time swallowing them. I think of my behavior over the last few months: lying so callously to my parents, always with a flimsy excuse for it; not being there for Beckett when he needed me; and now inviting Max here on the pretense that *he'd* enjoy the family time. I've made excuses for all of it by assuring myself it's in service of my work, my art—which, let's face it, is by its nature so all-consumingly about *me*. At an audition, I need to shine the brightest so that it'll be clear that I'm the only one who can play that part. But all the world is *not* a stage, and I can't go through it expecting to be the leading lady in everyone else's life. Not even, I think as I watch Baba tell Max some anecdote about the early days of Rate the Plate, my parents'.

When they stand to start clearing the table, I get up with them. I see Max start to stack plates too, but I put a hand on his and shake my head. "I gotta go talk to them," I say, indicating the kitchen. He nods and sits back down.

My last view as I turn to enter the kitchen is Max and Minu sitting across from each other, an awkward silence between them.

Maman is throwing out the scraps left on the plates while Baba is by the sink, rinsing dishes to put in the dishwasher.

They've already fallen into a comfortable rhythm, and a comfortable silence, which I don't want to break. But I have to.

I clear my throat.

They both look at me warily. For a moment, it's like we're setting the stage before the curtain goes up, each of us striking our opening poses. Then Maman puts out her hand to take the plates from me. I give them to her while I gather my courage.

"Can we talk?" I ask. My voice sounds scratchy, as though I haven't used it in a while.

"What's there to talk about?" Baba says, turning back to the sink. Maman is still looking at me, but she doesn't say anything.

"Well, first of all, I want to say again how sorry I am that I lied. I am really, really, really sorry. And if I can do anything to make it up to you, I will."

"How about you go to business school?" Baba says to the dishes.

"Anything but that," I say.

Baba finally faces me. "Why not? Is what we do so horrible that you're ashamed of it?"

I stare back at him. "Is that... Is that really what you think this is about?"

Maman sighs. "Of course he doesn't," she says, shooting Baba a look. He shakes his head and returns to the sink. "We want you to be successful, Nasrin, because we want you to have a good life."

"But what does success even mean if not, say, the show? Our numbers are incredible. We have over a million subscribers now. And once it's on Hulu, there'll be even more people watching. I'm getting paid...."

"It's not just about getting paid," Maman says.

"What, then? Don't you want me to make a living? Isn't that the point? Or do you just specifically hate show business that much?"

"We don't hate show business," Maman says just as Baba turns off the tap and puts the dish towel over his shoulder. "But we can't forget what you were like after you didn't make the cut for that play. How depressed it made you."

"But that was *years* ago," I protest. "I was only fourteen."

"Do you think it's going to be so different? So you have a Hulu show now, but what happens after that?" Baba asks. "How many child and teen stars get one gig, or two, and then just...disappear?"

"Maybe they disappear because they're filthy rich and don't need to work anymore," I mutter sarcastically. Maman stares hard at me, and I take a deep breath. "Do you really think I need a crash course in how hard this business is? Because I get that every day in my classes at Tisch. That's why I wanted to go. To hone my craft, but also to learn how to navigate it, as a *business*. So that I can deal with rejection and *not* fall apart." Saying it out loud like this is elucidating for me too.

"But why do something where rejection is such a huge part of the equation at all, Nasrin?" Maman asks.

"Because it's the only thing that makes me feel alive, like I have something special to give," I say, crossing my hands over

my chest. "The purpose you and Baba always talk about—"
I take one hand and fling it out in the direction of the wall
separating the kitchen and dining room, on the other side of
which the sampler hangs. "You claim it's not about money, but
that's what Baba meant when he worried so hard about me
waiting tables, wasn't it?"

"Of course not," Maman says crisply. "We just want better for you than what we had. We struggled a lot when we
first came here. Do you think we'd ever want that for our only
child?"

"But do you realize what kind of pressure that puts me
under?"

Baba shakes his head. "I guess we can't do anything right,
Samineh. Why do we even bother?"

"Ugh. The problem is you never listen," I say as I turn on
my heels and walk out of the kitchen. I sound and feel like a
petulant teenager, but I also don't know how else to act when
they're treating me like a child, like they know everything
about what's best for me. In their eyes, I'm only ever going to
be that devastated fourteen-year-old girl—not a young woman
with eyes wide open, who's fully prepared for heartache if it
means she gets to pursue her dreams. They have no idea the
rush I get when I'm on a stage, how I need it to survive—just
like I need food and shelter, all the things they're concerned
I won't be able to provide for myself.

And they'll never know it if they don't listen.

I walk back into the dining room, expecting to find Max
and Minu still staring awkwardly off into the distance.

Instead, Minu has moved over to Max's side of the table and they seem to be watching something raucous on his phone, a stand-up comedy set, I'd say, by the sounds of laughter emanating from both the phone and the two of them.

Max looks up when he sees me and gives an apologetic smile. "Sorry. It was kinda loud in there, and we figured you deserved some privacy." He indicates his phone.

"Right. Thanks," I say. I should be grateful that he's so thoughtful, but the sight of him and Minu sitting so close to each other just makes me feel weird.

Why, I wonder as I plop myself down in Minu's old seat, does nothing feel right lately?

"It's not fair!" I say. Or rather, Leila does.

I'm standing in front of Chaya, the actress who plays my mom. Her dark hair and pear-shaped figure echoes my own mom's pretty well. I guess I didn't say anything quite as clichéd to my parents the other night—but then again, it wasn't *much* more original.

"Cut!" Petie yells, and then stalks over to scrutinize both of us. "Something isn't quite working."

"The line?" I ask, somewhat hopefully.

"Nope, the line's fine. Let's take five and let me think on it."

Chaya and I nod, and both go to the craft services table to grab some waters. "You excited about Vancouver?" Chaya asks me.

She's clearly making small talk, not asking me for a

rundown of my extremely complicated life. So I just nod. "Mm-hmm."

"Me too. Though I'm a little worried about how cold it gets up there," she says.

"Yes. I've heard that." *I've heard that Canada gets cold?* Solid conversation. Still, it's more genuine than anything my real mom and I have said to each other lately.

Chaya steps away from me to peruse the vegetable platter. I notice she's looking at her lines on the pages Petie handed out to us about twenty minutes ago. That might be a good thing for me to do too. Maybe I can figure out why this scene isn't working.

LEILA

It's not fair!

AMAL

What's not fair is you lying this
whole time. Dancing? Singing?
That's not why we moved here.

Honestly, who needs Method acting when this scene is just a spoof of my real life? But I shake my head and look closer at the words. I've spent the last week arguing about performing being important, about wanting to be taken seriously. That means *I* need to take my own work seriously too.

I think of Clara teaching us Stanislavski's "magic if" method and the questions we're supposed to ask ourselves,

250

like "What does the character want?" and "What does she need to make the other character do to get it?"

What does Leila want? That's easy, because it's the same thing I want: to act, sing, and dance. To chase the energy that I get when I'm pretending to be someone else and whisking an audience away with me.

What does she need to get her mother to do?

That's a little trickier. The way it's written now, and the way I've been performing it, she's thinking about herself and not her mom—which, I suppose, isn't out of character for a teen.

But if I made her think about her mom, then what would Leila realize? That her mom is doing her best too? That her mom loves her unconditionally? That, underneath it all, her mom doesn't want her to live a life of rejection? But the irony is that Maman is rejecting any notions I have for my own life and happiness. I mean Amal is.

When Petie calls us back to the set, I step on my mark and decide I'm going to try playing it that way. Maybe Leila isn't saying it's not fair for her; maybe she's saying that it hasn't always been fair for her mom.

When Petie says "Action," I look into Chaya's eyes, searching them, and then I gently grab her hand and say softly, "It isn't fair."

Chaya looks confused for a moment but quickly recovers. "What isn't fair..." she starts.

"Cut!" Petie yells and turns to me. "What happened?"

"You said it wasn't working, so I thought I'd try something

different," I reply. "Maybe we need to see it from Amal's point of view. Maybe that's what Leila would try to—"

"That's cool," Petie says, "but I figured out what wasn't working already. It was the throw blanket in the back. Too bright green. The internet would go nuts green-screening crazy crap into my scene. Anyway, could you go back to playing it the way you were before? That was fine."

I hesitate for a split second and then nod. "Sure."

"And you know what?" Petie adds. "Why don't you stamp your foot too? It'll really bring the line home."

"Cross my arms. And stamp my foot. And yell 'It's not fair,'" I echo in a hollow voice.

"Exactly," Petie says. "And...action."

CHAPTER 30

Put on a Happy Face

✦

At the end of Tuesday night's shoot, Petie lets us know that the start date for Vancouver is officially three weeks away. "Which means we'll only be shooting here for two more weeks before we relocate. Also, you're all getting new contracts. Cheryl is handing them out now."

I take the manila envelope with my name on it and slip the thick stack of pages out just far enough to see the Hulu logo at the top before sliding them back in. Three weeks. I really need to make that appointment with Clara . . . again. I've been putting it off partially because I don't have the time . . . but really because that would make this so much more real.

"You should get an agent to take a look at that," Beckett says to me when I've shown him the intimidating envelope. "I can introduce you to someone at my agency. Not that you'll have a problem getting an agent with a contract in hand."

I nod, knowing I should be happy we're talking about agents and contracts and credits. Except I can't help but feel that I've somehow missed a step. And that maybe it's ultimately going to make me miss more than that.

Dinner with my family continues to be awkward and subdued. Without Max as a buffer, it's clear no one is talking to me—not even to ask me to pass some silverware; Baba gets up and walks all the way around the table to grab a fork from right beside me.

Maybe I should cancel again next week.

To fill the silence, my parents probe Minu for information on her classes for once. The reasons for her vague, one-word answers are obvious to me, but Maman and Baba don't seem to be catching on. Especially since she, unlike me, has been smart enough to have a parentally appropriate burner social media account this whole time. I move food around on my plate bitterly while Baba goes on and on about what a great school Barnard is. "Of course you know that," he says.

"Not if she doesn't go to class, she doesn't."

It takes me a second to realize that I was the one who said those words. Everyone's forks have stopped moving. Minu is shooting a laser death stare in my direction.

"What do you mean?" Baba asks, looking at Minu.

"Nothing," I say quickly. "Just an inside joke between us."

Baba turns to Minu. Evidently, his experience with me over the past two weeks has made him extra suspicious, because he goes so far as to ask her, "You *are* attending your classes, aren't you?"

"Of course, Amoo," Minu says. "Like Nasrin said, it was an inside joke. A stupid one."

She stares at me again, but I just nod and go back to my food. Everyone seems to drop the subject.

I don't intend to stay too long after we've cleared our plates. But just when I'm grabbing my coat, Minu asks if I can come to her room to help her out with deciphering a dense English essay.

"You want me to do more of your work?" I grumble as she shuts the door.

She turns to me, eyes flashing. "I can't believe you said that. After everything I did for you?"

"Everything you did for me?" I ask incredulously. "You mean blackmailing me to keep my secret?"

"I *covered* for you," she responds. "Loads of times. And I wasn't blackmailing. I was asking for a favor in return."

I roll my eyes. "You could've fooled me."

"You are such a spoiled brat, you know that?" she says as she crosses her arms and sits down at her desk chair.

My jaw actually drops at that one. "Am I the one wasting my parents' money by not going to the classes they're spending a fortune on?!"

"Actually, yeah, you are," she responds. "Because they weren't paying for the classes you were going to, were they?"

"At least I was actually going to school. Not partying."

"I'm not just partying," she says. "I'm experiencing life here."

"Oh please...save your bullshit for my mom and dad, okay?" I go to open her door to leave.

"You have no idea what it's like to see all these opportunities and freedoms on social media all the time and never have them for yourself." I hear a hint of a waver in Minu's voice. "It's so commonplace to you, being able to attend a show, or go on a date, or wear whatever you want, or have basic freedom of speech. You don't even realize it's a privilege. But it is."

I stare at the pilly blue-and-beige carpet on her floor, absorbing her words before I turn around to face her. "Okay," I finally say. "But do you know that it's a privilege to go to school too? How many other people dream of having that opportunity?" I realize, of course, that I'm echoing Max's sentiments to her. But even as I defended her to him, it's not like I didn't know that he was right.

There's silence. I'm expecting another glare or a roll of her eyes, but instead, she bites her lip, looking thoughtful. "You're...not wrong," she says. "I just wanted to experience everything. Who knows how long I have here? If I don't find a job pretty immediately after college, my student visa will run out without ever turning into a work one."

I pause for a minute. "And then you'd . . . have to leave?"

Minu nods and the thought gives me a pang, both for her and, I realize, for myself without her. "I wouldn't want that," I admit.

Minu gives me a small smile. "Me neither. But it's not

entirely up to me. So this idea of soaking up my time here while I can—maybe I got a little carried away. But the whole 'American college experience' thing is sometimes hard to resist."

"I mean . . . I can understand that," I say. "I'm worried that with the show moving to Vancouver, I'm going to miss out on the whole college experience, too. Including getting to experiment with my craft."

"Aren't you doing that with the show?" Minu asks.

I sigh. "Yes. And no. Something's missing. Like . . . that rush of performing for a live audience? But also, maybe, being a part of material that I believe in. But . . . like you said, I'm spoiled. And I'm complaining about a huge opportunity that any young actress would kill for."

Minu tilts her head. "But you're not happy."

Her words are so simple that it takes me aback how pierced I feel by them. How come I never stopped to think this myself: All my anxiety, and worries, and fears . . . there's a word for that. Unhappy.

"I'm not," I admit. "I hate having Maman and Baba so mad at me. And, let's be honest, I can't even blame them."

"And what about college? Does it make you happy?" Minu asks.

I pause. "My classes are really hard. Challenging. I don't always feel like I have a good grasp on what I'm doing. Which I'm really not used to, not when it comes to performing, anyway. Everyone at Tisch was the star of their high school, you know what I mean?"

"Sounds exciting," Minu says.

"Uh, I was going to say terrifying, but..."

"Isn't that two sides of the same coin?" Minu asks. "How can you have thrills without risks?"

"Maybe..."

"You didn't answer my question. Do these challenging classes make you happy?"

I pause and search my memory for my favorite moments of the past six months. Not a single image of *STD* runs through my brain. Instead I think of getting applause after the improv acting exercise. Bonding with Beckett over smoothies. Seeing Lucia's brilliant play in a tiny theater and then, even better, getting to work with her for half a second. Having someone as incredible as her tell me I'm talented too.

There's only one exception: Tru and her gorgeous songs. But then, I've always thought she was too good for *Small Town Dreams*.

Maybe I am too. Or maybe, at least, I can answer Minu's question honestly: "My classes do make me happy," I say. "Because they encompass everything about performing that I love."

"Well, there you go," Minu says. "What's the point of pursuing your passions if they aren't going to make you happy? You might as well be a business major, then, right?" Minu smirks and arches an eyebrow.

Maybe it's a jab, but it's one that's deeply rooted in something I've been avoiding for far too long: the truth.

CHAPTER 31

Those Magic Changes

✩

"Tie me down,
I'll just drown you out,
With my big and loud
Choice,
My voice,
And your noise,
Can't hold a candle,
Can't handle
My flame,
Know my name,
'Cause you'll never tame it,
You can only blame it,
When it blazes so bright
And shuts off your light."

I love this song that Tru wrote for me. I love getting to spit out its rhymes and belt out its big chorus. And right now, it's the only thing that's holding me together.

It's our last week on our little New York set. The energy feels like pre–opening night dress rehearsal. Everyone is performing at their best, saying their lines and hitting their marks like we're all swimming in an endless communal pool of adrenaline. The chatter in the air feels like the first birdsong of spring, the kind that heralds all the warmth and sunshine that's in your future. It's all the beautiful anticipation I always try—and fail—to explain to someone who's not a performer themself.

So there's no accounting for how I feel right now. Like I'm just watching instead of participating; like I'm in the audience, removed from the energy and emotions by distant seats and a thick curtain.

Cheryl has been collecting everyone's contracts. All day, as people have come in for their various call times, I've watched their eager faces as they hand in their manila envelopes. Mine is still in my bag.

The contract inside isn't signed. Beckett, true to his word, did hook me up with his theater agent, who took a call with me over the weekend since she knew the timeline was so crunched. Her name is Izzy, and she seems both highly knowledgeable and completely no-nonsense. I immediately liked her. After taking a quick look at the contract, Izzy told me she would like to speak to the Business Affairs office about a few points. Which is what I tell Cheryl now when she comes over to collect my envelope.

She looks at me blankly, since I'm clearly the first one to mention this to her. "You'll have to talk to Petie," she finally says when my request registers.

I nod, then walk over to Petie, politely waiting my turn behind Anouk, Morris, and Jeff. It takes him a while to get to me, but I stay put.

"What's up, Nasrin?" he says once he's done talking to them about their impending scene. "If it's about your scene, we can talk about it when we get to it, okay?"

"It's not about my scene," I reply calmly. "It's about my contract."

"Oh, you can just hand that in to Cheryl," Petie says, pointing her out as if I might not know who she is.

"Right. When it's signed," I say.

Petie hesitates. "Why wouldn't it be signed?"

"My agent wants to chat with someone in Hulu's Business Affairs department," I reply. *My agent. Business Affairs.* I have to admit, it feels good to be throwing around such professional terms.

It also finally seems to get Petie's attention. He frowns and looks at me like he's seeing me for the first time. "It's a standard contract," Petie says. "All the actors got the same one."

I'm sure that's not true. I'm sure, for example, that all the actors did not get the same fee . . . especially since Morris and Juliet have already been whisked away a couple of times to shoot social media teasers for the show. Either way, I don't back down. "She still wants to talk to them. She says there's some wording surrounding the merchandising and soundtrack sales that she doesn't love."

Petie huffs out a big sigh, but I just wait patiently. "Fine," he says. "Tell Liz to get you the contact info for their BA department. But also tell your agent that we need this signed by the end of the week, or we're going to have to recast. We're going to be shooting Leila in Vancouver in two weeks, with or without you."

He means it as a threat, obviously. But as he walks away, this other, very strange sensation creeps over me at the thought that they might be shooting Leila without me. It feels suspiciously like... relief.

"Max will be handing out your quizzes from last week," Professor Pham says at the end of Stats class.

I wait dutifully while Max makes his way around the classroom, getting to my row last. He places my paper facedown on the desk but flashes me a brilliant smile as he moves on to give my neighbor her quiz.

Turning the paper around, I stare at the small, neat *A* encircled in a perfect arc. I can't believe it.

I look up to catch Max's eye and see that he's still smiling at me. He gives me a thumbs-up.

I gather my belongings slowly, but it takes my brain a

minute to catch on that it's because I want to talk to him privately. There are only a couple of people left in the class by the time I approach him.

"Thank you," I say at the same time as Max says, "You killed it, Nasrin."

"Because of you," I reply.

"Because of your own hard work," Max says. "I knew you could do it."

"Since I have my dad's blood running through me?" I ask, half joking.

"Since I think you can do anything you set your mind to. Whether it's acting, or stats, or anything else."

I smile at him. "Thanks for that. I'm not sure too many people would agree with you these days, but thanks." I wave the quiz in front of him. "And thanks for this. Because even if I'll never love stats, you made me understand and respect it. And that, I think, is the hallmark of a great teacher."

"Will you be uploading a review for my website, then?" Max asks.

"Of course..." I say.

"Performed in song and dance?" Max asks.

I laugh. "Really?"

Max nods. "Gotta stand out from the field somehow."

"The crowded field of college stats tutors?" I ask.

"Listen, I know you're about to go Hollywood, but you want cutthroat, you should check out the competition. Have you ever taken a look at the OddsAre hashtag?"

"Can't say that I have..."

"It's better that way," Max says seriously. "The puns alone are enough to cause irreparable damage."

I laugh.

He smiles. "Anyway, I'm proud of you," he says as he lifts the strap of his satchel onto his shoulder.

"Thanks," I say. And as I watch him getting ready to leave, I get strange flashes in my mind. Of him and Minu laughing together over the comedy video. Of what I imagine they must have looked like sitting across from each other on their date. "Hey, Max." From my peripheral vision, I see Beckett hovering near the door, ready to head into Acting with me. The déjà vu comes on strong. But this time, I realize, I think I'm going to gun for a different outcome. "Are you free for a meal sometime this week? Maybe a dinner?"

"I'm sure I have some nights free. Did you find a new restaurant you want to try?"

I shake my head. "Not yet. But I did find a date I want to try."

"A date?" he asks hesitantly.

"A date," I reply firmly. "Would you like to go on one with me?"

"Really?" he asks.

"Really," I reply, and then, when there's another few seconds of silence, I backtrack. "But only if you want to. No hard feelings if not, I get it..."

Max grabs my hand, possibly to stop me from babbling.

"I'd love to," he says. "Text me to work out the details?"

"Yeah," I say, feeling oddly breathless as he flashes me that rare smile.

He gives my hand a light squeeze before he lets it go. "Hey, Beckett," he says as he walks past my friend and out of the classroom.

"Hey," Beckett says back, and then turns to me with his jaw dropped open. "Oh. My. God," he mouths as he puts his hand to his heart and pretends to swoon.

I shrug, but the self-satisfied smile on my face tells him all he needs to know about my true feelings.

CHAPTER 32

Some Enchanted Evening

✦

When I get out from Acting, I see that I already have a message from Max. How about tonight?

I'm grinning at my phone like I would be at him, and I'm sure I look like an idiot, but I don't care. Yes, I write back. Meet me in front of Third North at 7?

You got it, he writes.

It gives me just enough time to research restaurants. Despite all my complicated feelings about my parents, I go to my most trusted source first: Rate the Plate's blog. Maman has a team writing content for it, but I notice she authored the latest entry herself. I flash back to me as a nine-year-old, fixing some of my parents' English grammar and American idioms before they hit publish on their posts. That was right before the write-up in *Wired*, when Rate the Plate felt like a small family business and the three of us felt like one indestructible unit. Maman and Baba would give me little gifts or sometimes pay for extra dance classes as a "salary." That's where my stage curtain necklace came from. I bring my hand to it now; I never could've imagined that it would still be here when my parents themselves feel so far away.

I try to rein in my thoughts and focus on Maman's write-up, which is for a Peruvian restaurant in Tribeca. Her description of the food seems too good to pass up. Maybe, I admit to myself, going there is also a way to talk to her without actually talking to her. But I try to dispel any lingering sadness by instead embracing the excitement of my first real date.

Uncertainty takes over the moment I step in front of my closet to stare at my wardrobe.

I think I need a second opinion. Or maybe even entirely new clothes. But Beatrix is out, and Beckett is at an extra rehearsal for *The Walk-Up*. Finally, I pick up my phone and, after a split second, hit the FaceTime button.

"What's up?" Minu says once she answers.

"Um, hey. Hi. So...I have a date...."

"Oh! I would ask who with, but, like, I'm pretty sure I know the answer to that," she says, smirking.

"Yeah, yeah," I say.

"On second thought," she says, looking pensive, "I think I'd like to hear you say his name."

"Ha-ha," I reply sarcastically.

"No, seriously. Who do you have a date with? Is it someone

from your show? One of your classmates? A handsome stranger you met on the F train?" Minu bats her eyelashes.

"Minu," I say.

"Yes?" she asks innocently.

"It's Max, okay? Max," I reply in exasperation.

She grins. "Yes! My plan worked!"

"Your plan?"

"I figured you'd see him in a different light once *I* went on a date with him...."

"Minu," I say. "That is complete bullshit. You went on a date with him because you thought he was cute!"

"I mean, yes," Minu admits. "But once I realized there was no spark there, I switched tactics to fanning the flame of *your* sparks."

I roll my eyes. "Okay, sure, whatever."

"Anyway, is there a reason you called me?"

"I, uh, think I need a little wardrobe help," I mutter, taking one more hopeless look into my closet.

"Say no more!" she says, clapping her hands. "Makeover montage! I'll be there in forty-five minutes."

True to her word, my cousin shows up at my door with three hangers and a tote bag full of accessories. She's pulling the dresses out as I pace my dorm room in anxious figure eights.

"Damn," she says as she opens the bathroom door and hangs the dresses up on the curtain rod. "Were you even this nervous when you were about to audition for a huge web series?"

"Of course not," I reply. "What's there to be nervous about when they give you all your lines on a piece of paper?"

Minu raises an eyebrow. "That's one way to look at it, I guess. Okay, so what do you think?"

I look at the array of dresses Minu brought: There's a burgundy velvet dress with a matching belt, an emerald jumpsuit with a plunging neckline, and a black tulle dress embroidered with tiny silver stars. I walk over to touch that one first.

"I agree," Minu says. "I think this is the most 'you.'" She holds it up in front of me while I look in the mirror. "But also new to you, so you don't have any associated memories with it. You can make fresh ones."

"It's pretty," I say.

"Try it on."

Minu leaves the bathroom, and I shut the door. By the time I've come out, she's laid out a chunky silver cuff and a necklace of bright blue beads on my dresser.

"Gorgeous," she says when she sees me in the dress. "Twirl?" I do, billowing the dress's tulle overlay out. "How do you feel in it?"

"Pretty cute," I reply, looking into the mirror.

She raises her eyebrow. "*Pretty* cute?"

"Maybe just pretty," I say. "I feel pretty," I add firmly, and it takes all my self-control not to break out into the Bernstein-Sondheim number.

"Good." She hands over the jewelry. I put on the cuff but hesitate on the necklace, lightly touching my curtain pendant. I like the idea of a blank slate for whatever tonight's memories will be, but then again, the person Max seems to like is the Nasrin he's known all along.

"Unfortunately, I don't think we're the same shoe size, so I didn't bring any," Minu says. "But do you have some strappy sandals? That's what I usually wear it with."

"That's okay," I say, and take out my rainbow-checkered Vans. "I think I gotta look a little like me, right?" I take off the star-and-clapboard necklace, but leave the curtain pendant on.

Minu nods her approval. "Perfect." She gives me two kisses on the cheek and a spritz of perfume before she sends me out the door.

When I exit my building, Max is already there waiting for me. Though he's turned away from the door, I recognize the tall, slim plane of his back, clad in a soft sea-blue sweater. I also realize I already know that the color of his shirt matches the hue of his eyes perfectly—before he turns around at the sound of his name.

"Wow, you look beautiful," he says.

"You do too," I say. "You should wear that color more often."

He ducks his head. "Thank you," he says. "So, where are we going?"

"The subway," I say. "Come on."

He reaches for my hand, and I take it. It surprises me how natural it feels to walk down the streets of the Village, hand in hand with him. As we approach the West Fourth Street station, Max points out the high-octane basketball game going on at the courts right next to it. "I kinda have this tradition that I have to stop and watch for a minute every time I pass. Do you mind?"

"Not at all," I say. "I'm a sucker for traditions." We stand near the small crowd outside the chain-link fence, watching the kids inside run, dribble, dunk, and dodge each other like pros.

"These...aren't professional players, are they?" I ask. "They look young."

"Just kids for now," Max says. "But they could be. They're amazing, right?"

I nod. Though I don't know too much about basketball, I've spent enough years in dance to know athletic prowess and masterful choreography when I see it. "Do you play?" I ask Max.

"In middle school," he says. "I love it. But I wasn't ever tall enough to make the varsity team."

"That sucks to have something like your height deter you from what you love to do."

Max shrugs. "Yeah, but...I mean, don't all actors go through the same thing? How many roles are you denied not because of your talents, but simply because you don't look right for the part?"

"Touché," I say.

"And yet..." Max says.

"And yet?"

"You're doing it. And you're going to continue to do it. Because it's what you're meant to do, right?"

"I thought so," I say, watching a kid duck his way out from under the arm of a much bigger kid to score a basket.

"You don't still think so?" Max asks, surprised.

"I do, but also... someone recently pointed out that the show doesn't seem to make me happy. And I don't know if I'm meant to be at odds with my parents. It doesn't feel right."

"Yeah," Max says. "I can tell how close you guys are." He sounds a little sad when he says it, and I think of him and his family. I can't imagine feeling removed from my parents all the time like he does, having this knot in my stomach every day.

"I don't know how you've done it," I say, my fingers lightly grazing my pendant. "I'd be nowhere without my family's support. In some ways, I'm so spoiled," I say, thinking of Minu's words. "So privileged."

Max shrugs. "Privilege comes in different forms. I mean, I'm a straight white dude. Like, come on. My baseline is privilege."

"You're... not wrong," I say.

He laughs. "I know it. And it's important to me to know it and to try to use it to make the world a little more equitable. My folks... they haven't always seemed to understand that. They don't want to see some of the ways they've had things handed to them that others just haven't. Because they're not rich or anything, and nobody says they haven't worked hard too.... I don't know. Where their mind first goes when talk like this comes up is to feel personally attacked. Sometimes, it's hard to reason with abject defensiveness. But your folks..."

"I know. You love them and they're perfect," I say.

"No," Max says. "I mean, yes, I do kinda worship them."

I nod. "The marble bust you're chiseling of them in your free time might have given it away."

Max smirks. "What I wanted to say is I think your parents are great. But I don't think they're in the right here."

I raise my eyebrows. "You think I was, for lying to them?"

He hesitates for a moment. "Not exactly..."

I laugh. "Good. If you'd said yes, then I'd know you were just blowing smoke up my ass."

"But I do think you love each other. And you respect each other. And armed with those things, you'll work it out."

"I hope you're right," I say, my hand instinctively going to my necklace again.

"Actually," Max continues, "hanging out with your family...it made me decide to call my own folks again. To ask about graduation."

My jaw drops. "Max! That's amazing."

He shrugs. "You once called me out for expecting perfection from everybody and...that might be true. My mom kept telling me she'd feel uncomfortable sitting with a bunch of college graduates, and I kept hearing it as an excuse. But then I realized, she thinks *I* look down on her. I was so angry they didn't seem to hear me, I never realized I wasn't really hearing them either."

I chew on that for a minute. "Seems to be a common thread these days. Anyway, what did your parents say? Are they coming to graduation?"

The corner of his mouth goes up. "Yeah."

I clap my hands on his shoulders. "That's awesome, Max. I'm so happy for you."

He shrugs, turning back to the basketball game. "I mean, they still have plenty of time to back out, but...I just wanted to thank you. I would never have taken the time to listen if it wasn't for you." He reaches out and lets his thumb lightly brush the back of my hand.

I turn to look at his profile, the constellation of freckles on his nose. He must sense me staring because he turns to face me too, blue eyes looking into brown without breaking contact.

I let my instincts take over, sweeping my thumb gently down the slope of his nose and across his cheek, following a line of freckles that goes all the way to the tip of his ear. "Sorry," I whisper. "I've wanted to do that for a while."

His eyes brighten. "You have?"

"They're like a galaxy of stars," I say.

He runs his hand gently down my waist underneath my open wool coat, lingering on each tiny silver embroidery on my dress. "I like these stars," he says, stilling his hand on my hips and looking into my eyes. "I like this star."

I bring my face closer to his, until his freckles are blurry, and right when I can't make them out at all anymore, I close my eyes. I don't know which of us actually closes the gap between our lips. I just know that it feels like a dream or, more aptly, like a version of life I didn't know could be real. This is my first non-stage kiss, I realize. And as much as I've been honing my craft to feel connected to the characters I play...

there's nothing about this that I could ever have re-created. Not, anyway, how it's lighting me up, like all the embroidered stars have ignited, casting me in a glow that shines from the inside out. And it's in that moment that I realize there are some real-life things I've been missing out on, being so focused on the imitation of them.

"Wow," I say softly when we break apart, our noses still touching.

"Wow," Max replies dreamily, and the energy radiating between us is palpable. Almost like a buzzing.

Oh, wait, no. That's the real vibration of Max's phone; I'm close enough to him that I feel it too.

"Sorry," Max says as he quickly takes it out and glances at the message. "Tutoring stuff. I don't need to be dealing with this right now." I watch him put his phone in Do Not Disturb mode.

"You're packing in your tutoring business now that you got the girl?" I tease.

"For the night," he replies. "I just want to be completely present. Here with you."

My cheeks flush before I take my phone out and duplicate the gesture. And then I wrap my arms around his neck and we press our lips together again.

A loud coach's whistle right next to our ears startles us apart. The basketball players seem to be taking a break.

Max glances at his watch. "Oh no," he says. "Aren't our reservations in five minutes?"

I look at his watch. "They are."

"I'm sorry," he says. "It was my fault we stopped to watch the game."

"I'm not," I reply, looking around. "Wait right here."

"Where are you going?" he asks as I cross the street.

"You'll see."

Five minutes later, I'm back, my arms laden with two hot dogs and two sodas. Max rushes to take them from me once he sees me struggling to keep everything upright.

"Thanks," I say. And then I indicate the basketball court. "Dinner and a show. What could be better?"

He grins and puts an arm around me as the kids get back into the game. I take a bite of my hot dog and know that I could easily write a thousand-word blog post about it, and how the warmth of the boy sitting next to me is making it one of the best culinary experiences I've ever had.

CHAPTER 33

So Long, Farewell

✦

Max kisses me good night in front of Third North. My lips feel numb and swollen from all the times they've been touched by his tonight. But I don't mind one bit.

When I get up to my room, Beatrix is already asleep, so I try to move around quietly. I finally take out my phone and see that I have several missed calls and texts. My parents called twice. Beckett texted to ask about the date. And there's a missed call and voice mail from Izzy the agent.

"Hey, Nasrin. Just wanted to let you know that I've been speaking to the Hulu people, hammering out the details. There are a few things they say they won't budge on, and after speaking with some colleagues, I don't think they're going to. But I did manage to up the royalty percentage on both soundtrack sales and merchandising. Give me a call back when you can.

I think we're really close to finalizing, and you should be able to sign this by end of day tomorrow. Talk soon."

It's past eleven p.m. Too late to call her back. But, really, I think it's all for the best. I want to spend a little longer savoring this Max afterglow.

My phone buzzes with a text from Minu. How was the date?

I give my phone a deep, contented sigh before I write back: Wonderful.

Good kisser? she asks.

Great kisser. Great listener. Great everything.

Minu sends back a little devil emoji.

Thanks for the dress, I type as I unzip the side and step out of it. It made me feel like a million bucks.

I'm glad it worked out, Minu writes. Maybe I'll wear it on my next date. Since it seems to have such good romantic karma.

I'll even get you your own pair of Vans, I write as I hang the dress neatly over my desk chair. I'll get it cleaned before I give it back.

I get ready for bed and then lie awake for a while, thinking of Max, touching my hand to my lips. But after a while, my thoughts turn to Izzy's voice mail. I'm close to signing the contract. Which means I'm close to leaving New York. My dorm, and Beckett, and Max. And... my classes. My drama exercises. The opportunity to work with someone like Lucia.

I toss and turn all night, getting only an hour or so of sleep.

At 8:30 a.m., I deem it an okay time to return Izzy's call. She picks up on the second ring, luckily sounding chipper, like she started her morning hours ago.

"Hi, it's Nasrin. I got your message last night."

"Hi, Nasrin," Izzy says. "So, yeah, basically the contract is pretty much done. If everything I mentioned sounds okay to you, I think I can have them send you an electronic copy to sign this afternoon."

"Right," I say hesitatingly.

"Is there some other section you want me to look at?" Izzy asks. "Something that's giving you pause?"

"Um, the whole thing is giving me pause," I respond.

"I know it can seem overwhelming. And the legalese is enough to make anyone's head spin. But it's not a bad contract, honestly. I just wouldn't be doing my job if I didn't try to fight for a bit more on some of these points, you know?"

"It's not that," I say. "Well, yes, I'm overwhelmed. But not really about the details of the contract." I pause again.

"What is it?" Izzy asks.

"I just...I'm not sure that I want to sign it at all. I'm not sure I want to do this." The words buzz out of my mouth like bees, tangible and unavoidable. It's the first time I've said them aloud to anybody—and they are, frankly, terrifying. But that doesn't make them untrue.

"I see," Izzy replies calmly. "Well, I don't blame you. It's a big decision. You'd be moving to another country. Leaving behind your friends and family..."

I think of my parents, doing the exact same thing when they left Iran. But their reasons seemed a lot more sound than mine. They wanted—no, needed—more opportunities for themselves, and for me. I need opportunity too...just maybe not the one that seems like the obvious choice. "I'd be leaving school behind," I finally say. "I just feel like... not that I haven't earned this, exactly. But that I don't know enough about my craft yet. Not in the way I want to. Not in the way that would lead me to the parts and pieces I'd really feel passionate about." I hesitate, realizing how I probably sound to someone whose job it is to get me work. "I know I sound stupid."

"No. You don't, actually," Izzy says. "You sound serious about what you want. Let me just say that understanding your own end goal is probably the most important thing you can do as an artist."

My end goal. I feel like all I've done lately is lose sight of that. I was only supposed to lie to my parents until I found the right words to tell them the truth, and instead I kept grasping for excuses not to. And what was I even lying for, once I started phoning in my classes?

"I *am* serious," I reply. "I feel like I'd be an idiot to let this opportunity go. But... I think I'd feel more like an idiot if I let the opportunity of school go. Did you know that less than fifteen percent of applicants get into Tisch?" I smile slightly, thinking of myself almost exactly one year ago, trying to work up the courage to say the exact same thing to my parents.

"I did," Izzy says. "And I think you should follow your gut here. Most of the time, it's all you have to go on in this business."

"Thank you *so* much, Izzy. I really appreciate everything you did for me. And I'm so sorry if I wasted your time."

"Of course you didn't," Izzy says. "It's my job to scout out talent. And, hey, if you still want me to represent you, I'd be more than happy to."

I consider it. But then I realize an agent would be looking at gigs for me. And right now, at this moment, I don't want professional gigs. I need to put my life on Do Not Disturb and concentrate on school. "Can I call you in three years?" I ask.

"Absolutely," she responds.

I consider telling Petie my decision over the phone, but it somehow doesn't seem right. Besides, I plan to finish out the final online episode before the Hulu contract kicks in.

"I don't understand," he says to me after he's done conferring with Tru about a reprise and I've finally managed to get his attention.

"I'm not going to be signing the contract," I repeat. "I won't be moving to Vancouver."

Petie blinks at me. "Is this some sort of hardball? What do you want that they're not offering you? Fame and fortune? Well, this is the start of that, sweetie."

"That's just the thing. I don't want fame and fortune. At least... not yet."

Petie snorts. "So you think they're just gonna wait around for your schedule?"

I shrug. "I don't know. But I don't know if *this* will even equal fame and fortune. And you don't either, but the difference is you love this show. I...don't. I'm sorry. But if I'm going to disappoint my parents, I want to at least do it in pursuit of something that I'm passionate about. You know what I mean?"

"No," Petie says flatly. "I have no clue what you're talking about. But I do know that I can recast your part in a heartbeat. So if this is some kind of ploy..."

I shake my head. "No ploys. No gimmicks. I know you're going to find another Leila. It just can't be me."

"Okay, whatever," Petie says. "Good luck," he murmurs as he walks away. I'm not sure anyone has ever meant those two words less.

"You really did it," a breathless voice comes from beside me. I turn around to see Tru.

I smile at her. "Yeah. But I'm going to miss you. A lot."

"Not as much as I'm going to miss you. In *Canada*..." She looks around the set. "I can't believe you really did it. You gave it up. That takes some serious guts."

"I just had to follow it. My gut."

Tru nods. "I can't pretend that I haven't worried about it too, that maybe this isn't the best vehicle for my talents."

I gently take her by both arms. "I can tell you in all honesty that your songs are the best thing about this show. And it's been an absolute honor to sing them."

"Thank you," she says. "The opportunity feels too huge to pass up," she adds with a shrug.

"Absolutely." I smile at her. "And I hope the show is a mega success and you're lauded as the next Menken and Ashman, Rodgers and Hammerstein, and Lin-Manuel Miranda all rolled into one."

"But with a little more Truism?" she quips.

"Definitely."

She leans in to give me a hug. "The best thing about you, Nasrin, is that I know you mean that. Wanting the show to be a success for my sake."

"Why wouldn't I?" I ask.

Tru leans back and smiles. "Because you're not Hollywood. At least, not yet." She winks at me as Cheryl starts calling everyone to their places.

This turns out to be my last-ever scene for *STD*. I'm lucky that I get to sing a few of Tru's genius bars. I'm lucky that I had this opportunity, that I got to experience a real set. But, most of all, I'm lucky that I ultimately made a decision that's not giving me pause, no matter what it looks like from the outside. I know I'm doing the right thing for me.

When I wrap, I say goodbye to Petie, who just waves at me dismissively. I make the rounds then, saying my goodbyes to everyone else: Liz, Anouk, Chaya, Juliet. When I get to Morris, I see him leaning against the wall and chatting up a familiar face.

"Beckett," I say, my head tilting in surprise. "What are you doing here?"

He turns around and holds out a bouquet of miniature pink roses. "I had to get you something for your curtain call."

I smile as I take them. "You shouldn't have."

"So it's really true, huh?" Morris asks. "You're not moving with us?"

"It's really true," I say. "But hey, break a leg. You're going to be amazing."

"Thanks," he says just as Cheryl calls his name. "Looks like I'm up. So I'll talk to you later?" he asks Beckett.

Beckett holds up his phone. "Definitely."

"Cool," Morris says.

When he's far enough away to be out of earshot, I turn to Beckett. "Did you just get his number?"

"Why, yes. Yes, I did just get the hot boy's number."

"And you *do* realize he's moving to Vancouver in a week?"

I watch Beckett as *he* watches Morris's jeans-clad ass walking away. "I mean, maybe I can make long distance work... this time."

I have to laugh.

"What?" Beckett says. "I promise I'll be more communicative!"

"Come on, you hopeless romantic," I say, dragging him away. "Before you break out into song."

CHAPTER 34

Don't Rain on My Parade

✧

I'm standing outside my parents' apartment building with a bouquet of flowers and a box of rice flour cookies from the Persian bakery. This time I've come with a plan. And a script, of sorts. It's time to stop hiding behind anger and disappointment. It's time to own up to what I did, but to be honest with them about how we got here too.

When they open the door, I immediately hand my mom the flowers and my dad the box of cookies. "I'm sorry," I say simply. "From the bottom of my heart, I am so very sorry."

Maman takes one look at the flowers she's holding, and I can already see the tears forming in her eyes. Baba kisses me roughly on the cheek, his mustache tickling me. "Okay," he says.

I feel a small sense of relief after my mom hugs me and tells me dinner will be ready soon. But I also know there's more I have to say. "Where's Minu?" I ask when I walk into the empty living room.

"Out with friends," Maman says. "Just the three of us tonight."

The three of us. I was going to have this conversation with my parents whether my cousin was here or not, but something about having it just be the three of us—the Mahdavi unit that's the root of everywhere I've been and everywhere I'm going—feels right.

Maman is about to head back into the kitchen when I place my hand on her arm and ask, "Can we talk before dinner?"

She looks at me a little oddly but then says, "Sure. Let me just turn the heat on the rice down. Nader, can you get a vase for this?"

I sit on the living room couch while I wait, doing the latest breathing and visualization exercises that I learned from Acting II.

And who said drama school did nothing to prepare you for life?

When my parents finally come in and settle down on the couch, I take one more second to think of my word of intention: "self-aware." This is about me and all my facets: from my passions to my flaws. It's about everything my parents gave me, but also everything that was always there inside me—the whirlwind of nature and experience that makes me who I am, and brings me to my decision about where to go next.

I look my parents in the eye, first Baba, then Maman. "I want you to know that I really am sorry," I say.

"We know," Baba says. "We accept your apology. Thank you for the flowers and the cookies."

"I'm glad you accept the apology," I continue. "I really am. But I need you to accept more."

Baba raises an eyebrow and leans back. "So it's an apology with a condition?"

I shake my head. "No. The apology is genuine. I never should have lied to you. But *this* is the conversation I should have had with you a year ago, when I first got that acceptance email from Tisch." I turn to look at my dad. "I know you only want the best for me. I've known it with every fiber of my being, my whole life, because you have always put me first, above everything. I am your jigar talah, after all." The old nickname elicits a small smile. "When I overheard what you said, Baba, I really thought it meant you'd be ashamed of me if I was waiting tables."

"Of course it didn't," Baba says. "I just don't want you to struggle, jigar talah. Like we did."

"I know that. And that you want to save me from heartache. But I also know that...you can't. Nobody can. Life is heartache and hard times and disappointments."

Maman sighs. "We realize that, Nasrin. But when you pursue something like acting, you're setting yourself up for disappointments tenfold. Maybe it sounds glamorous to be a 'starving artist,' but trust us, there is nothing glamorous about starving. Nothing. We've been there."

I nod. "I know. And I know you've sacrificed so much and left behind your culture, your language, your *family*, to come here. And that a lot of it was for me. But the thing is, if you came to America for opportunity, for me to have all the country's opportunities, isn't the biggest one of all to have choices when it comes to my career options?" I turn to Baba. "You believe that great minds have purpose, and others have wishes. But can't a wish, a dream, be a purpose? Of course I have to make a living...but I also have to live, Baba. No one can predict the future. I just have to pursue my happiness now, the best way I know how: doing the thing that I believe will let me make the most of my life."

Baba sighs. "And being in this streaming show is it, huh?"

"Actually, no," I say. "I quit the show."

Maman stares at me. "What? I thought it was going to be on Hulu and become a hit. Did it already get canceled?"

"It didn't. And it probably is going to become this massive hit. But...that's not why I do what I do. Maman, do you code because it makes you money? Baba, do you analyze business trends and theories because of your bank account? I know financial security is a happy by-product, but I honestly don't think it's *why* you do any of it. You have passion for it. And I really believe, with all my heart, that your success is in large part due to that passion. That it couldn't exist without it, even if you had all of the same skills and intellect."

Maman and Baba share a glance over my head.

"Nasrin, we know you're talented," Maman says. "We've never doubted that for a second. It's just..." She looks over at Baba. "Maybe we'll feel like we failed you as parents if we don't try to keep you from avoiding our mistakes."

"But I don't want to just avoid your mistakes, Maman. I want to embrace what makes you so good at what you do too. Can't you see that?"

Maman bites her lip, nodding. "We just want you to be happy."

"I know you do," I say. "That's why you have to believe me when I tell you, drama school is what will make me happy. Maybe not every second of every day, because nothing can do that. But at its core, it's where I'm meant to be. Because it's not just about talent. It's about hard work and studying the history of my craft. I want to learn, and grow, and honor how important the arts are to the human experience. How much plays and movies and shows and music have made all of us understand this wild world better. Do you see what I'm saying?"

"You're saying you want to stay at Tisch."

"No," I say. "Well, yes. But I want to do it with your full knowledge, your blessing. And I don't mean I expect you to embrace this as the ideal life for me. I just want you to embrace me. And trust me. I desperately want you to trust me again. Maybe I'll fail, and of course I'll have disappointments ... but because of everything you've taught me and everything I've learned from your examples, I'll also be able to pick myself back up. If I know I can always come to you when I need help."

"Of course you can," Maman says sharply. "Was that ever in question?"

I shake my head, smiling. "No. And it never should have been. I was too scared to have this conversation with you before, but I should have told you that this is who I am and what I want...and asked for your support. Because I know, no matter what, I've always had that. And I'm so lucky that I have."

"Okay, Baba jaan," Baba says. "It's our blessing you want?" He looks over at Maman, who nods at him. "Then that's what you have."

I grin as I get up and give them each a huge hug. "Thank you. And I do have two other pieces of good news. One for each of you." I turn to Baba first. "I spoke to my adviser this week and I can minor in the Business of Entertainment. At Stern."

"Really?" Baba asks hopefully. "Stern?"

I laugh at his eager expression. "Yes. And I promise I'll share my real coursework with you."

"Oh, maybe we can look into some entertainment-based mock proposals," Baba says.

"Maybe," I reply. "I mean, don't expect me to go on CNBC anytime soon...."

Baba's face immediately brightens. "But with your performance background and your business acumen, that might be perfect for you! Do you think we can call our contacts at *Mad Money* now?" He turns to my mother, eyes gleaming.

"Maybe in a little bit, joonam," Maman says.

"I'll just forward Nasrin the email," Baba says, picking up his phone. "Just so she has it."

Maman shakes her head as she leans in to whisper, "Is this the type of support you had in mind?"

"Yes," I say with a shrug. "I'll save disappointing him on becoming the next Suze Orman for another day."

She laughs. "And what was your piece of good news for me?"

"Oh," I say, a smile creeping over my face. "Well, I finally went on my first real date. With Max."

"Max?" Baba says, looking up from his phone. "That's wonderful!"

"I *knew* he was more than just a friend!" Maman exclaims, clapping.

I laugh at their elated faces. "Guess I was the last to know."

CHAPTER 35

I Dreamed a Dream

✫

"Oh, and Ali?" I say sweetly.

"Hmm?" Beckett asks, turning around.

I narrow my eyes, and my voice drops an octave to say, "Take out the damn trash."

There's a collective roar of laughter from the audience as the lights go down. Beckett and I scramble into position as the rest of the cast comes out from the wings. When the lights are back up, we all hold hands and bow. My parents are in the middle of the second row with Max and Minu. They're all on their feet, and my mom has put thumb and pointer into her mouth to produce her signature whistle. I beam at them. I found out just about an hour before the curtain went up that I'd be understudying Shauna's role in *The Walk-Up* today, and all of them managed to make it to the performance. It marks the first time Beckett and I have gotten to perform the play together for real. We look at each other and grin, knowing we nailed it.

Lucia greets us in the wings as we get off. "Chemistry," she says as she gives me a hug.

"Brilliant material," I say into her hair.

The Walk-Up is only running for one month, and I know this is likely the only time I'll get to perform it. But I also know better than to take that for granted now.

There's only two weeks left in my freshman year at Tisch, and I don't take anything for granted. Not running from a grueling dance class to an intense voice lesson. Not mining my emotions to make myself as vulnerable as possible in the name of an authentic performance. Not how Stats suddenly makes sense to me, or how Max and I spend most of class trying hard not to stare and grin at each other. Our general ratio of success is, uh . . . Look, it's not great. But hey, we're down to only, like, two to three times per class. That's something.

Most of all, I don't take for granted that my parents are here. That I'm not lying to them about anything anymore, that we can talk openly about our lives again. It feels like the biggest weight has been lifted from all parts of me: my shoulders, my heart, my gut. My stomachaches have all but disappeared too.

Small Town Dreams is premiering in just a few weeks on Hulu. There have been billboards for it all over the subways and ads popping up before almost every other show on the streaming service. I smile every time I see Morris and Juliet and hear them sing Tru's songs. The girl who's playing Leila now is Sunny, the one I first met at the audition. I'm glad she seems to have gotten over her nerves. Or at least, I *hope* she's not barfing before shooting every scene. Tru and I have stayed in touch, and she keeps me in the loop about what's happening—including Petie's every meltdown. But she also seems genuinely happy, and I'm so glad of that.

I worried a little that maybe I would regret letting the opportunity go, especially once I started seeing the show everywhere—but I'm happy to report that I don't. The rush that I get from Lucia's play, from performing work that feels meaningful and right...I feel like that's the only reason to pursue this impossible dream. Success as measured by fame or fortune is elusive. But success measured by my own standards, by continuing to grow and improve and be passionate about what I do...*that* is something I can always strive for. I'm in control of that.

"Wonderful, jigar talah," Baba says as he rushes out to embrace me as soon as I enter the lobby. Maman and Max are both holding bouquets. Max politely waits for Maman to give me hers first as she kisses me on both cheeks.

"That was hilarious," she says.

"Thank you," I reply, beaming.

"Loved it," Minu says. "Also, is the guy who plays Harry single?"

I laugh. "No idea, but I'm sure I can find out for you."

Max leans down to kiss me on the cheek as he hands me his own bouquet.

"What did you think?" I ask him.

"That you're brilliant, of course," he says.

I nod. "Congratulations, you've aced this pop quiz."

"There's just..." He hesitates.

"What?" I ask.

He looks around at my family. "Oh, nothing. Never mind. It was great."

"If you have a criticism, you can say it, Max. I've dealt with internet trolls *and* elite drama school professors. I can handle anything."

"It's just..." He bites his lip before looking back at me. "There was kind of a dearth of lassoing scenes, you know what I mean?"

I burst out into laughter. "Um, I'll be sure to let Lucia know that her Queens-set play is lacking some rope tricks."

"Please do," he says as he grabs me by the waist and pulls me in for a hug. "I'm so proud of you, you know that?" he whispers in my ear.

I smile. "Thank you," I whisper back, looking over his shoulder and seeing the same pride reflected in my parents' faces. Best of all, I know it's reflected in mine too. I'm proud of myself for dreaming a dream, knowing its challenges, and persevering anyway. I know that fire can keep me going even in the lowest times. That fire and my family, the people who love me and want the best for me.

I'm pretty sure I've finally figured out exactly how to succeed.

ACKNOWLEDGMENTS

First and foremost, I have to thank my editor, Rachel Stark. It's been a blast setting this stage with you. Your insightful notes always made me dig deeper and find more and better ways to bring out the best in Nasrin and in me. I'm so grateful to have been on this journey with you.

I also owe a huge thanks to Mahita Penke and Kieran Viola, who helped this project find its way to me, and who have been an absolute pleasure to get to know and work with. And a big thanks to everyone at Hyperion, including Elanna Heda, Augusta Harris, Ann Day, Matt Schweitzer, Holly Nagel, Danielle DiMartino, Dina Sherman, Guy Cunningham, Jacqueline Hornberger, Jenny Langsam, Sara Liebling, and Marybeth Tregarthen. Finally, enormous gratitude to designer Zareen Johnson and illustrator Sara Alfageeh for a cover that made *me* break out into song and dance.

Thank you so much to Victoria Marini for all your patient, diligent work getting this project off the ground. And thank you to Ashley Herring Blake for dealing with my freak-out emails with such grace and patience.

A big thank-you to Talia Mariani for sharing so many of your experiences from the Tisch musical theater program with me. And thank you to Terry Hadjiivanova for looking over my stats homework.

I've loved musical theater with my whole heart for as long as I can remember. For that, I have to thank my parents for showing me my first-ever movie, *The Sound of Music* (dubbed entirely in Farsi) and for filling my head and heart with a steady diet of classic musicals growing up. I also have to thank Ms. Hulley, my theater teacher in elementary and middle school, who incongruously sparked a love of performing for an otherwise painfully shy kid. I owe so much of all that is wonderful about my life to the Walt Whitman High School theater department, who not only gave me some of my best teenage memories, but also my dearest lifelong friends. We go together—Katie Blackburn, Karen Donofrio, Amy Sommer, Sharon Baldwin, Terry Hadjiivanova, Caitie Wagstaff, and Zarina Hora—like rama-lama-lama ka-dinga-da-dinga-dong. I love you all immeasurably...or at least 525,600 minutes/year.

A huge thank-you to my family for putting up with my occasional bursting out into show tunes. And especially to Graig, Bennett, and Jonah for singing along and bringing me one step closer to fulfilling my dream of becoming a Von Trapp Family Singer. Or, maybe even, a Madrigal.